JOURNEY TO THE THRONE

JOURNEY TO THE THRONE

VANI MAHESH

HarperCollins *Publishers* India

First published in India in 2022 by HarperCollins *Publishers*
4th Floor, Tower A, Building No. 10, Phase II, DLF Cyber City,
Gurugram, Haryana – 122002
www.harpercollins.co.in

2 4 6 8 10 9 7 5 3 1

P-ISBN: 978-93-5629-327-4
E-ISBN: 978-93-5629-331-1

This is a work of fiction with some parts based on historical fact. All situations, incidents, dialogue and characters in this novel, with the exception of some well-known historical and public figures, are products of the author's imagination and are not to be construed as real. They are not intended to depict actual events, or people or to change the entirely fictional nature of the work. In all other respects, any resemblance to actual persons, living or dead, is entirely coincidental.

Cover illustrations and design:
Harshad Marathe

Typeset in Sabon 11.5 pt/16 pt
by Veena, Bookwatch

Printed and bound at
Thomson Press (India) Ltd

Contents

To
Akshara, Neethi,
and my wonderful readers

Author's Note

My interest in ancient and medieval Indian history made me look for literature written during that era since I wanted a different view of the society as it existed back then than books of facts. My quest led me to the play *Devichandraguptam* by Vishakhadatta. This play is partially lost, but it brings out an exciting event that transpired in the Gupta clan.

The Gupta era is heralded as the golden period of Indian history. However, most of us know only about the rule of two illustrious kings, Samudragupta and Chandragupta, from the dynasty. The play *Devichandraguptam* is about an incident from Chandragupta's childhood, which could be part truth and part fiction. It is mainly about the turbulent relationship Chandragupta shared with his elder brother Ramagupta.

Not much is known about Ramagupta except for the coins found in central India attributed to him. On the other hand, there are several inscriptions, an account by Chinese traveller Fa Hien, as well as coins that detail the life of Chandragupta. I have woven the story of *Journey to the Throne* by combining the available factual information with the event described in the play.

1

'We live like nomads for a week and then head back to the palace. What's the point of this silly expedition?' eighteen-year-old Rama, the elder son of Emperor Samudragupta, complained for the umpteenth time. 'Father wants us killed, not trained,' he muttered under his breath. The soldier next to him marched stoically, not daring a reply. Concurring meant he would be disgracing his king, and differing would offend the young prince.

'The point is battle-readiness. Forests pose dangers; palaces don't.' Rama's younger brother, Chandra, regretted his words as soon as they were out. They were sure to further irk his brother.

'Do you always have to be pretentious? Try talking like a normal fifteen-year-old for a change.' Rama kicked at the leaves that kept getting inside his shoes. The dry leaves that poked his feet like pinpricks left him seething.

'Go on. Tell me that I should be noiseless when I walk in the woods. You seem to know it all somehow.' Rama looked Chandra in the eye, as if challenging him to respond.

Chandra stared back, secretly glad that he was now a good head taller than his brother. He decided not to prolong the discussion, which had the potential to turn into an argument and perhaps a full-blown fight. Chandra joined the soldiers who strode ahead of him. These tough men were better company than his bickering brother any day.

'Let's look for some deer, Prince.' One of the soldiers smiled warmly at Chandra as he fell in step with them. 'They make a tasty meal, in spite of our cooks.' The soldier guffawed at his joke, and the others joined in.

The old cook chuckled good-naturedly. Having been an army cook for decades, he knew better than to take these jibes seriously. 'You expect a gourmet meal in a forest? Also, don't you know Prince Chandra is vegetarian, like his father?' There was a familiar solemn look on the cook's face at the mention of the king. Most people in the kingdom thought of his father as God, which Chandra found comical.

Chandra heard another soldier take a dig at the cook. 'Look at our prince – nothing but skin and bones, thanks to your cooking. The queen may throw you into the dungeon for this crime against her son.' There was more laughter.

'They are only joking.' Chandra tried to be nice. 'I love your cooking.' He had lied convincingly, or so he hoped. The truth was, the man's cooking was so terrible that every dish tasted like dry twigs.

But the cook was visibly thrilled with the compliment. 'I'll cook a special vegetarian meal just for you tonight, Prince.'

Chandra walked on with an encouraging nod and a smile, wondering what awaited him that night. Then again, food was not the only hardship on these week-long camping trips that their father made them take twice a year. They had to get up well before dawn when the morning chill bit into their skins. Their breakfasts and lunches were so inadequate that Chandra had forgotten how it felt to be full. Dinner was another story: sumptuous but tasteless. Add to that miles and miles of walking.

However, he didn't hate these trips the way Rama did. There were benefits to them – spotting the odd cheetah or a fox; a soldier who taught him knife-throwing skills; another who knew how to tell stories, especially about war (though Chandra suspected the authenticity of the soldier's heroics in those tales).

Chandra adjusted the heavy rucksack that sat like a boulder on his shoulders. Since they never halted at the same place twice, they carried their supplies when they walked.

'Shall I carry it for you, Prince?' offered a soldier who noticed Chandra fiddling with the bag. Chandra refused the offer, though it was tempting. His father was firm that they had to be like the other soldiers at the camp.

'I'm fine. How far are we from the campsite?'

'Another hour. We will halt as soon as we cross this part of the forest. People have spotted lions around here, so we better walk fast and get out,' the soldier replied.

'That is a good idea. We don't want to be a lion's dinner. Are we heading home tomorrow as planned?' Chandra asked. He wanted a hot bath and good food.

Then, he planned on sleeping for two days straight in a soft bed.

'That is what Commander Kritavarma says,' replied the soldier. Accompanying them on these camping trips was none other than the Chief Commander of the king's army, Kritavarma. He was also King Samudragupta's childhood friend, which made him overprotective towards the princes. It was a little too much protection, Chandra often felt, but the commander laughed it off, saying it was a break from work for him to go on these trips.

Chandra heard the soldier next to him speak again, 'Tonight, we will camp at the edge of the forest closest to Pataliputra. Tomorrow morning, the stable hands from the palace will bring the horses for us to ride back home.' The soldier smiled. 'The ordeal will soon end for both of you.'

Pataliputra was their capital, a city Chandra had grown up in and loved. The Gupta empire covered most of Bharata, but Pataliputra was the city chosen as the capital for its abundant resources. In fact, since the time of the Mauryan kings, for almost six centuries, Pataliputra had been the capital of several Magadhan kingdoms.

'Snake! A snake!' a terrified scream from Rama echoed through the forest, making Chandra instinctively run towards his brother. Rama stood frozen in place, his face ashen, staring at a dark, sinewy 'snake' hanging in front of him. His fear of the slithery creatures was not new to anyone.

2

Chandra went closer to the object that had terrorized his brother. Unlike Rama, snakes fascinated him. Pulling Ajeya, his dagger, out of its sheath, Chandra gently poked the dangling thing. 'I don't think it's a snake,' he declared in a mildly disappointed tone. 'Just a vine of some kind.'

Kritavarma hurried towards them, hearing the commotion. After a poke at the hanging object with the edge of his long sword, he too declared that it was just a vine. 'But, Prince Chandra, you are not to approach anything suspicious without protection. You have to control the urge to rush at things headlong.'

'My body seems to act on its own at times, Commander.' Chandra grinned at Kritavarma. 'Next time, I'll mind my body.'

'This could have been a snake, and it could have killed me. Anything can happen in these godforsaken forests.' Rama's voice rose in anger. 'And I don't need you to protect me, Chandra. Who asked you to rush to my aid?' Rama snatched Chandra's dagger in rage from him and threw it into the woods.

Chandra was livid. Everyone knew how much that dagger meant to him. It had been a gift from his grandfather on his tenth birthday. When he had named it Ajeya, the invincible, there was considerable ridicule. Even his usually understanding father had laughed at his obsession with the weapon, but Chandra had remained undeterred. He always carried it on him, except when he went to bed. At night, he kept it right next to him. At first, he kept it on his bed. Later, he kept it on a table close by, when his mother insisted that he might end up poking himself with it while sleeping.

'You are horrible. How dare you throw away Ajeya!' Chandra screamed and rushed into the thicket to fetch it.

Huffing in anger, Rama strode down a random path. 'It is just a silly knife. It doesn't change into a magical object just because you named it.'

'Prince Rama,' Kritavarma almost shouted in alarm, 'that is not the path we should be on. Come back.'

'You all go wherever you want to. Leave me alone.' Rama kept walking. 'I don't matter to you anyway.'

Chandra, who had found his dagger by then, was dumbstruck by what Rama had just said. *He cannot be in the forest by himself. He could become the next meal of a predator!* Chandra was in a panic. *I promised Mother that there would be no fights between us this time.*

He looked at Kritavarma, hoping for a miraculous rescue from the situation. The commander, who looked as stunned as him, stood staring at Rama's back. Then, to Chandra's relief, he shouted orders to his men, 'Change of direction. Follow me.'

As Kritavarma started walking briskly behind Rama, Chandra caught up with him. 'Commander, do you know where this path takes us?' Worry gnawed at him. They could become food for the wild animals in the forest.

Kritavarma sighed. 'No, Prince, I don't. We are on a journey to an unknown destination.' His frustration showed despite his best efforts. Kritavarma didn't like disobedience or uncertainty.

'I'm sorry for all this trouble,' Chandra said softly. He was.

Kritavarma smiled wryly. 'Not your fault, Prince.'

Rama heard Kritavarma. 'Nothing is his fault, ever.' Though he didn't raise his voice at the commander, his face displayed anger.

Not my fault because I'm not an idiot who doesn't follow orders in a forest, Chandra wanted to shout at his brother but decided to remain silent. It was better that way for everyone. As a child, he had never understood his brother's anger towards him, but now he did. Rama flew into a rage whenever he felt outdone by Chandra. *I've better things to do than to make you look bad.* Chandra had tried to convey that sentiment in many ways, but Rama refused to believe him.

Now, without an end in sight, the walk seemed more difficult than ever. After a good two hours of walking through the forest, the sun was about to set. Kritavarma's anxiety was evident in the way he was snapping at everyone.

The forest was abuzz with noises – screeching insects, chirping birds, hissing winds and rustling leaves. Add to that the scary barks and growls of wild animals. Chandra wished all the noises would vanish and there would be silence.

'How far are we from the campsite?' Rama stopped to ask Kritavarma.

'We may not be able to camp since we could soon be eaten by a pride of lions,' Chandra snapped.

Before Rama could say anything, Kritavarma, hoping to avoid another scuffle between the brothers, said, 'I'm not sure where we can halt on this path, Prince. We must look for a riverbank. That would be the only safe place to pitch our tents.'

'Are we really in danger like this genius is saying?' Rama tried to sound unfazed, but no one was fooled.

'We're not at all in danger, Brother. Being stuck at night in a dense forest amidst wild animals is absolutely safe.' Chandra couldn't resist the sarcasm.

'If you don't shut up, I'll feed you to a lion myself.' Rama tried to sound fierce, but his voice had lost its bite.

3

Despite his apparent bravado, Rama's heart sank in fear. *What if I have put everyone's life in danger, including mine?* Why did his brother bring out the worst in him? Everyone who seemed light and jovial around Chandra clammed up the minute they saw him – as if he was a thorny obstacle they had to walk around carefully.

But now, it was not just Chandra who was making him feel so harrowed, it was the camp itself. Rama had always hated these trips, but this one was especially gruelling. His best friend, Meghanad, who usually went with him on these expeditions, hadn't come because he had been sick. His other source of solace, his dog Kusha, wasn't there either to elevate his spirits. He missed his mother. He missed venting to her. The only good thing about the forest was that he was away from his father.

With the darkness slowly spreading, Kritavarma decided to camp wherever they were even if it was in the middle of the dark, dank forest.

'It's risky to camp here, but it's riskier to walk on,' Kritavarma said. Rama thought that he'd rather be killed by a wild animal than face his father.

After a few moments, they heard the unmistakable bubbling and eddying sound of the flowing river. 'Let's follow the sound of the river and get to the bank before the darkness blinds us.' Rama had never been happier to hear the commander's words.

The wide bank of the river Ganga looked perfect for camping. Rama sighed in relief and looked around for approving nods. Was anyone going to show him gratitude? *Well done, Prince. Thanks to you, we have found a new spot for camping. You gave us a grand adventure, Prince.* The sight of Chandra sitting on a rock jutting out of the river irritated Rama. 'He is the one crazy for misadventure, and I'm the one always in trouble,' he grunted to himself in annoyance.

Once the tents were pitched, the fire was lit and the cooks got to work. The drums started rolling and the bugles began screeching. The soldiers' patriotic hurrahs for the king and the kingdom echoed through the wilderness. Soon, sura (cheap wine) and ganja were out. Kritavarma permitted some indulgence on the last leg of the camp. Rama, without a glance at the commander, joined the soldiers in their celebration. Before long, they were past caring about anything or anybody.

* * *

Chandra stared at the river absently. *What a dreadful night! Why is Rama so unpredictable and volatile? Why does he hate me so much?* These questions had haunted him since he had begun to realize that Rama's anger towards him was deep and intense. It was not like the squabbles other siblings had.

'He is complex, Chandra. But he's your brother. You have to be considerate towards him,' his mother had said the night before they had set out on their trip. 'He feels everyone prefers you over him, especially your father. That upsets him a lot.'

'Then, start telling everyone to like him better, Ma!' Chandra was irritated. Her constant insistence that he be the kind and considerate one had begun to irk him lately. 'Or, better, tell him to hate me a little less.'

'He is angry and upset with everyone, not just you. He has craved acceptance from your father for years, but now he has given up on that and turned a little rebellious. Let's—'

'Ma!' Chandra cut his mother off impatiently. 'He does not attend any training sessions or classes. It has been ages since anyone saw him at a council meeting. And, he speaks rudely to everyone, including you and Father. Are you surprised that Father does not accept him?'

'Rama has hated strict schooling since he was a child. But your father refused to change the way he was taught.' She gave Chandra a hurt look and pleaded with him. 'We can't give up on him. We have to help him find his strengths.'

Chandra agreed with her to calm her down, but he had no clue how to help someone who hated the very sight of him. Chandra felt drained. He looked at the soldiers who were busy laughing, arguing and shuffling clumsily, which passed off for dancing. Most of the men were already intoxicated, and his brother was getting there fast.

Lost in thought, Chandra heard a roar, a faint one, but indeed a roar. *A lion? A tiger?* Chandra sprang to his feet and hopped across the rocks to reach the group around Kritavarma.

'Is that a lion, Commander?' Chandra was almost breathless with worry. 'Do you think it's alone or are there several of them?'

Kritavarma patted Chandra on the back to calm him down. 'It sounds like a lone lion. But let's hope it's not keen on having dinner with us.' The commander's forced lightness did nothing to reduce Chandra's anxiety.

Cupping a hand to his ear, Chandra listened. 'It's headed this way. The growls are getting louder. It wants us for dinner.'

4

Within minutes, the lion thundered into the camp, alerting even the intoxicated soldiers. Fear spread through the camp. All of them knew the havoc a wild lion could wreak.

'Split into two groups and escort the princes to the river,' Kritavarma's voice boomed in urgency. 'Fast.'

Even in their drunken haze, the small platoon obeyed. They split into two: one escorting Rama, the other Chandra. The brothers were urged away from the wooded area and towards the river. Even as they ran, the sharp rustle of dry leaves from behind, followed by louder roars, indicated that the lion was getting closer.

Rama teetered and wobbled as he ran. Chandra kept flashing worried glances at his brother, fearing that he might fall when the lion approached them. Thankfully, he didn't, and they made it to the bushes that rimmed the water.

Kritavarma now gave orders in a quieter tone, 'Dive into the river if the animal gets close. Lions don't swim well.'

Now that they were relatively safe, Chandra, along with the others, ventured a look at the campsite and gasped. Facing the growling lion were their two cooks, who had gone looking for herbs. They were going to be the unsuspecting victims of the hungry beast.

'Commander, we have to rescue those men,' Chandra whispered urgently.

Kritavarma whispered back, 'We can't help them, Prince. Now, be still. Let's not draw attention to ourselves.' He put a finger to his lips, indicating silence.

Kritavarma's reply made Chandra gape in shock. *Are we going to let those men die?* He jumped back in horror when the lion pounced on the men with an ear-splitting roar. The old cook fell to the ground. The other cook ran for his life, tripping and stumbling.

Chandra looked on in a daze as the animal planted a massive paw on the fallen man's chest. The man was now screaming gut-wrenchingly, 'Help me, someone, help me!'

Undeterred by his screams, the lion took a large bite of the man's shoulder. Nausea coursed through Chandra. He couldn't bear it any longer. He couldn't be a mute spectator when one of their men was dying. As everyone watched, Chandra pulled his sword out from its sheath and rushed towards the lion.

'Prince, stop ... stop! Come back!' cried Kritavarma. When Chandra was mere inches away from the lion, he jumped on it with a scream, as if possessed. He pushed his sword through its gut with all the force he could muster. The lion, puzzled at first, stopped its feast. But as the sword sank in further, the beast went berserk. Letting out a cry of pain and anger, it lunged at Chandra.

* * *

Rama looked on, first in alarm and then in horror at the scene unfolding before him. When the lion's paw struck Chandra, Rama screamed at the soldiers surrounding him, 'Go, help him. Why are you standing?' He couldn't believe what his brother had done.

By the time Rama got his bearings, Chandra had sidestepped the lion and was now stabbing the beast maniacally with his dagger. The screams—from the soldiers, the lion and Chandra—filled the air. After a few moments, the lion collapsed, its roars turning into low moans.

Rama walked towards Chandra, who sat shivering through a thick blanket wrapped around him. Concerned faces hovered around him and voices rose in incoherent chatter. His face covered in scratches, probably from the lion's claws, Chandra looked dazed. He seemed to be oblivious to the events around him. When their gazes met, Rama didn't know what to say to his brother. For that matter, they hadn't said anything substantial to each other in months.

'He's in shock. He'll be all right soon,' said one of the soldiers, whose tone Rama found irritatingly condescending. Some soldiers were busy inspecting the dead lion and the injured cook. Rama averted his gaze when he saw the man's half-eaten shoulder. *Will this injured man survive?*

As he wandered, he felt he had yet again become invisible to everyone, with Chandra occupying their attention. Feeling nauseated, from sura, ganja and all the action, he slumped down on a fallen tree branch, overcome with exhaustion. *Can some people at least stop all this fuss and arrange for food and bed?* Rama's concern and sympathy for his brother slowly turned to anger. *Is this drama necessary? Why did Chandra have to put so many lives in danger to rescue one man, who might not even live?*

5

'Ma!'

Rama's voice jolted Queen Dattadevi, who had been lost in her thoughts. Relief washed over her like warm waves to see that he was safe.

'Are you praying for Father's long life? You should pray for mine instead,' Rama joked, but he looked distraught. 'Ma, what came over me to scream the way I did? Father will kill me today. He's asked me to meet him in the afternoon.'

The previous evening, the troops had entered the king's court with the soldiers carrying Chandra on their shoulders, cheering maniacally for him. His father had come down from the throne, which he never did when the assembly was in progress, to congratulate Chandra. When the hurrahs had died down, Samudragupta had turned to climb the steps to the throne.

Rama had exploded, 'What Chandra did was brainless. He put all of us at risk to save one man, and now he's a hero?'

Samudragupta had glared at his son. 'To a member of the royal family, every life should count. A prince is expected to help those in need.'

Rama had lashed out again, 'Chandra is not half as great as you are all making him out to be. There's a big difference between real bravery and a mere display of it.'

Rama now sat on a stone bench that faced their courtyard garden, a riot of colour after the rains. Breathing in the fragrant breeze, he wished all his problems would disperse like the clouds in the sky. Kusha curled up under his feet contentedly. Rama was jolted out of his thoughts when he heard his mother saying, 'Your father didn't say anything to me last night. He might have forgotten about it.'

Biting into a piece of the sweet his mother offered him, Rama laughed. 'That is true, Mother. He has asked me to have a drink with him!' He continued in a serious voice, 'Ma, can you please come too? I hate talking to him alone. It'll be the same old how-I-need-to-improve-my-ways talk.' Rama fed the dog, who jumped up and down excitedly for his share of the treat.

'You know your father. He won't like it if I show up uninvited, Rama. You speak to him. He is strict, but he's a just man. Make sure not to lose your temper.'

Rama rolled his eyes. 'You've given me the same advice ever since I was born. And it has never worked.' Rama hugged Kusha, who was now settled comfortably next to him on the bench. 'I'll go with cotton in my ears to tune him out. Don't look so worried.' He got up to leave. 'I'll live.'

Dattadevi smiled at her son. He was so dear to her. If only he could control his temper. She patted him on the shoulder and said in jest, 'Go with armour too. In case your father draws his sword.'

'Now that may be your best advice to date.' Rama left with Kusha at his heels.

At the door, he stopped and turned to his mother, 'But, Ma, I do think Chandra is just an attention seeker. What he did was foolish – to rush headlong at a lion.'

Dattadevi remained silent, instantly triggering Rama's anger. 'So, even you think he was a hero? How can he fool so many people? Am I the only one to see through his façade?'

As his mother looked quietly into the distance, Rama could feel his temper rising and quickly exited.

* * *

Feeling a familiar dread, Rama clambered up the wide marble stairs lined with imposing teakwood railings. His head still reeled from the wine he had had with Megha a few hours ago. Walking through the well-lit corridor that led to several official chambers on either side, Rama stopped outside his father's office. He was about to knock on the door when he heard his mother's voice. So she *was* there! His ears perked up when he heard her say: 'You are unnecessarily harsh on Rama.'

'You know I'm not.' Samudragupta's voice was gruff. 'I've warned him often enough. Who will trust a king who can't even control his own children? If he does not improve his ways, I'll name Chandra the heir apparent to the throne.'

Rama's head spun, and the ground seemed to cave in. He leaned against the wall to steady himself. *What is Father saying? Will he snatch my birthright and make Chandra the king?* Rama felt numb.

He turned around and walked away. The last thing he needed was a talk with his traitorous father.

6

'Don't read too much into the conversation, Rama. I'm sure your father said that in anger,' Megha tried to calm his friend for the umpteenth time. They had been sitting by the river for hours now, but Rama's angst showed no signs of abating.

Rama launched into yet another tirade against his father and Chandra, 'You know why I quit those training sessions, Megha? Because of the way the teachers gloated over Chandra's brilliance. Nobody, mind you, nobody has said anything good to me, ever.'

Rama continued his monologue, 'What is there in training with archery or swords? It's just practice. I want to be a good statesman. But does my father approve of that? No! For him, being a prince is all about wielding swords and wringing necks.'

'Then attend council meetings and speak up there. Get noticed. You are a good statesman,' Megha suggested as he'd done a hundred times before. Rama did possess good political acumen. He had topped the strategy and political education classes.

'It's frustrating that I have to prove myself to claim what is my birthright.' Rama threw a stone into the water. 'This is war now, Megha. I tolerated it when Father gave Chandra a better sword or a horse, but I won't sit back and watch him give away the throne.' Smoking his last ganja roll, he got up. His head reeled, and his feet felt like wool. 'Even if it means doing the old man's bidding until he dies.'

'Don't talk about the king dying!' Megha sounded hurt.

'How can you be my friend and like my enemies?' Rama shook his head disapprovingly.

'Your father and brother are not your enemies.' Megha laughed. 'And I may like them, but my loyalty is to you,' he vowed solemnly.

Rama smiled at his friend's words. 'I know it is. But I still wish you didn't like them.'

* * *

When Rama showed up at the council hall for the evening assembly, the guards bowed to him but hesitated to open the door. The king didn't like latecomers. Knitting his brows severely to show his displeasure, Rama walked towards the door. Two large bronze lions on either side of the wide door greeted him. Rama pushed open the door.

He hadn't expected the massive door to creak loudly and announce his arrival. Hundreds of oil lamps and lanterns in every nook and cranny of the enormous hall made the place look as bright as day. There went his plan to blend in anonymously!

With every eye trained on him, Rama cast a furtive glance at his father, who was staring at him blankly. He looked around and found an empty chair at the back of the hall and collapsed into it. The chieftain, who had been speaking before Rama entered the hall, resumed his speech.

Samudragupta's three childhood friends—Prime Minister Harisena, Finance Minister Lakshmidhara, and Chief Commander Kritavarma—had taken their seats right at the front. He felt a wave of anger when he spotted Chandra sitting next to Kritavarma, where Rama always sat. Calming himself, Rama tried to focus on the issues under discussion.

‘Maharaj, excessive rainfall has destroyed our crops. Please help us tide over this period with a loan …’ said a chief of a vassal province.

Rama did not like it when his father granted an exemption. *Why can’t these farmers learn to manage droughts and rains?* Megha’s voice rang in his head, ‘Speak up, get noticed.’ He decided he was going to talk the next time there was an opportunity.

‘The highway roads have been ravaged by rain. Our caravans can’t move past the Vindhyas to the southern regions. Can you please have the roads repaired?’ said the guild-head of the merchants.

‘We spent a lot of resources on the roads after the last rainy season. We don’t have the budget to spend on it this year,’ replied Lakshmidhara in his barely audible voice. *Why can’t he speak up a little?*

Rama raised his hand. He had a point to make, and he was going to do so. Samudragupta looked surprised but nodded. Rama started to speak, hoping he would not stutter. ‘Why don’t we ask …’ Rama stopped to collect his thoughts. As his father looked at him impatiently, he continued bravely, ‘Why don’t we ask the southern kings to repair the roads? They need the crops and spices we send from here.’

There was silence all around, making Rama wonder if he had said something foolish. He sighed with relief when Harisena supported him. ‘Prince Rama has made a good point. Most southern kings are our vassals, and we have let them rule without paying taxes. So, we can demand this of them.’

Rama felt happy. He had made a valid argument!

The next to speak were the heads of the priests' guild, gold guild, artisans' guild among others. Rama's head started pounding as he waited for the meeting to get over. It took some effort to stifle the yawns that were threatening to escape.

The meeting finally wound up an hour later. With the royal band playing the drums and bugles, Samudragupta ceremoniously descended from the throne and the attendees stood up. Rama joined his father as he walked down the runner with a large entourage of guards trailing him. Speaking above the loud chants of the priests, Rama managed to ask, 'Father, can we talk now?'

Samudragupta stopped and adjusted his finely embroidered shawl across his shoulders. 'We were supposed to do that hours ago, Son.'

Rama hung his head briefly and then forced himself to ask his father, 'Can we please talk now?' He entertained no hope that his father would agree, but luck was on his side.

Samudragupta consented after a pause. 'Walk with me to the garden.'

That night, after a brief talk with his father, Rama left the palace a determined man. He had promised his father that he was going to reform and refrain from smoking and drinking. His father had only nodded with a neutral expression, but Rama was happy. At least his father hadn't dismissed him like he usually did. From the next day, Rama began to attend every training, class and council meeting. He was ready to prove to his father that he was a worthy heir to the throne.

7

Three months into Rama's transformation came the hunting day, the one activity Rama enjoyed. He had got his father's approval. The day began on a good note for the royal hunting party. Although Kritavarma couldn't accompany them, he had made sure there were enough trained soldiers and huntsmen in the group to protect the princes. The sturdy horses imported from Persia took the hunters to the thick jungles north of Pataliputra in less than four hours.

And hunt they did! Mules, buffaloes, cheetahs. Chandra allowed Rama the first shot at any animal for two reasons. The first was that he was determined not to rub his brother the wrong way and the second was that he was not fond of hunting the way Rama was. Riding and trekking were his passions rather than killing animals. But his father insisted that hunting was one of the essential skills of a royal.

Rama was having a good time. He had Megha for company and a jungle full of animals he could seek, chase and kill. 'His aim with arrows and spears gets better when he hunts,' mused Chandra.

'We should have brought buffaloes to bait the tigers. We have come to the land of tigers, but we're returning without a single one,' Chandra heard Rama complain to Minister Guna, who had accompanied them. There was always something to disappoint Rama. Chandra quietly listened to the conversation without interrupting.

'To hunt tigers, we'll have to camp a few nights. But we should end the day now,' said Minister Guna. 'It's about to get dark, and we still have a good four to five hours of travel back home.'

'Then, I want at least one last hunt,' said Rama adamantly. 'An easy one by the riverside. We will wait behind the trees and aim at the animals that come to the river for a drink.'

That is not a real hunt. That is a cheat hunt! Chandra was tempted to say, but he controlled his tongue with great difficulty. The day had gone well thus far, and he didn't want to jeopardize it with a negative comment.

The entire hunting party knelt behind the trees that lined the raised river bund. Soon they saw a cloud of dust: a herd of some kind was emerging through the haze.

'A herd of bulls, I think,' said a huntsman next to Chandra. He was right. Huge, long-horned bulls, at least twenty of them, came into full view.

'Don't shoot. I'll round up a bull from the herd. Stay back. I want to do this on my own.' Rama's words made Chandra almost fall off the bund in surprise. The soldiers were as taken aback by this order as Chandra.

Chandra silently pleaded with Megha to intervene. True, he didn't like his brother much, but he didn't hate him enough to see him get mauled by bulls! To his relief, Minister Guna said to Rama, 'Prince, these bulls are too ferocious to be rounded up. They can gore one to death within minutes. I think you should hunt them from here.'

Rama shrugged off the minister's words and continued resolutely towards the river with a lasso rope.

'Prince,' Megha tried to reason with Rama, but Rama stopped him. 'Megha, stay back. Let me do this.'

Chandra, though tempted to say something, kept quiet. It was unlikely that Rama would pay any heed to him. Instead, he watched his brother approach the herd, hooting and yelling.

Rama trailed the herd that had now moved to the narrow path between the river and the forest. He succeeded in making most of the pack disappear into the woods. Then he charged at the remaining few, swinging the lasso rope above his head. At the end, there was a lone bull, the slowest and the bulkiest of the lot. Rama, with the gait of a victor, threw the rope around the beast.

Chandra breathed a sigh of relief. His brother was going to live after all! But the relief was short-lived. The lasso fell short by a few feet. Rama looked momentarily perplexed but quickly began swinging the rope again. The bull, which had been trying to escape, suddenly seemed to change its mind. It stopped, grunted and charged at Rama.

Panic spread through the soldiers. They slid down the bund, their spears drawn and pointing ahead. Chandra joined them, but he knew it was futile. They couldn't throw spears from that distance. There was a good chance that they would hit Rama instead of the beast.

8

Rama took to his feet when the bull charged. However, the tenacious bull chased him, closing the gap between them quickly.

Rama was sure that that was the end of him, but he kept running. His breath caught in his chest, and he felt he was going to collapse, maybe die. *Where are the idiotic soldiers? Why aren't they shooting at the bull?*

Even after what seemed like a lifetime, the heavy thudding behind Rama continued. The bull was not giving up its chase. Rama's head started to feel heavy and his vision blurred. If he slowed down, he would die; he knew that. Still, he couldn't run anymore. As this realization hit him, he tripped over something and fell. He tried to get back on his feet but he couldn't move. He fainted with fear and exhaustion.

* * *

Those running behind Rama could only see the back of the speeding bull through the thick cloud of dust it had kicked up. It was safer to get closer before shooting at the animal. But, by then, Rama may well be under its hooves or over its horns. Still, the soldiers hesitated to shoot. Nobody wanted to take the risky shot.

Chandra drew an arrow and strung it to his bow. He was going to take a chance and shoot at the bull. Wiping the beads of sweat on his forehead, Chandra took his stance and pulled the string. Just before he let the arrow fly, he stopped in confusion. The bull had halted! He realized that Rama had fallen. The beast seemed to be contemplating its next move.

Without blinking an eye, Chandra shot arrows at the

bull. As the animal hit the ground, the soldiers erupted in joy.

* * *

Rama slowly awoke to see an anxious Guna and Megha hovering over him. Men were fanning him and sprinkling water on his face. *I'm alive!* As the thought sunk in, Rama's eyes opened wide. He tried to sit up. His body ached as though an elephant had trampled over him. He felt sick and feverish, but relieved.

Sipping the tender coconut water offered to him, he stared at the bull that looked like a gigantic porcupine with countless arrows sticking out of its body. 'Thank God for our expert archers,' he sighed and smiled at Megha. Then his eyes fell on Chandra, who was bending over the bull, picking off the arrows.

'Who shot those arrows?' Rama asked the soldier next to him with a creeping suspicion. Chandra was very possessive of his arrows, and even during practice, he would retrieve them from targets whenever he could.

The soldier, unaware why Rama had asked that question, replied proudly, 'Prince Chandra did! If he hadn't shot them so expertly and quickly, God knows what the bull would have done.'

'Why did you all wait for so long before killing the bull?' Rama's loud voice and stony demeanour belied the rage that was building inside him. 'You wanted my brother to have his last hunt? Is that why? You were sent to protect us, not for entertainment at my expense.'

Before the bewildered soldier could reply, Rama stumbled to his feet and strode towards Chandra, pushing aside Megha's hand on his shoulder. 'Who asked you to help me? I'd have preferred death over rescue by your hand.' Rama's voice spewed venom. 'What if you had missed an arrow and hit me? Your recklessness could have taken my life. Or, maybe that's what you wanted. To eliminate me.'

Chandra looked startled. 'You had fainted, and the bull was ready to gore you. Instead of being angry with me, you should be thanking me. By the way, if I had killed you, Father would have sent me to prison, not given me the throne!'

'There were enough archers who could have saved me. You shoot arrows from behind like a coward, and now you are the champion?' Rama stormed off towards his mount. It was supposed to be his moment of glory, not his brother's yet again.

He rode behind the entourage with Megha next to him. Everyone was quiet. Rama felt even more depressed as the sound of the flowing river and the nightly noises from the forest started to fade. They would soon reach the city, where he would have to face his father. Shuddering at the thought, Rama dismissed his guards and rode further down along the riverbank instead of entering the city. Megha duly followed him.

'Chandra doesn't even like hunting. Why did he come along?' Rama threw a stone into the water in rage. 'I had almost roped in that bull, but now all of that is forgotten. Why did I risk my life? All because I wanted to prove to Father that I too am capable of bravery!

Why should I work this hard to prove my worthiness, Megha? The throne is my birthright.'

'Who are you angry with, Prince?'

Rama stretched out on the sand. 'Who am I angry with? Everyone who ruined my childhood by ridiculing me, ignoring me, and casting me out like garbage.'

'Prince, I don't think anyone did anything deliberately to humiliate you, especially Prince Chandra. He is not malicious.'

Rama shook his head. 'You don't understand what I go through. Chandra is my enemy, not my brother. I'm sure he instructed the soldiers to stop and let him shoot. He wanted to be a hero and reduce me to a nobody.'

Megha tried correcting his friend. 'Prince Chandra was the only one ready to take that risk—'

Rama cut him off, 'You can adore that two-faced cheat all you want, but be there for me when I need you. I don't have a lot of people I can trust.'

He got up and walked a little. Then he stopped and said, 'Megha, this is for your cousin's wedding.' He handed Megha a small cloth bag with gold coins.

Megha stared in surprise. 'Prince, I didn't tell you about the wedding expecting a gift. I'm sorry—'

Rama smiled. 'I know you never expect anything monetary from me. But let me share a little of your burden.'

Megha averted his gaze as his eyes moistened. 'You have a good heart, Prince. I hope you give your brother a chance to be in your life.'

9

Chandra went to visit his mother. Although it was late, he knew she would be awake. 'Ma, are you there?'

The door opened immediately. Chandra walked inside and sank into a luxurious settee. 'You have such comforts in your chamber, Mother,' he complained mockingly. 'It smells heavenly in here! Look at my chamber. All hardwood, and it smells like paint.'

'Your father wants to bring you boys up without any frills and fancies.' She smiled at him. 'What are you doing here at this hour? Aren't you tired? You should rest.' Though she was reprimanding him, he knew she was glad he was there.

'So you heard about today, Mother?' Chandra drawled, swirling the drink in the silver glass on the table. 'Is that why you are drinking yourself silly?'

This elicited a whack on his head. 'That is a herbal drink your father left behind! About today, what was all that drama, Chandra? A lion last time and a bull this time?' She rolled her eyes at him.

'Yes, Mother. Next time, it'll be a dog, a cat and then a rat. We have decided to lower our standards each time we fight.'

She laughed for a moment before saying, 'Rama hasn't come back yet. Do you think he's drinking somewhere? Or has he gone off hunting with friends?'

'Ma, let him be tonight. He is old enough to take care of himself. For now, I insist you focus on admiring your magnificent younger son.' Chandra puffed up his chest. He could not talk and joke with anyone else the way he could with her.

'What makes you think you are magnificent? Both of you are rogues,' she teased him back. That was good. It meant she was worrying less now.

'Are you joking, Mother? I'm the future Rajadhiraja, Raja Martanda Chandragupta and you are calling me a rogue?' Chandra dramatically jumped onto the settee and threw up his arm as if he were holding a sword.

Dattadevi laughed again till her eyes started to water. 'You skinny giraffe, get off the settee before you topple over! You don't want to be a Raja Martanda with broken bones.' He loved the way she laughed openly and freely like a child.

She looked towards the door and stopped laughing. Chandra followed her gaze. Looming large in the doorway was his brother.

'Rama! Come in, Son.' Dattadevi tried to sound cheerful, but Chandra knew it was contrived. He sat with his back to Rama, indicating that he didn't wish to be a part of the conversation his mother had initiated.

'Ma! You laugh when he declares himself king? All of you seem to have decided that he's the future monarch of the Guptas. When were you planning to give me the good news? That I'm to serve my little brother from now on?' Rama's voice croaked in angst.

'Does any of this look serious to you? Chandra was joking. Come here. Sit with us.' She walked towards the door to soothe her older son.

'You are no better than Father. At least he doesn't hide the fact that he hates me. Have a good time with your magnificent son.' Chandra heard a thud. He drew a sharp breath. What had Rama punched? Hopefully, the wall. The fading footsteps indicated that Rama was gone.

'How can we make him believe that we're not conspiring against him?' Dattadevi held her head in both hands, sinking into a chair next to Chandra's.

Chandra didn't attempt to soothe her. She had to be stricter with Rama and tell him that he was being unreasonable.

* * *

As Chandra walked towards his room, anger slowly rose in him like a storm. All he wanted were a few good moments with his mother, and Rama had to ruin that too. Chandra hated that she was always worried about Rama. As he neared his quarters, he saw Rama sitting on the porch of his quarters. At first, Chandra decided to ignore him and walk on. But then, he changed his mind. Someone had to break the ice between them.

'What do you want? Go away,' said Rama gruffly as Chandra approached him.

'Why are you so angry with me? Why would I even be considered for the throne when you are the first-born? Your imaginary ghosts are making everyone miserable, including you.'

'Don't play coy, Chandra. I know what you are planning. You dance to Father's tunes to ensure that you are the next king of the Guptas.'

Chandra stared at his brother. 'If Father likes me for who I am, I'm not complaining!'

Rama got up, looking furious. 'Why will you complain? I'm the one who should, for having a backstabber for a brother.'

Chandra glared at Rama. Angry words tumbled out of his mouth: 'I'm a backstabber because I work hard while you don't? When you go out and have a good time with Megha, I sit in the council meetings. When you catch up on your morning sleep, I get on with training. When you nap in the afternoon, I sit in the economics class. Have you ever thought Father might like me because I'm not a quitter?'

'Shut up and get lost. I know how to get the throne. You think you are smart, but I'm smarter.' Rama walked into his quarters, leaving Chandra angrier than before.

'Then start showing your smartness for a change. Why are you hiding it so well?' Chandra shouted after Rama. He headed back to his quarters. He felt foolish for having initiated a conversation with Rama. *Never again*, he swore as he collapsed on his bed, exhausted.

10

Chandra entered the parlour to the faint notes of the veena. With the usher gone, the richly decorated space was empty. The aroma of incense sticks and fresh flowers filled the air. But Chandra had no patience to enjoy any of that. He was eager to know why his father wanted to meet him that night.

Chandra walked towards the door left ajar at the far end of the parlour. Standing quietly in the doorway, he watched his father immersed in the music he was creating. His bare back bore signs of hard-fought battles, scars etched by weapons of all sorts – spears, knives and arrows. A warrior and a musician was a rare combination.

After a few moments, the king placed his instrument on the ground and prostrated before the large golden idol of Vishnu. He noticed Chandra when he turned.

'Chandra! Why didn't you come inside? Would you like to play a song for the Lord?' Samudragupta asked.

'Not today, Father,' Chandra said. After prostrating before the idol, he fell in step with Samudragupta as they walked out of the worship room.

'I heard you shot a bull under great pressure yesterday.' Samudragupta smiled approvingly at Chandra as they took their seats next to the window. The sprawling garden outside was pitch dark, except for the few lanterns and the fireflies that twinkled like stars.

'You did the right thing, Son. One who displays bravery when others hesitate is a true leader.' Chandra smiled modestly but beamed inwardly. Such high praise from his father was rare.

'Chandra, I feel it's time to move you from subduing lions and bulls to more intelligent beings – those who challenge your mind and intellect.' Chandra's heart thudded for a moment. What did his father have in mind for him?

'We are going to begin a war campaign in three months, a long and hard one this time. The aim is to conquer the independent provinces in the north.'

Samudragupta wrapped a shawl around himself to fight the cool breeze blowing in through the window. 'We can't let foreign tribes, the likes of the Kushans and the Shakas, conquer the smaller rulers and establish their power. We have to drive them out of Bharata, back to Persia.'

Chandra nodded but remained silent. There had to be more to the story. Was Father going to take him along?

Samudragupta came to the point quickly: 'I want you to be a part of the decision-making and governance in my absence. You are already attending public council meetings. From now on, attend the confidential ones too.'

Chandra stared at his father in disbelief.

Samudragupta smiled when he saw the bewilderment on his son's face. 'You are fifteen, which is a good point in life to become a man. We'll train you in the next few months in all the matters of state. Harisena, Guna and Lakshmidhara are the ministers we trust completely. And Commander Kritavarma, of course. We'll hold meetings with them every night till I depart. You must come tomorrow night to the meeting hall in the north wing. From there we will go to the 'secret room', as you used to call it!'

Chandra grinned. 'Oh, yes. The room with a hidden door! I was taken there once, and that too wearing a blindfold. I tried for months to find out where the camouflaged door was.'

'And, I know you found it!' Samudragupta smiled and got up. 'I'm not asking Rama to join the private council. He's not ready for the role. The council discusses matters that require discretion, and Rama speaks without thinking when he's angry or drunk. But your mother won't hear of it. So, you can't tell her about your involvement.'

Chandra nodded, but he felt panic rise. How would he keep things from his mother?

11

The next three months melted away like snow for Chandra. His days were full and exhausting with physical training, classes and the evening assembly. He also attended intense late-night meetings. His father and the ministers argued and discussed highly interesting and exciting issues, but they often left him with a headache.

Samudragupta spoke to him on the night before he left for his campaign. 'Chandra, be at the royal chariot at the first prahara. We will visit the temple of Lord Vishnu,' he instructed, as they got ready to disperse for the night.

'Let the boy sleep, King. He can join you when the farewell festivities begin,' said Harisena.

'I agree, let him sleep. I can barely keep myself awake at the first prahara,' said Kritavarma with an exaggerated yawn. Since Harisena and Kritavarma were the king's childhood friends, they had no hesitation in voicing their opinions before him.

'Do you all plan to be asleep when I'm leaving on a war campaign?' Samudragupta shook his head in mock disapproval.

Kritavarma bowed. 'Apologies, King. We will sit right here and go over the tax details with Lakshmidhara. Then again, that will also put us to sleep.'

'Next time, when you ask me to release war grants, I'll sanction goats instead of gold,' the usually mild Lakshmidhara growled. The finance minister was the quietest of the four friends.

Samudragupta eased out of his chair. 'Enough entertainment for one night. Let's get some sleep. Chandra, I do want you to come tomorrow morning with me. We're a prosperous kingdom only by Lord Vishnu's grace.'

* * *

Standing before the life-sized gold idols of Vishnu and Lakshmi, Chandra prayed hard for his father's safe return. Though he had seen his father leave on war campaigns before, he was too young then to understand the magnitude of danger to the king's life in a war.

When the priest's mantras reached a final crescendo, the bells rang, indicating that the prayers had ended. That meant his father would leave soon. Chandra's heart sank with anxiety and an unknown fear. Samudragupta, as if sensing his son's angst, strode out of the temple with an arm around Chandra's shoulders.

'You're as tall as me now, Chandra,' Samudragupta remarked, genuinely surprised. 'By the time I'm back, you'll be taller than Kritavarma.'

'I hope so, Father. One of my life goals is to be taller than the commander.' Chandra smiled, feeling pleased. His father knew how to divert his mind.

As they neared the chariot, the dozing charioteer got up instantly, fully alert now. Unlike the large retinues at other times, only four soldiers on horseback would follow the chariot today. With a soldier on one end and Kritavarma on the other flanking Samudragupta and Chandra, the chariot started. As soon as it moved, Chandra felt his father's weight on him and heard him scream, 'Get down, Chandra.'

On the floor of the chariot, the only things Chandra could hear were a thud, a neigh and a death-scream from behind. A soldier was dead. As Chandra crouched, his body held down by his father, his head spun from shock and confusion. The chariot raced ahead.

* * *

'Who, other than us, knew about our visit to the temple?' Samudragupta paced around the meeting room. He looked at the faces around him – Harisena, Lakshmidhara, Kritavarma, Queen Dattadevi and Chandra.

'Minister Guna and Prince Rama. We hadn't told the charioteer, the bodyguards or the priest beforehand,' Kritavarma replied gravely. The worry lines on his forehead had deepened into grooves. It was only an hour ago that the king had spotted the killer atop the temple aiming an arrow at him – just in time.

Samudragupta turned to the queen. 'Where was Rama last night? Who told him about the visit to the temple?'

'I was supposed to tell him but never got a chance,' she replied hesitantly. 'He was asleep when I went looking for him.'

Samudragupta's lips pursed slightly. 'Must have been drunk,' he muttered. The queen's eyes narrowed in disapproval, though she didn't respond to the comment.

'I have to start the journey in a few hours. Let's keep this attack a secret. We don't want people to panic. Investigate everyone who accompanied us – the soldiers, the charioteer and the priest. Find the culprits as quickly as you can.'

'There's just been an attack on your life. Do you have to go on the war campaign now?' Queen Dattadevi exclaimed, aghast.

'More reason to get out of town, don't you think?' Samudragupta's laughter did nothing to change the queen's disapproving look.

'My Queen, don't worry about the king. He is the best warrior out there with a well-trained army at his disposal. And I'll be here to safeguard the kingdom,' Kritavarma tried to soothe the queen.

'If everything is so safe, why was there an attempt on the king's life today?' Dattadevi's voice was polite, but not her words.

12

Three days after Samudragupta left Pataliputra, Chandra made an extraordinary discovery. He couldn't wait to share it with the ministers and the commander. The first one to arrive for the meeting that night, Chandra paced the room impatiently. All he wanted was for the door to open and people to walk in, but all he heard instead, for what seemed like an eternity, were the anklets of the female attendants in the passageway. Just when anxiety threatened to consume him, the door was flung open. To Chandra's relief, it was not just Kritavarma who entered but all four of them together.

Chandra began to speak even before they were done with their greetings and settled in their chairs. 'I've found out something important about the attempt on Father's life.' He saw the look of surprise on his listeners' faces.

'I found Commander Vijaya at the priest's house two nights ago. I thought he was there to question him. But, he visited the priest at midnight again. I found it suspicious.' Chandra stopped for breath. 'So, I followed him around today. He met some people on the outskirts of the city. They are gathering at his house tonight.'

Everyone was quiet for a few moments before Harisena spoke, gently but disapprovingly. 'Prince, this is a useful lead. But you put yourself in danger.'

'What business did Vijaya have with the priest?' Kritavarma knitted his brows. He sounded grave. Vijaya was a junior commander under him, and someone he trusted. Chandra knew he was going to start pacing soon, as he always did when anxious. He moved out of the commander's way.

Walking up and down the small room, Kritavarma spoke in a clipped tone, 'Vijaya was in charge of recruiting soldiers. If he's a traitor, then I have to weed out his recruits too.' Chandra was pleased that Kritavarma had taken him seriously.

Kritavarma took out an arrow from a leather case he was carrying. 'This was the arrow shot at the king. It is the same as the ones we use for long-range shooting. Vijaya must have provided these to the enemy.'

Chandra felt bewildered. He hadn't connected Vijaya to the assassination attempt so directly. After a few moments of silence, Harisena sighed. 'I feel Vijaya is only an accomplice. There must be someone more powerful behind him. We have to stop them before they cause any real damage.'

Kritavarma stopped and said, 'Oh, I will. If I kick Vijaya's backside hard enough, the truth will fall out of his mouth easily.'

Chandra chuckled. But his mirth disappeared quickly. *What truth will they discover from Vijaya? Who had tried to kill Father in his own city?*

* * *

That night, a guard in the Magadha security uniform walked towards a small, abandoned roadside temple. It was eerily quiet, except for the sound of the river Ganga flowing in full force a little distance away. He knocked on the closed door of the temple.

When the door opened, the guard tried to peer inside. Kritavarma blocked the door from the guard's view with his massive frame.

The guard said, 'Sir, someone has just arrived at Commander Vijaya's house. My tent is ready for you. There are two good horses within reach, as you'd instructed.' The man, a night guard at Vijaya's house, waited for Kritavarma's reply.

Kritavarma shoved a few gold coins into his hand. 'Shut your mouth about tonight. Or else you won't live to enjoy this gold.'

The guard nodded in agreement and left. As soon he was out of sight, another man stepped out of the shadows.

'Why are you here, Prince?' Kritavarma said as he rubbed his hands together to warm them. The cold air pierced his skin like sharp needles. 'Go back to the palace and get some sleep. I'll take care of these brutes.'

'But this is far more thrilling than sleep,' replied Chandra, dismissing the commander's suggestion.

'Well then, get ready to brave the cold and some snitches.' Kritavarma patted Chandra on the back. He might be the prince of Magadha, but to Kritavarma, who had never married himself, Chandra was like a son. He had known the boy since the day he was born. He had taught him to ride his first horse, swing his first sword and shoot his first arrow.

From a distance, they could see the tents silhouetted in the dark across the street from Vijaya's house. The night guard's tent was in the middle. As he had promised, two sturdy horses were grazing close by.

Pushing the flap aside, they entered the tent cautiously. Once their eyes adjusted to the darkness, they crouched on the floor, watching Vijaya's house through a tiny crack in the flap. Nothing happened for a frustratingly long time. All they could see were occasional shadows of people in the draped windows.

Their wait ended with a burly man waddling out of Vijaya's house, clutching a bag. He clumsily mounted a horse that an attendant brought up to him.

'Let him ride a little distance before we go after him. Just in case someone is watching from inside. Given his riding skills, it won't be hard to catch up with him,' said Kritavarma.

As the man struggled to ride with his burly body squeezed on horseback, a tall and lithe hooded figure materialized from a side alley. There was a swift exchange: the burly man waddled on after handing over the sack and the horse to the new man, who rode off.

'I'll chase the man on the horse, Commander. You take care of the other one.'

'No, Prince. I will chase—'

Before Kritavarma could complete his sentence, Chandra dashed towards the horses. Soon he was chasing the man, who was quickly disappearing from view.

13

Chandra was determined to catch the man and seize the sack. For all he knew, it could just be a bag of rice, but it was equally possible that there was valuable information in it. A few more minutes of the chase brought him to a rough, muddy track that ran between farmland and a stream.

Chandra threw a sharp spear at the rider. The man slowed, turned around and started towards Chandra.

When he stopped before Chandra, there was a look of surprise on the man's face. 'A prince of Magadha chasing vagabonds at night? Are you too poor to even hire patrolmen?' the rider drawled in the Magadha dialect of Prakrit, but it was apparent he was not a native speaker. The way he spat out words betrayed a lack of sophistication.

'Who are you?' Chandra ignored the man's words, though he hadn't expected to be recognized.

'Not a nice man.' The rider came closer to Chandra. 'Lad, go home. Don't mess with my business.'

'I'll go if you give me the sack,' said Chandra, with a braveness he didn't feel. He knew he had to keep the man talking until Kritavarma found them. The man seemed to be a seasoned criminal. He didn't even seem to register the blood oozing from his ankle where Chandra's spear had struck him. He had strong biceps and a face crisscrossed with scars.

'This is not playtime, kid. I kill people for real.' The rider smiled crookedly and came even closer to Chandra. 'Go home to your mother. You are too young to die.'

Then, the man struck Chandra—not with the sword but with his hand, straight across the face—once, then twice. While Chandra reeled under the assault, the man stabbed Chandra's horse in the belly, making it howl and collapse. That proved to be Chandra's lucky break. The shrieks from Chandra's injured horse confused the rider's horse. It started neighing and bucking. As the rider tried to steady his mount, Chandra thrust his sword into his thigh.

The man cursed and grunted and fell from his horse. 'You leave me no choice but to kill you, you young devil.'

Chandra's grip on his sword tightened as he saw the man stagger towards him. The man swung his sword at Chandra, but he sidestepped to escape the blow. Unfortunately, Chandra's foot hit a small boulder, and he tripped and fell flat on his back.

Chandra panicked as the gigantic sword neared his throat. Summoning every bit of strength in his body, Chandra held his sword above his head and blocked the thrust. Though he continued to resist the sword, he knew it was only a matter of time before his arms gave way and his head was separated from his body.

Then, suddenly, the pressure on his arms eased. The man, threatening to slit his throat a moment ago, was now staggering. Chandra looked up to see what had caused that miracle. Kritavarma held the rider's neck in a death grip.

* * *

The interrogation chamber looked deadly. There was a variety of instruments of torture, from spiked iron boots to leather belts hanging on the windowless walls. Chandra stared at the men in front of him – the brute who had accosted him, the burly man who had carried the sack, and Vijaya.

Vijaya and the brute had warrior-like scars on their bodies. The burly man had a large stomach and a thick gold chain around his neck.

Kritavarma was talking to Harisena in hushed tones as they pored over a palm-leaf document they had found in the bag of Chandra's assaulter. Chandra caught the commander's gaze and nodded slightly to indicate that they should start.

Kritavarma flashed the letter before Vijaya. 'Who are you helping, traitor? This document has details of all the fifty fort walls and their security protocols. And, it has a route map of the king's war campaign. Who were you sending this to?' Kritavarma's voice grew angrier. Vijaya remained unaffected. Kritavarma punched him in the stomach.

Harisena intervened. 'Commander, don't hurt him yet. Let's give him five minutes.'

'Where are you from?' Harisena asked the other two. His polite question did not get an answer.

'Wait a minute,' said Chandra, walking up to the brute. Something had caught his attention. 'Lift your left foot,' he said to the man. The man twitched his nose and acted as if Chandra didn't exist.

'They don't understand words,' Kritavarma muttered and shoved the man to the ground. Chandra lifted his foot to inspect a tattoo that started on the sole and spread to the ankle – the image of a crouched lion.

'A Shaka soldier.' Kritavarma's eyes looked murderous as he turned to Vijaya. Kritavarma dug his thumbs into Vijaya's throat. Vijaya looked like his eyeballs were going to pop out.

'You've sided with our worst enemy. I want to kill you right here, right now.' Kritavarma's fingers dug deeper into the soft flesh of Vijaya's throat. 'But I need answers. Are you ready to talk yet?'

After a few more hours of private time with Kritavarma, Vijaya divulged a name – Shashi, a junior minister who worked under Lakshmidhara in the finance department. At the sight of the knife near his throat, the burly man squealed that he was a Shaka strategist. His work was to formulate a plan to attack the Gupta fort using Vijaya's information. The brute had been heading to Sourashtra to deliver the document to the Shaka king, Rudrasimha.

'There's someone else in the picture here. Shashi and Vijaya couldn't have put together all this information on their own,' Harisena concluded firmly.

14

The next day, it was back to the interrogation chamber, with only Minister Shashi facing them. Chandra hadn't slept a wink the previous night thinking of the rot festering inside their trusted circles. Shashi and Vijaya (and who knew how many more), who had taken an oath to protect the kingdom, had turned traitor. The disloyalty they had uncovered had frightened Chandra at first, but now all he felt was rage. He couldn't wait to destroy the traitors.

'Who is backing you, Shashi?' Chandra's voice had a harshness nobody had heard before. The bar with protruding nails that Chandra twirled menacingly made Shashi shiver visibly.

'You are too young to underst—' Shashi began to speak, casting a nervous glance at the sinister-looking stick.

'No, he's not too young to understand traitors. Answer him!' Kritavarma's angry words made Shashi jump in fright.

'Nobody is backing me. I collect information from Vijaya and a few others to pass it on to Rudrasimha.' His voice croaked and his hands shook.

Chandra pulled out his dagger and ran it down Shashi's thigh. Shashi wailed like a baby. He sobbed and said, 'The Shaka king is planning an attack on our city, but I don't know any details. I've given him information about our military, our king's campaign ...' He lowered his voice and added hesitantly, '... and a little about our finances.'

Chandra wanted to plunge the dagger deep into him, but he controlled himself.

'You are certainly not capable of putting together this strategy. You are protecting someone,' Harisena said firmly, flashing the palm-leaf document before Shashi. 'Who is it?'

Shashi continued to wail but didn't say a word. There was no use talking to him any further. Someone had bought his silence with either money or a threat, probably both. Kritavarma signalled the guard to take him away.

'Do we have enough forces if the Shaka king attacks?' Chandra asked Kritavarma after Shashi had left.

'Sourashtra is more than a thousand miles to our west. It'll take the Shaka army at least two months to get here. Our scouts haven't told us about any activity along our borders. So, his forces aren't anywhere near us yet. But we'll have to be vigilant,' said Kritavarma.

Chandra's head started to pound. He had had enough of the claustrophobic interrogation chamber. He thought of going to his mother, but almost immediately dismissed the idea. Guilt tore at him for hiding things from her. He headed to the wrestling ring instead. Throwing a few punches would help ease his frustration.

* * *

Atma stared out of the window of his house. It was night, and Shashi, who was supposed to meet him that afternoon, still hadn't turned up.

'I think something is wrong, Vidura. Shashi should have come by now,' Atma said to Vidura, his assistant for over two decades.

'Can he get you in trouble, Sir? Don't worry. I'll take the blame on myself.' Vidura wanted to show his loyalty.

'It won't come to that.' Atma shook his head. 'I made it clear to Shashi that his family will be safe only as long as he protects me.'

'How about Vijaya, Sir? He looks like a trouble-maker.'

Atma dismissed Vidura's concern. 'Vijaya doesn't even know I exist. He thinks Shashi is the mastermind.'

Vidura nodded in agreement. 'Should I check with Shashi's wife?'

'Why are you so thick? There may be people watching that idiot's house if he's in trouble.' Atma continued in a tone of disgust, 'Vijaya put together that failed plot to assassinate Samudragupta. Shashi convinced me it would work.'

Atma stretched his legs. Though he was seventy years old, his mind was sharp as a knife. Nothing would stand in the way of his agenda of exacting revenge on Samudragupta.

15

Chandra read the scroll Harisena gave him. It was a letter from his father.

'Minister Harisena, an attack on us by the Shaka king is a joke, so don't panic. He's too bankrupt to wage war against us. However, find out who's behind Vijaya and Shashi. There's no need to bother the queen with any of these details.

The news from here is that, except for King Matila, all the others have submitted without a battle. We have defeated Matila too, despite the support he had from the Naga kings. Tomorrow we will head north towards Gandhara.'

Chandra scowled after reading the letter twice. 'I don't understand Father. How can an imminent Shaka attack not cause panic?'

Kritavarma agreed with Chandra and tore the letter to shreds. They couldn't afford to have it end up in the wrong hands. 'If we don't stem the rot now, it may be too late.'

Harisena disagreed. 'Let it be for now. We have to make the renegade believe that the case is closed with the arrests of Vijaya and Shashi.'

'But we still don't have a clue about the identity of the main traitor,' said Chandra. 'Minister Harisena, you are the one who keeps saying there is someone powerful behind Shashi and Vijaya. Aren't we better off hunting down the man helping our enemy?'

'The plot will unfold with time, Prince.' Harisena patted Chandra on the back. 'Now eat these fluffy pooris before they become cold. I don't know how the commander stays fit with all this rich food,' said Harisena, helping himself to a mouthful. They had met that morning in Kritavarma's sparsely furnished, brightly lit dining area. The commander employed very few people, one of them a great cook, making his house ideal for meetings.

'My life is hard,' said Kritavarma with mock gravity. 'Once I retire, I want to eat all I want for at least a month. Something you've done all your life.'

Harisena laughed. 'Focus on crimes and traitors, Commander. Not on what I eat.'

Chandra envied their easy friendship. He had never had a close friend, except for Pranava, a pleasant fellow who studied with him.

'Why should we keep this a secret from Mother? She may have good insights into the matter,' said Chandra unhappily, as he walked out with Harisena an hour later. The summer heat felt like lava against the skin. He missed the carefree days when he could escape to one of their summer palaces.

'He doesn't want to worry your mother.' Though this sounded like a poor excuse to Chandra, he didn't press for details. He decided to take a break from the political mayhem.

'I'll go riding with Pranava today. Can you please tell the commander?'

* * *

Pranava was the son of a senior commander who had died in a battle five years back. Samudragupta had provided accommodation for him along with his mother inside the palace fort. Pranava went to school along with the princes and the other ministers' children. Chandra liked Pranava's natural wit, friendliness, and the fact that he rushed headlong into things, much like him!

As they waited by the river for a few others to join them, Pranava asked, 'Prince, I don't see you in the evenings anymore. What is going on?'

Chandra smiled. 'If I told you, I'd have to kill you!'

'Try me.' Pranava grinned, as he circled on his horse. He could never stay still.

Chandra laughed. Pranava treated him like a friend, not like a prince.

'I'll tell you some other time. By the way, who's joining us today?' asked Chandra, changing the topic. Pranava always gathered a group of three or four people, so that they could camp at night.

'Wait till you see them.' Pranava flashed a mysterious smile at Chandra.

'Oh, no ... I don't want an experimental crowd today,'

Chandra groaned. Last time, Pranava had brought two of their classmates, who had bored Chandra to death with their tales.

Soon, they heard hoof beats. Four horses came into view. Two of the riders were familiar to Chandra. They were the sons of senior commanders. Chandra had never seen the other two before. They were about the same age as him, but they had fair skin and light golden hair! Where had Pranava found them?

'Good evening, Prince Chandra. Thank you for inviting us.' One of them bowed and spoke in perfect Magadhi Prakrit. So, they were locals. Chandra smiled politely and looked at Pranava, waiting for an introduction. The two boys looked a little tense.

'Prince Chandra, this is Soma and this is Sura,' Pranava introduced them. 'Twins. Their ancestors were Greeks.'

'We don't see your community here. But you speak our language quite well,' Chandra remarked as they started riding, following Pranava's lead.

'Our ancestors came here when Queen Helena married King Chandragupta Maurya. About two hundred of us live a few miles from here. But we're no longer purely Greek,' Soma, the chattier of the two, replied.

Chandra was relaxed during the rest of the hour-long journey into the forest.

'Soma is a great slinger. He can catapult anything he can see or hear,' said Pranava, visibly proud of his friend.

Before Chandra could get off the horse, a small wild berry fell on the ground and splattered into a purple pulp. Then another one, and another. As everyone watched in amazement, Soma catapulted small stones at the tree, and soon, there was a mountain of berries around them.

'That is amazing! What speed and accuracy!' Chandra exclaimed. 'You have to teach me at least the basics of catapulting.' Turning to Sura, he said, 'Are you an expert slinger too? Or do you have some other mind-blowing talent of your own?'

Sura laughed. 'I'm the boring twin. I study the similarities and differences between Indian and Greek astrology.'

Chandra nodded. 'That sounds very interesting too. You both should visit us at the palace. We can exchange ideas.' Chandra was always eager to make new friends and learn from people.

'You're kind, Prince. It would be our privilege to visit you at the palace.' Soma and Sura bowed to Chandra with a smile.

16

'A letter from King Samudragupta,' King Pushyavarma exclaimed, opening the letter handed to him. He was the ruler of Kamarupa, a small province in north-eastern Bharata. He had known Samudragupta long before they both became kings.

'What does he say?' The queen was incredibly proud of her husband's long-time friendship with the mighty Gupta monarch.

'He has asked us to keep an army of ten thousand foot-soldiers and five thousand horsemen ready, in case Pataliputra asks for help. I guess he senses a threat while he's away.'

'But why's he still out waging wars? He practically has all of Bharata under his control! I feel sorry for Queen Dattadevi. I'm sure it's not easy having a husband who is always playing with danger.'

'He is not an ordinary king. He's waging these wars for the good of our country.'

As the king got ready for a nap, his fourteen-year-old daughter barged into the room, panting. Chasing her was her nine-year-old brother.

'Father! Rahula is tearing my book,' squealed Dhruva, stopping before her father. Pulling her gently by her shoulder, the king settled her on the settee next to him. 'Father, that's my teacher's book. I'll be in trouble if this silly boy tears it.'

'She keeps teasing me that I'm brainless. I want her to stop saying that if she wants her book back.' Rahula, all flustered, fanned the palm-leaf book dangerously.

Dhruva smirked at her brother. 'Why do you get offended if someone speaks the truth?'

Holding his son down, Pushyavarma took the book from his hand. 'Don't you both have sword practice now?' the king asked, hoping to drive them out so that he could nap.

Dhruva pouted. 'I don't want to go. I don't want to use weapons against anyone.'

Rahula, now seated in his mother's lap, seized the opportunity for payback. 'But, Father, she doesn't need a weapon to kill someone. She can bore them to death by just talking.'

Pushyavarma intervened before the kids could start bickering again. 'Dhruva, you must learn at least the basics of using a sword. One day, you'll be a queen. You should be able to command an army if you need to.'

'Father! I wish I were a commoner who could learn the scriptures and lead a life of peace.'

'You are learning the scriptures, Dhruva. But you must also fulfil your father's wishes,' the queen reprimanded her daughter and turned to her son. 'And, you, Rahula, have you been attending the scripture lessons?'

'He missed them last week, Mother,' Dhruva said. 'At this rate, he'll be a cowherd cutting grass with his sword, at best.'

Rahula tried to pounce on his sister but was pulled back by his mother. He hurled another insult at her instead. 'You'll only be a sanyasin and not a queen, ever.'

* * *

The Shaka king Rudrasimha's new scroll to Atma had been anything but pleasant. The king had given him an ultimatum – either Atma should come up with a plan to defeat the Guptas, or he would lose his connections with the Shakas. Atma had to act fast. Rudrasimha was his only hope of avenging Samudragupta. He couldn't afford to sever ties with him.

Atma did not have any access to confidential information since Shashi and Vijaya were arrested six months ago. That evening, he was out on a mission to recruit a new informant.

'Why don't you wait right here, Sir?' said a concerned Vidura. 'I'll bring the boy to you. Where we're going is not a good part of Pataliputra.'

Atma shook his head. 'I can't risk anyone seeing me. Bring him to the river.'

They were on a street that was getting increasingly busy and filthy. Soon, there were loud voices everywhere – hawkers peddling their wares, drunken men brawling, women shouting at their kids, dogs barking and crows cawing. A thick, revolting stench hung in the air. It was the eastern edge of the city, where poverty reigned and cheap taverns ruled the neighbourhood.

As Vidura walked towards a tavern, Atma limped alone, with only his thoughts for company. He relived the events that had got him ousted from Samudragupta's council. Atma had been the prime minister and advisor to Samudragupta's father for decades. But, Samudragupta, after taking over Magadha, had refused to take Atma's financial and military advice.

Atma had reasoned with Samudragupta patiently in a meeting, 'If you win wars, you must bring home the wealth. Protecting Bharata from foreign invaders by uniting it under your rule can't be the only reason to go into a battle. I don't see why you should dishonour your father's sound practices.' Samudragupta had been quiet.

Then, one morning Atma had heard the heartbreaking news that Harisena had replaced him as prime minister. Atma was demoted to being one of the king's many advisors. Furious, he'd confronted Samudragupta. 'You can't make a novice like Harisena the prime minister of a large kingdom just because he's your friend. You've stripped me of my position only because I opposed your plans. A sycophant is not what a king needs as his right-hand man.' Atma knew he was in trouble as soon as the words were out of his mouth.

Samudragupta had formed a small private council of ministers and commanders, and Atma was not a part of it. Atma had then gone on to gather a covert group of people to protest against Samudragupta's war policies – not out of malice but with the sole aim of making Samudragupta change his mind. Unfortunately, the wimpy protesters he'd recruited had squealed that Atma was the man behind them. That had marked the end of his career as a political leader. Samudragupta had banished him from the court completely.

You'll pay for this, King, you'll pay for this dearly, Atma had vowed silently. He'd eventually sided with the Shaka king, Rudrasimha, a man who harboured a similar hatred for Samudragupta.

17

Rama raised a brow quizzically at the man who approached him. Nobody spoke to anybody in the tavern. Everyone just drank, smoked and ate.

'Prince,' Vidura bent closer to Rama and whispered. He was cautious not to let the others hear him. But he need not have worried given the din, with everyone talking at once and the tavern-keeper yelling at those who didn't pay. 'Minister Atma is waiting for you outside. Please follow me. Only you.'

Rama heard the impudence in Vidura's voice. Instead of anger, he felt panic. *Good God, the man knows who I am.* His head reeled. He always got away with his disguise in that tavern. Everyone else there was too drunk to notice him.

What does the old minister want from me? He looked at Megha, who appeared as taken aback as him. Vidura was already walking out of the tavern.

'Go with him,' Megha urged Rama. 'I think that's Vidura, Atma's assistant. You have to meet the minister, now that he knows you're here.'

'Father will feed me to hungry lions if he hears that I'm here or that I'm meeting that old traitor.'

Rama followed Vidura. The horse wagons rattling on the narrow, cobbled street threatened to knock him down. 'Where are you taking me? Couldn't you find a place with better roads?' Rama snapped at Vidura when there was nobody around them. He had planned to visit the dancer Urmila after a few drinks. *I am meeting an old owl instead.* Rama cursed his fate. Finally, the street ended in a narrow dirt road that led to the river.

'Wait here, Prince,' Vidura stopped Rama and signalled him to sit on an abandoned stone bench.

'There're bird droppings all over. Where do I sit? Whatever it is that your old master has to say, it better be good.' Rama winced in pain as he sat down. There were blisters on his feet. He'd gone barefoot to the tavern to merge with the crowd.

'Prince.' Rama was startled to hear a voice behind him. Atma, in the guise of a commoner, walked around to face him.

'Why are you in disguise, Minister? Planning to visit the tavern with me?' Rama tried to hide his nervousness with a joke.

Atma ignored Rama's words. 'Have you seen yourself lately, Prince? Do you look like the future king of Magadha?'

Stung by Atma's reproach, Rama glowered. 'Look who's talking! The man who got kicked out of the king's council.' Rama got up to leave. 'I've been taught to respect elders. Don't make me cross the line of civility.'

'Sit down and listen to me if you want to become a king. Your brother represents your father in the court in his absence. Do you understand what that means?' He did not wait for an answer and continued, 'The king has chosen Prince Chandra as his heir, not you.'

Atma's words pierced Rama like a knife. Managing to control his raging emotions, he said, 'How do you know that? Even if it's the truth, why're you telling me? Whether Chandra becomes the king, or I do, how does it matter to you?'

'Your father was unjust to me, and now he's being unfair to you. I want to help you because I want fairness in the Gupta kingdom – as it was during your grandfather's times. If you trust me, meet me here tomorrow at the same time. Otherwise, feel free to suffer your fate. Don't discuss this meeting with anyone, not even with your mother or your friend.'

Rama watched Atma limp away holding Vidura's shoulder. *Should I trust this man?* As Rama spent the night tossing and turning, a thought kept haunting him. *If Father appointed Chandra as his representative, why didn't Mother tell me about it?* The more he thought, the more he felt he was alone. No one supported him. Atma was not a friend, but at least he was offering to help him become the king. The old man's ulterior motives were irrelevant; all that mattered to Rama was that he should become the next king of Magadha. By the end of the night, Rama had made his decision. He was going to accept Atma's offer.

18

The Shaka king, Rudrasimha, read aloud the letter from Atma.

'*Prince Rama, the elder son of Samudragupta, is not on the best terms with his father, which will work in our favour. Please give me a few months to make him useful. He will undoubtedly bring about the demise of the Gupta empire. Then, I'll make sure the Shaka flag flies high in Magadha.*'

Rudrasimha crumpled the letter and threw it away. The chair that seated Rudrasimha's bulk creaked as he shifted. His pockmarked face looked murderous. 'Atma is old and delusional. I'd told him that Pataliputra should be ours before Samudragupta returns. But the old goat is still making these elaborate plans.'

Taking another swig of his drink, Rudrasimha grunted like an angry animal. He had been waiting for years to avenge the humiliation meted out to him by Samudragupta. When Atma had come forward to help him in his mission, he had become hopeful. But thus far, Atma had only made empty promises.

'You don't seem to feel the rage I do.' Rudrasimha knitted his brows in irritation at his minister Kedara. The minister, a tiny man, shrunk in his chair.

'A coup has to be carefully plotted before it is executed, King.' Kedara's voice was almost a whisper. 'Atma seems to have a good plan for a change.'

'Minister, are you suggesting that we wait for that dim-witted prince to help us? Let's attack Pataliputra before Samudragupta heads home from his war campaign.' Rudrasimha's voice rose so high, it squeaked.

Kedara replied, 'Marching east as far as Pataliputra from here is not an easy task. Samudragupta's vassals and allies are stationed along the route. Our small force will be destroyed before we reach there.'

'Stop being so pessimistic!' Rudrasimha snapped at Kedara. 'Think instead. Allies and vassals always want freedom. Send them a message asking them to join hands with us.' The Shaka king threw his silver cup against the wall. It fell to the ground, and the red liquid spilt all over.

Rudrasimha's face contorted with anger as he thought of the time Samudragupta had ambushed his beloved city of Ujjaini. Many southern invaders had already ravaged Ujjaini, but Samudragupta's attack had come as a shock to him, because there had never been any bad blood between them.

Rudrasimha had to take his army from Sourashtra and head to Ujjaini, which was a good six hundred miles away. In the first three days, it was a closely fought battle between him and Samudragupta. Having fought dozens of campaigns in the northern Bharata, Samudragupta didn't have a big army. However, by the fourth day, the Gupta army had grown ten times with the aid they received from an ally. Rudrasimha had no more resources left. He had been forced to concede and call a truce. But when he met Samudragupta and proposed that the Shakas and the Guptas become allies, Samudragupta had laughed.

'An ally is someone who is an equal or a friend. You will be my vassal. You can rule your land by paying us taxes and by following the rules we set.'

Rudrasimha had lost his temper. 'In this part of Bharata, I am a powerful ruler. Don't invite trouble for yourself by waging war in my homeland.'

'Your homeland is Persia, not Bharata. Let's continue the war. When I win, you have to leave your throne and head back to your real home,' Samudragupta had derided.

It was true that the Shakas were a nomadic tribe in Persia. However, they had been ruling over western and northern Bharata for close to four centuries now. How could Samudragupta still taunt him as a foreigner?

Short of resources, Rudrasimha had swallowed his pride and accepted the status of a vassal. Samudragupta had humiliated him further by throwing a pity tax exemption at him for five years. But in return, Rudrasimha had to swear his allegiance to the Gupta empire.

'The Shakas must not wage wars against the Gupta empire or its allies,' Samudragupta had dictated, while his ministers inscribed the terms on copper plates. 'I won't invade you as long as you abide by the rules. If there's even a tiny whiff of doubt about your loyalty, you're finished.'

Pulling himself away from his thoughts, Rudrasimha spoke to Kedara, 'Samudragupta knows that we plotted to kill him. If we don't conquer Pataliputra before his return, he will butcher us.'

19

Atma looked at the Ganga making her way through rocks and ravines. The chill of Margashira was unbearable as he waited for Rama. It had been three months since Rama had started collaborating with him. In the three months, Atma had achieved a near miracle: he had convinced the inherently lazy and supremely adamant Rama to attend classes, training sessions and public council meetings. Now in the groove, Rama was doing well. That evening, Atma planned to push Rama into Harisena's inner circle.

Rama was never late, but he took his own time before he spoke. Atma knew this was power play. Rama obeyed him for the most part but didn't trust him completely.

Soon Rama arrived. When he got off his horse, his dog came panting after him. Rama ignored Atma and gave the dog water and food. Working with Rama required the patience of a saint.

Atma observed his prodigy while he waited. Rama had lost weight and looked fit. He looked nothing like the man who hid in a tavern and drank. As soon as Rama was done tending to the dog, Atma got to the point. 'I've an important piece of news. But you have to be cautious in using it to your advantage.'

He explained the plan to Rama.

* * *

The next night, Rama walked with Harisena towards a building that housed the meeting halls. He'd told Harisena after the evening assembly that he wanted to attend their private meeting that night. The surprise on Harisena's face was unmistakable. Rama wondered if it was because he knew about their secret meetings or because he'd asked to be a part of it.

Settling down on a soft, feather-cushioned chair, Rama realized that he had never been to this place before. Somehow, he didn't regret it. These halls and the people who gathered here suffocated him.

As they waited for the others to join in, Rama only exchanged a polite smile or a nod when his gaze met Harisena's. Neither of them tried to break the silence. Rama had distanced himself from the minister a long time ago because of Harisena's closeness to Chandra.

Their wait ended as Kritavarma and Chandra walked in together, laughing about something. A wave of jealousy washed over Rama at the comfortable relationship his brother shared with these men. When they saw Rama, they stood still for a puzzled moment.

Chandra took the chair farthest from him, while Kritavarma greeted him, 'Prince, good to see you.' Nodding at Kritavarma, Rama looked at Harisena, impatient to get the conversation started. The sooner it was over, the better.

'Prince Rama is here to share a matter of importance,' said Harisena without preamble, sensing Rama's unease.

Rama got to the point directly, 'I found pieces of this scroll by the riverside. I glued them together. It looks like there is a plan to attack Pataliputra.'

He handed Harisena a letter that was torn but crudely patched up. Atma had given it to him and coached him on what to say. Now, as Rama parroted the rehearsed words, he wondered if he sounded convincing. As Harisena read the letter, Rama recollected his conversation with Atma.

'There may be an attack on Pataliputra,' Atma had told him, showing him the tattered letter.

Rama had panicked. 'We must report this to Kritavarma right away.'

'We can. But then, Chandra will be the one working with Kritavarma to contain the attack. What will you gain from this, Prince? How long do you want to wait for others to take you seriously? And, if I can be blunt, none of them ever will, especially not your father. You must be assertive and lead the army in case of an attack.'

'Are you joking, Minister? I can barely hold a sword, leave alone lead an army into battle! Are you helping me or sending me on a suicide mission?'

'You have to take risks if you want to rule Magadha one day.' These words had made Rama bring that ludicrous offer to Kritavarma that night.

Rama snapped out of his thoughts when he saw Harisena pass the letter to Kritavarma. To Rama's disappointment, the minister betrayed no emotions. He had expected a more animated reaction than that.

'This letter certainly calls for immediate action,' said Kritavarma carefully, further deflating Rama's mood.

'We appreciate you bringing this to our notice, Prince. We will station more men on the northern borders where the enemy seems to be planning their entry,' said Kritavarma. Before he could pass on the letter to Chandra, Rama snatched it.

'Commander! I am not a scout who brought you information. Stop dismissing me like I don't matter.' He controlled his temper and added, 'I want to be involved in the efforts to counter this attack. And ... I want to be a part of running the state in Father's absence.'

Harisena intervened before things could get out of hand: 'Prince, it would be our privilege to have you as one of the decision-makers. We all want only the best for our kingdom.' He paused for a second. 'Let me send a scroll to the king asking for his permission. I am sure he'll be delighted that you wish to get involved with stately matters.'

Atma was right. It was Father who'd included Chandra in the private council, throwing me out. Rama's stomach tightened with hurt, rejection and rage.

* * *

Chandra was dumbstruck when he'd heard what Rama had to say. He asked Harisena as soon as his brother left, 'Why would someone scatter pieces of an important scroll at the riverbank? That too in a manner that it could be put together meaningfully?'

Harisena nodded. 'The circumstances under which the scroll was found are certainly suspect.'

Kritavarma agreed. 'Prince Rama has been putting in tremendous work lately. Let's encourage him by investigating the information he's brought us.' He added after a pause, 'Even though it's probably fake.'

Harisena said, 'We will soon know if this information is real or not. Let's be alert.'

Why had Rama changed so drastically in the last few months? It bothered Chandra, but he decided not to act on his suspicion – at least for the time being. *There may not be an attack at all.*

* * *

As it happened, there *was* an attack within a month of Rama delivering the scroll. Kritavarma asked both the brothers to accompany him to the troubled area. However, the attackers turned out to be a small band of outlaws from the land of the Nagas, their archenemy. A few hours after the Gupta army had counter-attacked, the enemy vanished.

'Forget us, these hooligans didn't even deserve a high-ranked soldier,' quipped Kritavarma as they rode back to the city.

'Wonder why the Nagas planned this joke of an attack,' agreed Chandra.

Hearing Chandra's words, Rama's temper rose, but he refrained from lashing out. Something else was bothering him. The assaulters had been abnormally kind towards him. *Did Minister Atma stage the attack? Was he making a mistake by trusting the old minister as Megha often said?* He shrugged off the thought. *Atma knows what is best.*

20

Rama met Atma in bright daylight in a crowded marketplace. They sat next to each other on a stone bench, pretending to be strangers waiting for a wagon.

Rama looked at his feet and said, 'Father has left Katripura and—'

'And now he's going towards Ahichatra,' Atma interrupted Rama. 'Prince, I have a map of his war campaign. Tell me something that I don't know.'

'I'm not a part of Harisena's secret cult, and I'll never be. I can only tell you what I know, not what you want to know,' Rama snapped. He hated it when Atma spoke in a tone that said, '*You need to improve so much more.*'

After fuming for a few minutes, Rama remembered something. 'A scuffle broke out in the assembly yesterday morning.' He told Atma about the Atavikas, a cluster of tribal kingdoms in the Vindhya mountains, who hadn't paid taxes. 'Other vassals were angry that we're letting the Atavikas go free.' Atma did not interrupt Rama. 'I think the Atavikas are rebelling.'

'How did Harisena handle them?' asked Atma casually.

Rama shrugged. 'He changed the topic.'

That night, in the dim light of an oil lamp, Atma wrote a short, crisp letter to the Shaka king. Then he went to bed.

* * *

Chandra entered through the door that was built into the wall and closed it behind him. He ran down the flight of stairs. Now that Rama attended their nightly meetings, the group met in the secret room whenever they needed to discuss anything privately. Samudragupta had asked Harisena to exercise caution when Rama was around.

'Am I late?' Chandra inquired sheepishly, running his hand through his hair. The ministers and Kritavarma had already seated themselves in the dimly lit room. He was sure he looked like an urchin with his uncombed hair after riding. He had planned to end the ride half an hour earlier to get ready for this meeting, but as always, that had remained just a plan.

'You're not late. We're early.' Harisena smiled to put him at ease. Chandra wished there was something to eat or drink, but the secret room was off-limits to servants. *If I had a little time to spare, I could have bathed and eaten something,* Chandra ruminated inwardly. He determined yet again to be more efficient with time.

'What should we do about the Atavikas? What if more vassals start refusing to pay the taxes?' Lakshmidhara asked. His voice sounded strained to Chandra. 'The war campaign is already taking a toll on our finances.'

'We have asked the Atavikas politely, warned them harshly, and now, the only alternative left is to send the army,' said Kritavarma.

'Given our resource crunch at the moment, we should avoid a battle,' said Harisena.

For a while, nobody spoke. Chandra tried to look at the problem differently. 'How many of them have refused to pay the taxes? Who do you think is leading this rebellion?'

Kritavarma, pacing up and down the room, said, 'I am sure Deva of the Kotatavi province is their leader. He has always been a troublemaker.'

'All nine forest kingdoms haven't paid any taxes in the last three months on their income and the trade they have done in our provinces.' Lakshmidhara showed the palm-leaf accounting book he always carried to the meeting.

Chandra pondered on that information for a few minutes. 'Can we negotiate with Deva? We can make him in charge of collecting taxes from the others and exempt him for a year or two.'

'That's your inner Chanakya speaking, isn't it?' Kritavarma teased Chandra, knowing his obsession with Chanakya Neeti. Then, he added seriously, 'It's not a bad idea. If all Deva wants is tax exemption, then what you are saying might work. If he's aspiring for freedom, then we have another war on hand. I'll have him brought here.'

21

Rudrasimha handed Kedara a scroll. 'Will this turn out to be another futile attack on the Gupta kingdom?' His face looked more sinister than ever with his mouth open, and a cheek turned up. He was using a nail to get at the meat stuck between his teeth.

Kedara adjusted his small frame in the large chair and went over it one more time. 'If what Atma says is true about the Atavikas, then it's good news. It may be worth inviting Deva here for a talk.'

Rudrasimha was grave as he glanced around his meeting hall – peeled paint on the walls, chairs that wobbled like an unsteady old man, carpets whose good days were long gone. Plagued by a three-year drought and relentless attacks from the southern kings, Rudrasimha had no resources to maintain the palace. He did not want anyone to see his decrepit state.

After a pause, he said, 'No, I don't want anyone here. We will meet in Deva's province.'

* * *

The next few days flew by in a whirl of activity for the Shakas and the Atavikas. Rudrasimha landed in Deva's province with Atma and Vidura. At first, Deva was unwilling to listen to Atma. Harisena had called upon him, and he had been exempted from paying taxes for two years. He had negotiated hard to get the others' charges waived for six months too. He was about to convey the good news to the other Atavika kings when Rudrasimha paid him a surprise visit.

However, the lure of freedom quickly dissolved Deva's initial resistance. *Why a tax waiver of a measly year or two? You'll be free forever when we win this war. We'll appoint you the Rajadhiraja, the king of kings, of the Atavikas.* Atma's words had convinced Deva to withdraw his allegiance to the Guptas and join hands with Rudrasimha.

Nine forest kings and three other vassal kings were backing Rudrasimha in his war against the Guptas. The foresters were not sophisticated in the use of weapons, but they were large, strong men and made great foot-soldiers. Deva's province became the chosen centre for their operation, given its proximity to Pataliputra.

That night, Atma addressed the Atavika leaders in a clearing in the middle of the forest. The men sat on thick wooden planks. Most of them looked sceptical and some looked frightened.

Atma began, 'First of all, rest assured that we're going to win this war. We've planned this so meticulously that there's no scope for error. I know all of you earlier surrendered your freedom to Samudragupta without a fight. Now is the time to get your land back and be sovereign. You are no longer helpless small provinces. The powerful Shaka king, Rudrasimha, is backing you.' Atma paused for a moment and then dramatically lifted his arthritic arms with clenched fists. 'Atavikas, are you all with us to fight this battle for freedom?'

After a moment of silence, a few arms went up, and then some more. Atma waited until the crowd roared and a unanimous decision was reached. After a few minutes of cheering, Atma asked for silence. 'Thank you, Kings. Now let's see how we're going to execute this attack. The annual horse fair starts in Pataliputra in a week. Vassal provinces are allowed to send in a hundred horses and twenty men each for the trade. So, all of you should send your best soldiers and the best horses, which will be roughly two hundred men and a thousand horses. They can officially stay in Pataliputra three days before the fair, once you obtain the trade permit.' Atma paused.

People seemed clued in, so he continued, 'Another thousand men must infiltrate the city slowly and join those in the trading grounds. Magadha allows free movement of people as long as they are not in large groups. Send men who can speak Magadhi Prakrit. They can blend in without arousing suspicion. Let them enter during the daytime. Late entrants are scrutinized more thoroughly.'

Atma stopped. He was feeling breathless. He looked at Rudrasimha, who sat in a corner wearing an unreadable expression. Ignoring him, Atma asked the Atavika men if they had any questions.

There were plenty – the best way to enter the city, places to stay, and ways to avoid trouble with the guards. Atma answered them all calmly. Soon, there was not a single doubter left in the gathering. As the wine flowed freely, there were loud cheers everywhere: *victory shall be ours*.

Rudrasimha stood up and announced, 'The Holi festival this time will mark the beginning of a new era for us and the end of the Guptas!' The crowd cheered until they were hoarse.

22

Chandra stood next to his mother on a raised podium. For a moment, he felt bewildered at the cheers. There were at least a thousand people in that giant stadium, all going berserk. This was not a new sight for him on the day of Holi, but it was always his father who presided over things. Chandra had assumed that it was Father who was the crowd-puller. This time, it was Rama, Mother and Chandra on the dais, but the buoyant crowd was the same as the previous years.

Dattadevi took a handful of vermilion and threw it into the air signalling the start of festivities. Within minutes, colours filled the air, as if a thousand rainbows had descended on earth at once. Faces dripped red, green and yellow. Hands were busy spraying colours and water. People were laughing, slipping and falling on the ground that quickly turned muddy. The child in everyone had been let loose.

According to tradition, the queen dabbed a little vermilion and turmeric first on Rama's face and then on Chandra's. Until a few years ago, she had to force them to play Holi with each other. Chandra was glad when she had finally given up. He was more than sure Rama was too.

Soon, Rama left. The queen stood with Chandra smiling at the crowd.

'Don't you want to play with colours?' she asked.

'Sure!' Chandra took vermilion and blew it gently on her saree.

'Chandra!' the queen sounded exasperated. 'You've ruined my saree! Go play with someone your age, you troublemaker!'

As the euphoria gained momentum, the queen was escorted to the palace. Chandra spotted Kritavarma in a corner and strode towards the commander, dodging people who tried to drag him into the grounds. Pranava walked towards him from the crowd.

'You can't be here!' said Kritavarma seeing Chandra. 'Play inside the palace fort.'

'And let you have all the fun?' Chandra shook his head and smiled. 'I'll stay here for a little while.'

Before he could finish, Pranava, joined by a few others, threw colours at Chandra. Soon there was a crowd of sprayers surrounding them. Kritavarma threw murderous looks at the boys. 'I came here to escape this,' he groaned, pointing to his clothes drenched in colour.

Before long, the noise began to exhaust Chandra. Turning to Pranava, he said above the din, 'I'm going back to the palace. Let's meet at the riding trail in an hour.'

As soon as he turned to head back, piercing screams ripped the air. It took him a moment to realize that people were shouting in agony, not joy. Then he saw battle-quality arrows finding their way into the crowd. As he watched in horror, bodies started piling up on the ground. Many tripped on those who'd fallen, creating more chaos. What had been a joyous celebration had turned into a battle scene.

'Head back to the palace.' Kritavarma almost shoved Chandra towards the bodyguards. 'Pranava, go with the prince. Provide a cover for him.'

But Chandra wasn't going to hide behind guards and head home like a coward! Not when people were being butchered. His eyes caught the source of the lethal arrows. Pointing at the trees, he shouted in panic, 'The trees ... on the trees ... shoot at the trees ...'

Pranava and Kritavarma understood what Chandra was trying to say. 'Shoot at the trees,' Kritavarma bellowed at the soldiers who were stationed to control the crowd. The assailants were shooting from the top branches of the tall sal trees that lined the grounds.

Snatching a bow and quiver from a sentinel next to him, Chandra joined the soldiers in shooting at the trees blindly. The attackers began falling to the ground, some splitting their heads and some lucky ones only breaking a few bones.

'I think almost all the attackers are dead or wounded,' said Kritavarma to Chandra as they took a break. 'There aren't any more arrows flying from the trees.'

Sweat-soaked and weary, Chandra gazed at the people writhing in pain on the ground. 'Who are these barbarians?' He was furious at those who'd turned the festival ground into a graveyard.

Pranava, along with a few soldiers, had already started lifting the wounded onto makeshift stretchers. Chandra joined them. He felt depressed and anguished when he saw a toddler bawling in pain, an arrow stuck in his chubby thigh.

'Let me help,' he said to the distraught mother and plucked the arrow out. As the child cried even louder, he tied his silk scarf around the wound. Then he swore to Pranava, 'I'll kill each one of those who planned this attack. They don't deserve to live.'

* * *

As it turned out, the attack in the morning was only the beginning. There was a massive ambush at the horse fair. Within hours, the Shakas had thousands of thoroughbred horses in their control, as they scared away the sellers who had come from all over the country.

Atma gave Rudrasimha a smile of satisfaction. If everything went as planned, Pataliputra would be theirs within days.

23

Kritavarma swung into action. He had every city gate shut within an hour. Chandra followed the commander everywhere. Borders were fortified. Sentries were posted on the ramparts to pour hot oil on the enemy. Citizens were instructed to stay inside the houses and report strangers loitering around to the authorities. Messengers were sent to the ally provinces Vaishali and Champa to send in their troops. Kritavarma and a few commanders were back on the watchtower every hour for a vigil.

'How many of them? They seem to be doubling in number with each passing minute,' Chandra observed anxiously, looking at the sea of enemy soldiers outside the gate that opened to the battleground. Shaka flags, red with the picture of a crouching tiger, were flying everywhere.

Kritavarma replied gravely, 'One of the men we captured in the morning is an Atavika commander. He says they are supporting the Shakas. They have fifty thousand infantry, twenty-five thousand cavalry and a hundred elephants and chariots.'

'So they outnumber us,' said Chandra. 'What do we do if help doesn't arrive?'

'We will fight on our own until help arrives. Let's hold a meeting. We need to plan quickly,' said Kritavarma before getting off the stairs. 'You might get to sleep only for an hour tonight!'

Chandra smiled weakly. 'I don't want to sleep. I just want them all gone,' he said, pointing at the camped enemy soldiers.

* * *

Late in the evening, Rama took a stealthy swig of drink with Megha. Kritavarma had given him strict instructions not to stir out of the palace fort, which meant that they could only sit by the pond and hope they wouldn't be noticed. His father would have him whipped if he caught him drinking in public.

'Two days into the battle now. What is going on?' Megha asked.

'As of today morning, the battle continues. We got help from the allies and have an army the same size as the Shakas. But a lot more elephants.' Rama got up to leave. 'I'm going to meet Atma.'

'So the old owl is back from his pilgrimage.' Megha spat in disgust. 'Just in time for all the action. I hope someone kills him during the battle. Don't you have to attend the meeting with the ministers?' Megha asked.

'Atma is helping me to the throne. Why are you so against him?' asked Rama. 'See you tomorrow – same time, same place. I'll go to the meeting with the ministers after checking in with Atma.'

* * *

It was the third day of the battle and their forces, now fortified by the army sent by the ally kings, were putting up a brave fight. Chandra, tired of being cocooned inside the fort and getting battle news from others, had ventured into the ground with Pranava. Pranava had managed to get them soldiers' uniforms. Pretending to be sentries, they had walked up to the edge of the battleground and watched the battle. They had got so carried away that Chandra had almost forgotten about the meeting with the ministers.

He rushed into the meeting hall, cursing himself for being late again. The ministers were already present there and so was Rama. Everyone looked visibly worried. They hadn't seen Kritavarma for two days now. Chandra hadn't seen him at the ground either, but, then again, the chances of recognizing anyone in that melee were slim to none.

'What if more forces are joining the Shaka army?' Lakshmidhara voiced his concern.

'I went over the list of our chieftains and vassals. I don't think there are any more traitors,' replied Harisena.

The door creaked open, and Kritavarma walked in. 'Didn't want you all to write me off as dead in the battle.' Smiling wryly, he sat on the cushioned settee and stretched his legs. Picking up a glass of wine, he downed it in one go.

'Don't joke about death at a time like this, Commander,' Harisena reprimanded Kritavarma. 'Anyhow, since you seem to be pleased with yourself, can we believe the battle is going our way?'

Kritavarma grimaced. 'The enemy is getting weaker by the day, and their numbers are steadily decreasing. But they are not going to surrender soon.'

'Can't we attack their tents and food supplies at night? That should make them retreat,' said Rama.

Really? Have you been attending any of the war-ethics classes? Chandra wanted to ask his brother but controlled himself.

Kritavarma said politely, 'That is unethical, Prince. We should not resort to such means when we can fight fairly.'

'Isn't it better to end the war quickly, even if it's through unethical means than to lose more lives?' Rama persisted.

Kritavarma refilled his glass and took another long swig. 'We are a moralistic kingdom, Prince. We abide by values and righteousness.'

Chandra sensed that Rama was gearing up for an argument to prove he was right and Kritavarma had no time or patience for that. He quickly changed the topic. 'What is their strategy, Commander? Keep fighting till they die?'

Kritavarma narrowed his eyes and looked at Chandra. 'A soldier said he spotted you and Pranava on the battlefield today. Please tell me he was wrong.'

'Well,' Chandra drawled, 'that brings me to what I wanted to tell you.'

'So you were there!' Kritavarma sounded aghast. 'We have enough trouble already. Don't add to it by risking your life, Prince.'

Chandra decided it was as good a time as any to propose what he had in mind. 'Commander, I am joining you in the battleground tomorrow. I hate sitting inside the palace when I should be fighting.'

24

'So, Chandra wants to fight?' As Atma repeated what Rama had just said, his head spun with plans.

'Do you have a hearing problem? That is what I said, and you've repeated it three times.' Rama snapped. 'I thought Mother would disagree, but she too has consented. His choice, if he wants to die in battle.' Rama shrugged.

'It's not that simple, Prince,' Atma drawled. 'If he survives the battle, do you realize people will treat him as a hero?'

'Let them.' It was evident to Atma that Rama hadn't given it any thought all.

'If Chandra fights and you do not—'

Rama cut off Atma, 'It'd again be the case of chivalrous-Chandra cowardly-Rama. I am fine with it.'

'Fine, then. That will make your brother the uncontested heir to the throne.' Atma dropped the script he was holding with a thud on the table. 'Why then should I work with you?'

Rama's head reeled as he understood what Atma was saying. 'So, what are you suggesting?' he asked suspiciously.

'If he fights, you fight too.'

As Rama staggered back to his room after that dreadful meeting, his heart fluttered with fear. Should he consider going into the battle as Atma had insisted? The very thought was bile-raising. He hated the stress of even the practice battles, where everyone surrounded him, and he had to fight his way out. *Why should a king fight? Why have an army if the king had to offer his head on a platter?* The more he thought about it, the sicker he felt.

* * *

'You are going to the battleground to fight?' Megha's voice held alarm. 'Your brother craves adventure. Let him have his fill. You shouldn't go.'

'I can't let Chandra be an uncontested hero. Even if it means I die.' Rama's face turned grave in the way it always did when Chandra's name came up. 'He has been waiting for an opportunity to make me look like a loser. And now that it has come, he's grabbed it like a hungry dog grabs food.'

'Well, Prince Chandra might genuinely want to go into battle, fight and save the world. He is that kind of person. But—'

'Stop, Megha. Are you my friend or his?' Rama hated the way Megha always defended Chandra. He hated that Megha liked Chandra at all. 'I know that schemer. He can fool anyone, including you, but not me.'

Kusha whimpered, sensing his master's foul mood. Rama held his dog closer. 'If I die, take care of Kusha. This time, I may not come out a victor, but I'll make sure that Chandra doesn't either.'

'Is this Atma's plan?' asked Megha.

'No, it's my own. Do you think I can't make any decisions on my own?' Rama hated the fact that Megha distrusted Atma so much. There was nothing wrong in what the old minister had said.

* * *

'This weighs a ton, Commander! Please give me a lighter one,' Chandra protested as Kritavarma fastened iron armour around him.

Kritavarma smiled but continued undeterred. When he picked up iron headgear, Chandra jumped back in horror.

'That thing will bake my head to a crisp. Have mercy, please!'

'The enemy has no mercy, Prince. We need your precious head well protected. Now bend down a little for me.' Kritavarma placed the helmet on Chandra's head and gave a satisfactory nod as it fitted snugly.

'I feel like a heavy iron statue!' Chandra complained, despite knowing how futile it was. The commander, who had already turned to Rama, would have none of it. Though the royal dresser was waiting to clothe the princes, Kritavarma had chosen to do so himself.

'Let's remember what we talked about yesterday. There will be two generals on either side of you. You'll be riding our regular chariots and not the embellished ones the king uses. Your presence has to be kept a secret for as long as we can. These closed chariots will provide you with enough cover but only as long as you are inside them. Don't make any decisions on your own, please.'

'Where will Pranava be?' Chandra asked. His friend was as eager as him to fight it out.

'Far away from you! The two of you together will be trouble.' Kritavarma smiled. 'I'll keep him with me.'

'Keep me with you too!' exclaimed Chandra, feeling genuinely disappointed. He wanted to be with Kritavarma in the thick of the battle.

Kritavarma paused for a moment. 'The enemy will bay for your blood, not Pranava's. Please listen to me.'

Rama snapped, 'Shut up for once, Chandra. Nobody needs your mindless heroics here.'

Chandra glared at his brother and murmured, 'That is such great advice, Big Brother. But save it for yourself.'

Kritavarma intervened, 'All right, Princes. Let's start. The soldiers are very excited to have you with them.'

Chandra bent down to touch Kritavarma's feet to take his blessings. He was glad when Rama did the same. He hated it when Rama was arrogant with Kritavarma or any of the senior ministers.

The Commander blessed them, 'Vijayee Bhava, return victors,' and handed them the swords. Chandra felt a thrill course through him as he hauled his bow over his shoulders. He hoped he was going to be useful on the battlefield.

* * *

Atma handed a scroll to Vidura. 'You have to find a way to give it to the Shaka king.'

The scroll had roughly drawn pictures of the princes and a note that said, 'Look for the Gupta princes on the battlefield.'

Atma hoped Rudrasimha was intelligent enough to understand that if he captured the princes, the war was over.

25

The battle frenzy began the moment the conches were blown from both sides. As Chandra watched in dismay, thousands of foot-soldiers from both sides ran headlong into each other, letting out guttural battle cries. The cavalrymen raced with swords held high, expertly controlling their mounts. Commanders Nakula and Satya were on either side of Chandra. They had drawn their bows and were now aiming their arrows.

'Prince,' Commander Nakula, the chatty one of the two, was trying to speak above the din, 'take in the scene around you but hold up your shield.' He smiled. 'Not to scare you but do remember that death here is only an arrow away.'

Chandra nodded numbly. He thought of replying to Nakula with something witty but felt too overwhelmed to think. He felt dizzy as their chariot sped alongside a sea of elephants, horses and other chariots. Mounted soldiers buzzed around them like a swarm of bees. The air smelt of a strange mixture of animals, earth and people.

Despite a queasy stomach and a foggy brain, Chandra forced himself to concentrate. He had come to the battlefield to fight, not to entertain himself. The Guptas were known for their intricate and impenetrable military formations, which they changed every day. That day, based on their discussion the previous night, they would construct a variant of the famed chakra vyuha, the one that had trapped Abhimanyu in the *Mahabharata*.

Chandra recollected Kritavarma's words, 'All of you in the chariots and on elephants will stay at the centre of the formation. There will be seven circles of cavalry around you. If an enemy soldier is brave or foolish enough to break into the formation, he will be surrounded, trapped and killed the way spiders ensnare their prey.'

Chandra tried to identify the seven concentric circles of cavalry that Kritavarma had mentioned. It was a lot more complicated in reality. Each chariot and elephant was circled by horsemen. Every ten such groups were again surrounded by horsemen. Chandra tried to count the spirals, but he couldn't get beyond two; they seemed endless like the ocean! Chandra marvelled at how everyone was moving all the time without colliding with each other.

He saw Rama a few chariots away. He too had two high-ranked generals on either side of him and seemed equally dazed. Everyone else atop chariots and elephants was firing arrows and throwing spears.

Now the enemy's weapons had started to land closer to them. Most of them hit either the shields that the soldiers held up or the metallic walls of chariots. Both made deafening clanks. Then, an arrow buzzed close to Chandra's ear, startling him out of his thoughts. Before he could understand what had happened, arrows were hissing all around them. Holding up his shield instinctively, he ducked.

'Stay down,' he heard one of the commanders scream at him. He had assumed that it was too early for any real fight to start. How wrong he was!

Within minutes, there were shrieks of agony from both people and animals. As he kept himself low in the chariot, Chandra heard a constant clang of the arrows hitting the walls of the chariot like a hailstorm. He felt fear like he had never before. He knew that if he stood up, one of those arrows could kill him instantly.

How are the commanders even fighting, he wondered and braved a look upwards. Nakula held up shields for both himself and Satya, while the latter shot arrows. An arrow hit Nakula's helmet at full force, making Chandra jerk back involuntarily. But the generals fought undeterred.

Then he heard a horrific scream close to him. Chandra went on his knees to peek outside. The charioteer of the vehicle next to his was drenched in blood. The general was taking over the reins, nudging the wounded man aside. As Chandra watched in horror, the blood-soaked charioteer fell off the chariot, with nobody sparing a moment to save him.

'Do you feel all right?' Satya asked Chandra, lending him a hand to stand up. There seemed to be a momentary lull around them.

'What just happened?' Chandra asked, looking at the devastation all around. There were bodies on the ground, many mutilated beyond recognition, and some still writhing in pain.

'They rushed in through our cavalry with their elephants, probably to get to our chariots. There's some damage, but we made them retract easily.'

Nakula then spoke to the charioteer, 'Let's move a little ahead. Otherwise, we'll run over the bodies.' The commander's unemotional words sounded strange to Chandra. But he kept quiet.

Soon, the frenzy started picking up again. Horsemen charged with their swords and foot-soldiers clashed against each other, chest to chest, weapon to weapon. Chandra spotted a gigantic Shaka horseman ruthlessly hacking the Gupta foot-soldiers with his axe.

'He is attacking our footmen from horseback!' Chandra nudged Nakula urgently. 'That is so not right!'

'Then, make it right. Shoot him,' said Nakula, handing Chandra an arrow. Chandra did not hesitate. He touched Ajeya for good luck before stringing his bow. His shaft found its target and the giant Shaka rider, menacing only minutes ago, tumbled from his horse. He was killed immediately by the Gupta soldiers.

After that, Chandra waited to find his targets – a group of enemy soldiers butchering the Gupta elephants, an evil-looking horseman aiming his arrow at a Gupta general, a giant of an Atavika soldier wringing the necks of the Gupta men. Chandra hunted the enemy the way people hunt animals in the forest – wait, watch and shoot. Most importantly, don't miss the shot.

After almost two hours of battling, Chandra stopped to drink the water the charioteer handed him in a leather bottle. His throat felt as parched as desert sand. He felt grateful to the many soldiers on foot and horses who provided him with cover and protected him. He wondered how the men on the field coped. They could be dead and gone any minute. Chandra looked around, not finding anything he hadn't already seen – rushing horses, dying men, wounded animals, dead bodies that had started to attract vultures. Then, he saw something shining in the far corner of the battleground. He looked again to confirm his suspicion. He was not wrong! 'By the name of Lord Vishnu!' Chandra muttered, before slapping Nakula on the shoulder.

26

Nakula and Satya looked in the direction Chandra was pointing. A few Shaka soldiers were arranging their elephants into a formation. The elephants had swords tied to their tusks! When they were unleashed, they would tear the Gupta army limb from limb.

'The nerve of the Shakas!' Nakula grunted.

Chandra asked urgently, 'What do we do? We need to counter them right away.' There was a nod from Nakula and a thoughtful silence from Satya.

'Let's take a small platoon and launch a surprise attack on them,' Nakula declared.

'Good plan. We'll kill the elephants too. Losing war elephants will cripple them,' said Chandra.

Satya stopped Chandra with his hand. 'Sounds like a good plan. But, Prince, you are not going anywhere. Stay here with Nakula. I'll lead the attack with sharp-shooters.'

Chandra dismissed Satya's suggestion. 'I'm going with you. I know how to make a flash attack. Let's not waste time arguing.' He tried to sound firm. He didn't want to be left behind.

Nakula and Satya looked at each other. There wasn't enough time to consult Kritavarma, who had led a battalion to the frontlines. Then Satya, the senior of the two generals, decided. 'Prince, you have to promise us that you'll attack only from the chariot. No horseback.'

Chandra nodded in agreement. He was impatient to get on with the attack. The charioteer manoeuvred the vehicle past the circle of horses that surrounded them. The chariot raced, kicking up dust and reducing everything around it to a blur. A set of soldiers, assigned to protect the chariot, followed it.

As expected, the Shaka men looked bewildered to see a chariot racing towards them. They were not ready for the attack – not yet. Before they could recover from the initial shock, arrows rained down on them. It was the long-range Gupta shooters in the act, with Chandra joining them. When he saw a set of their horsemen closing in on the Shakas for close combat, he itched to join them. However, he knew that Satya would oust him from the battlefield if he pulled any such stunt.

'The elephants are still tethered. Let's attack before they decide to unleash them on us,' Chandra heard Satya say.

As spears struck them in their legs, the elephants let out ear-splitting roars. The Shaka men began to move their precious animals to safety. Within minutes, they had disappeared behind the boulders that lined the field.

'That is enough damage for the day!' Satya flashed a rare smile. 'Now back to the battle, boys.'

Chandra looked at the enormous boulders and wondered who else hid there. They turned around. As their chariot started to pick up speed, a spear whizzed past them. The Gupta horsemen began to fall, struck by spears and arrows. The horses, now deserted by their riders, started running amok, adding to the chaos. Soon, a large group of Shaka soldiers surrounded them from all sides.

'Attack!' screamed Satya. The Shakas clearly outnumbered them now. 'Prince, stay down!' Satya shouted in panic.

Chandra ignored the commander's instructions. He started unleashing arrows at the enemy soldiers. In the melee, Chandra caught sight of a man standing only a few yards away, aiming an arrow at him. The next thing Chandra knew, the arrow had hit him squarely in the chest. Though it didn't pierce his armour, Chandra staggered under its impact. While he struggled to regain his balance, another one almost dislodged his helmet.

Chandra's head spun from the blow. He took off his headgear and leaned against the wall of the chariot. Nakula and Satya were too busy to notice him.

'*Har har Mahadev*,' a loud cry rang in his ears. It jolted Chandra out of his confusion. The man who'd shot him was now balancing his horse on its hind legs and peering intently at Chandra's face.

Then the man screamed again, now in triumph, 'The Gupta prince!'

Nakula, now alerted, swung his sword at the screaming Atavika general but only got his arm. The general, clutching his bleeding arm, turned around and shouted at his men, 'Capture the prince and get fifty tolas of gold in reward!'

Chandra sprung to his feet, putting the helmet back on. *What is happening?* The announcement of a hefty reward by the general had its effect. The enemy men were now all around the chariot, beady-eyed with greed. Some of them started to climb into the chariot to grab Chandra.

There was no time to draw arrows. Taking out his dagger, Chandra struck the hands of the men clawing at the chariot wall. Nakula and Satya attacked them with the hilt of their swords and their spiked boots. As the wounded soldiers let go of the chariot, screaming in pain, a fresh crop of men tried to grab Chandra.

The enemy soldiers were now swarming all around the chariot, like flies. The Gupta soldiers attacked from behind.

Though the enemy started to dwindle, they were unrelenting in their mission to capture Chandra. Satya decided to stop the fight and escape on their sturdy chariot, with the help of the thoroughbred horses tethered to it.

Satya instructed the charioteer, 'Ride away, past the horses and men, ours and theirs.' He spoke to Chandra in the same breath, 'Stand steady and hold up the shield.'

Chandra nodded in agreement, but he could feel his heart palpitating. Even if one of those four horses failed to cope, he would be eating his next meal in a Shaka prison.

* * *

Rama half stretched on a boulder alongside the river. Taking a swig of the homemade wine Megha had brought, he took a handful of his favourite tangy, spicy peanuts from his friend's hand.

'Not half as strong as our regular wine, but this will do for the night,' Rama smiled, casting a sideways glance at his friend.

'You are not to drink at all during the battle, Prince! We both need to cut down on our drinking and smoking. I can feel my liver rotting and my brain turning into mush. You don't want to be a brain-dead king, do you?'

'I don't mind being any kind of king!' Rama inhaled the ganja. 'I'll give it all up when I become the king. Don't nag me like my father.'

Rama's battle-weary nerves started to calm down in the silence of the night. He had skipped Kritavarma's night meeting. He could not bear any more talk of blood and gore that night. Especially not about how great Chandra was.

'Now will you tell me what I am dying to hear? How was your day on the battlefield?' asked Megha eagerly.

Rama sighed. The last thing he wanted that night was to recap his day, but he owed it to his friend. 'I was the usual coward in people's eyes and Chandra the hero. What is new in that, Megha?' Rama narrated Chandra's encounter with the sword-fitted elephants.

'Forget what your brother did. How was your day, Prince?'

'Well, let me see. For a long time, I sat demurely like a bride in the chariot while a lot of mad chivalry unfolded around me. Then I threw a few lances and shot some arrows. All that would have been just fine if my brother hadn't been bent on overshadowing me, yet again.'

'You did what you could. You were part of a real battle where people kill for real! Now, that's something,' said Megha.

'You are the only one who doesn't think me a complete failure.' Rama stared into the sky, taking the last sip of his drink. Then he threw the cup as far into the river as he could. *Wish I could throw my brother into the river the same way.*

'Prince! You polluted the sacred Ganga with the dirty cup.'

'It's a cup made of leaves, not of iron!' Rama protested. 'If I ever become the king, I'll throw you into a dungeon for being rude to me.'

'Then who will you meet by the riverside at midnight?'

'That is true. I'll bear with your insolence for just that.' Rama laughed. Megha was the only person in the world who seemed to like him for who he was.

After a brief pause, Rama said, 'Megha, this battle proves what I've always believed. A king should not stick his neck out in war and risk getting killed. There are qualified soldiers and commanders in the army for the job. A king can perform other, far more important, duties. If he's alive, that is!'

'Then why do you want to go to the battleground? Why do things that don't match your beliefs?'

'I can't quit now. Anyway, don't worry. I'll stay safe and be my non-heroic best.'

27

The war showed no signs of abating even after five days. A mood of melancholy pervaded the Shaka army. They'd lost more than three-quarters of their men. They knew that they had no hope against the Guptas. Their days were numbered.

The soldiers' despair was not lost on Rudrasimha. That night as he chewed on a piece of chicken, his demeanour oscillated between surly and vicious. He sat in the sweltering heat with Kedara, Deva and a few other Atavika generals, warding off flies and mosquitoes. The smell of decaying flesh from the battleground was getting unbearable with each passing day.

'The Gupta princes are fighting in the battle,' said Rudrasimha. 'If we kill them, the war is won. That's what Atma told us on the first day of the battle. Why haven't we done that yet? Especially today, when one of them was right at our doorstep begging to be killed, or at least captured.'

'Today, we were unprepared. Tomorrow, we'll drag the princes out of their circle of safety and capture them,' said an Atavika general.

'Don't make these useless plans when your thick-skulled men can't even think straight.' Rudrasimha spat out a bone. The generals, except Deva, stormed off. They had had enough of Rudrasimha treating them like his slaves.

'Your men were fools not to capture the prince today. Actually, I am the fool who thought your nomadic tribe could fight,' Rudrasimha directed his fury at Deva.

'I never promised you a well-trained army! You came begging for my support. Remember?' said Deva. 'Now, I've lost most of my men. I'm heading back by dusk tomorrow, win or loss.'

'You traitor! Coward!' Rudrasimha hissed at Deva, keeping his voice low. A fight with Deva was unwise. It was true that the Atavikas were untrained. But he still needed these burly men to make up the numbers.

'Don't scream at me. I'll leave when I want to leave.' Deva stood up and started towards his tent.

A volcanic rage surged through Rudrasimha. *If Deva left with the Atavikas, he would certainly lose the war. His only chance to take revenge on Samudragupta would be gone.* Blinded by desperation and anger, Rudrasimha followed Deva to his tent, making sure none of the guards was watching. Taking out the knife from his waist-pouch, he stabbed Deva from behind. He then covered Deva's mouth and stabbed him again. He pushed Deva's limp body aside and walked away.

28

It was still dark in that pre-dawn hour. The battle was a good two hours away, but the loyal Gupta chiefs were already in their battle gear. They'd assembled at the fort gate to strategize the day.

'We have to change our plan today.' Not a man given to useless chatter, Kritavarma got to the day's agenda quickly. 'We have to focus on ending the war quickly. Their forces are down to a quarter so we can be more aggressive. We will go in with the same formation to protect the princes but with a slight variation. Half the commanders who are assigned to the princes will today face off the enemy at the outer rim, and the other half will continue as usual.' Kritavarma quickly laid before them a complete plan of action.

Rama felt a distinct discomfort. *Only half the commanders for protection?* He didn't voice his thought since his brother seemed to have no problem with the plan.

At dawn, the soldiers joined their chiefs filling the air with loud battle cries – Jai Bajrang Bali (Victory to

Lord Hanuman), Maharaj ki jai (Victory to the king), Yuvraj ki jai (Victory to the princes) and a few incoherent ones. As soon as the royal band on the ramparts blew the trumpets and beat the drums, the iron gate opened, signalling the beginning of another day of the battle.

Soon, three massive men from the Shaka camp, mounted on sturdy stallions, raced past the frontline soldiers towards the Gupta battalion. Rudrasimha, with two Atavika generals, had set out to study the Gupta strategy for the day. They had an ambitious plan of their own, but it depended on what their opponents did. The grief-stricken Atavikas, after learning from Rudrasimha that the Guptas had killed their beloved leader Deva in his sleep, were vying for revenge.

Anxiety creased their brows as they rode closer to assess the Gupta army. They kept looking back to check if the other generals were following them as instructed. Satisfied that they were behind them, they rode on, moving past the infantry, and reached the part where the vyuha or the military formation of the Gupta army began. The gods were finally benevolent to them! There were elephants in the outer rim of the formation – a sight Rudrasimha had long waited to see. All those days, the Gupta elephants and chariots had been nestled well inside a sea of cavalry. But the three men knew it was hardly the time to rejoice. It was only the beginning.

Rudrasimha nodded to his soldiers and generals behind him. In the next few minutes, the Shakas brought in their own elephants to face off the Guptas. Every senior Atavika and Shaka commander was atop an elephant, taking on a Gupta leader.

Rudrasimha chose Kritavarma. 'Mark your end, you doormat. You've hidden behind your king for long!' Rudrasimha screamed above the din as he threw his spear at Kritavarma.

Catching the spear in his hand, Kritavarma shouted back, 'Try throwing the next one at me, you moron.'

'You'll soon see who the moron is,' Rudrasimha muttered to himself. Swords clanged, arrows were shot, javelins found their targets, men and beasts bellowed. The madness of the war was in full force when Rudrasimha beckoned to his chief commander.

* * *

'What is going on?' Chandra shouted in alarm, looking at the commotion breaking out ahead of them. Horses were neighing, and the elephants were trumpeting. Then he understood the devious plan of the Shakas. His heart sank in fear. The Shakas had brought in horses to which fake trunks had been attached. Since elephants never attack their young, the Gupta elephants were duly retreating, thinking they were facing baby elephants. With the elephants stepping aside, the Shaka men were moving into the centre of the formation – straight towards Chandra and Rama!

Nakula instructed Chandra to get off the elephant and get into a chariot. 'Take the princes away from here,' Nakula screamed at the commanders who were with Rama. As Chandra hurried off the elephant and into a chariot, his breath stopped at what he saw. One of their own generals, a large man whom Chandra had never seen before, was whipping the soldiers covering

Rama. As Chandra watched in dismay, the man pounced on Rama, who had just got off his elephant. The man pinned Rama under his boot.

'Move back, you Gupta slaves,' the man's demented scream pierced through the commotion. 'If you come up with any bright ideas, my sword goes straight into this prince of yours.' He held his sword at Rama's throat.

Everyone stopped what they were doing. Swords stopped mid-air. Everything went deathly quiet as the shocked Gupta soldiers watched their prince being captured.

29

'Rudrasimha! You low life! Fight like a warrior. Let the prince go.' It was Nakula. *So that's Rudrasimha disguised as a Gupta commander,* Chandra realized. Then his head reeled again. *How many Shakas are in disguise?*

Rudrasimha's face contorted into an inhuman snarl. 'Stop right there, you fool,' he screamed back at Nakula. 'Drop your swords, all of you, if you want this pitiable boy alive.' He laughed dementedly, grinding his boot on Rama's chest. Rama let out a howl.

'Retreat, you treacherous Guptas, retreat!' Rudrasimha pointed his sword at the stunned Gupta soldiers.

As the commanders stepped back, Rudrasimha's men, along with the Atavika kings, moved forward and surrounded Rama.

After a brief conversation with one of the Atavikas, Rudrasimha looked at the retreating commanders. 'Where is the boy who came to our camp? Bring him here.'

Kritavarma, who had just then arrived at the scene, spoke with seething rage, 'Rudrasimha, you are inviting your own peril. Let him go. Wage a real war if you are a man.'

'Kritavarma! You are hiding like a woman when your prince is under my boot. You must be getting old and senile.' Rudrasimha's laughter was vicious. 'Did you say war? When I last heard, war is over when you capture the king. Your king isn't here, but I have his son instead. That means the war is over! Time for us to rejoice. Don't you think so, commanders?' Rudrasimha looked at his men who nodded in agreement and grinned from ear to ear. They cheered Rudrasimha.

Kritavarma bellowed at the Atavika kings, who stood cackling around Rudrasimha, 'You cowards! Our king should have beheaded you all when he won your lands. You didn't deserve his grace. Rudrasimha, this is your last warning. Let the prince go.'

Rudrasimha's sword pierced into Rama's thigh, as if in response.

* * *

Rama felt faint with fear, shock and tremendous pain. Blood was now oozing out of his wound.

He heard Rudrasimha shout, 'Bring his brother here before my sword finds his heart.'

I am dead. Why would Chandra put his life in danger to save mine? Rama felt dejection wash over him. Tears rolled down his cheeks as he prepared himself for Rudrasimha's sword in his heart.

Then, he saw Chandra push aside Satya's arm that barred his way. His brother came forward. Hope kindled in Rama's heart. He might come out of this alive after all! The Atavika kings stepped aside to let Chandra get closer to Rudrasimha.

'Here I am. What do you want?' Rama heard Chandra's voice.

Stop being arrogant, Chandra. He'll kill me if you cross the line with him.

'Lay down your sword,' instructed Rudrasimha. 'Lay down the sword, I said.'

Lay it down. Don't try anything intelligent when I am on the verge of death, Rama wanted to scream.

* * *

Chandra stared into Rudrasimha's eyes and bent down to lay his sword. In that instant, he grabbed the ankle of the Atavika king next to him. The king fell to the ground like a tree. Chandra pinned the Atavika to the ground with his foot and held the sword to his throat, the same way Rudrasimha stood over Rama.

Rudrasimha laughed hysterically. 'Do you think I care enough about the life of this lowly Atavika to spare your brother? Kill him. Kill all of them, for all I care. I didn't bat an eyelid before plunging a knife through Deva!'

A stunned silence fell on the Atavika men, who had

been cheering for Rudrasimha until then. Chandra seized the opportunity and shouted, 'You heard Rudrasimha. He killed Deva. Capture the selfish traitor before he destroys you all.'

The Gupta spies who had seen Rudrasimha stab Deva had reported the incident to their camp the previous night. Chandra was hoping to break the news to the Atavikas and turn them against Rudrasimha. But the Shaka king had tightened the noose around his own neck!

In a flash, the Atavika kings pounced on Rudrasimha.

30

'Ma!' Dattadevi turned in surprise when she heard Chandra's voice.

'To what do I owe this surprise visit?' She smiled at Chandra.

'I came to see how you are doing in the king's chamber.' Chandra sat on a chair near the window. 'I like what you've done here. Well done,' he said in a tone of mock authority, cocking an eyebrow at the renovated room.

'Oh, really? I am honoured that you approve, Maharaj!' Dattadevi threw a cushion from the nearby settee at her son, and both of them laughed.

'Why are we laughing? Nothing we said is that funny,' Chandra remarked, still laughing.

'I'm happy that your father is coming back today.' Dattadevi sat next to Chandra, fanning herself with a gold-handled feather fan. 'I know he had to cut short his campaign because of the Shaka attack. But I am not complaining.'

It had been two weeks since the war with Rudrasimha had ended. Life had started inching back to normal in the city. People had begun to look less scared; children were allowed to play on the streets; and trade of all sorts, clothes to jewellery, had started to look up again.

Chandra parted the heavy silk drapes to let in the afternoon sunlight. But it was so hazy outside that the room remained nearly as dark as it was before.

'It might start raining soon. Monsoon is early this year, I hear. I hope Father escapes it.' There was concern in his voice as he took the cup of juice his mother offered. 'He has been riding non-stop for two weeks now. The last thing he needs is pouring rain.'

'Don't worry. Your father is a tough man. How do you feel now, Chandra?' Dattadevi asked softly. Soon after the war, Chandra had been plagued by nightmares of blood, screams, piles of dead bodies, the people he had killed and those who had almost killed him. To calm him down, Kritavarma chatted with him every night. They talked about varied topics, from horses to weapons to art. Chandra had begun to see a new side of the tough commander.

'I'm better. Pranava has been sleeping in my quarters, so it's not too bad.'

'How did he cope? It was his first battle too,' Dattadevi asked.

'He didn't witness as much horror as I did since he fell ill on the second day of the battle.' Chandra smiled. Then he asked hesitantly, 'How is Brother?'

'He is back in his room from the hospital.'

Chandra nodded. For a moment, he considered visiting Rama, but from past experience, he knew that the visit would bring no joy to either.

* * *

Samudragupta's homecoming was a grand affair. Everyone needed a reason to rejoice after the bleak days of the war. Houses bore a festive look with flower garlands and elaborate rangolis. People lined up on both sides of the street in the pouring rain and cheered until they grew hoarse. They prostrated on the ground when the king's chariot passed by, and many cried tears of joy. They loved their king. He was a good man who taxed them minimally and helped them amply in times of need. They wished he would never leave the capital to wage wars.

The events at the royal court were ten times more splendid. The queen had planned everything meticulously. Walking towards the throne, with Dattadevi on one side and Chandra on the other, amidst chanting by the royal priests, Samudragupta stopped and looked around. 'I had forgotten how flowers smell. I've been smelling only sweat, mud and blood for the past two years!'

Chandra smiled. 'Ma has been working non-stop to decorate this room.' He pointed at the lavish throne room, which had a fresh layer of paint, new silver lamps, carpets, and grandest of all, the brand-new life-size golden statues of Vishnu and Lakshmi.

Samudragupta smiled gratefully at his wife. He laughed when Chandra murmured in his ear, 'Beware, she may have emptied the treasury for this renovation.'

As the dancers, musicians and magicians put up great performances, Chandra wondered when they were going to address the issues that plagued the state after the war. His father seemed lost in the moment.

What would they do with Rudrasimha and the Atavikas who were in prison? How would they fill the royal coffers that were not looking too healthy? How were they going to compensate the people who had suffered losses in trade? A meeting was set for the next morning.

31

Chandra felt that his father had conquered not just the whole of Bharata, but sleep and fatigue as well! He had been riding non-stop for fifteen days after two years of incessant fighting. The previous night's celebrations had stretched way beyond midnight. Yet, his father had scheduled an early private meeting, for which he'd managed to reach earlier than anyone else.

They were going to decide the fates of the imprisoned Rudrasimha and the Atavikas. Stifling a yawn, Chandra took a sip of the hot drink kept for him.

'We will annex the lands of the Atavikas and employ our chieftains in those provinces,' declared Samudragupta. 'No more freedom for those traitors.'

'How do we find chieftains who speak their language?' asked Kritavarma.

Chandra chimed in, 'What they speak doesn't even sound like a language. Just high-speed murmurs.'

'I am sure there is a language hidden in the murmurs.' Harisena smiled before offering a solution, 'We will have to select one of the locals as an assistant to our chieftain. Someone who speaks their language, as well as ours.'

'I'll take a road trip to the Vindhya mountains. Haven't been there in a decade since we first fought them,' said Kritavarma.

'I am going with you!' Chandra said eagerly. How nice it would be to go to the Vindhyas! Which also meant escaping the daily routine for a while. 'Hope it'll be at least for a month.'

Samudragupta chuckled. 'Road trips can wait for now. What do we do with Rudrasimha?'

Chandra was surprised. 'The same as the Atavikas, right?' He pictured Rudrasimha working in their fields and washing their chariots.

To his disappointment, the committee decided that Rudrasimha could go back and rule as their vassal, but only after he'd compensated them for the war losses.

Samudragupta clarified, 'Saurashtra is too far away from here for us to rule. Also, since it has a seaport, the southern kings are perennially plotting a war against the Shakas. We don't want that headache.'

'Rudrasimha has access to the sea and a well-established port. He can trade with foreign countries and become the richest of all the kingdoms. Why isn't he doing that?' Chandra was curious.

'Well, because he is Rudrasimha!' Samudragupta laughed. 'His ego is larger than his size, if that's possible!'

'How foolish to let ego come in the way of prosperity!' Chandra shook his head in disbelief. Then again, Rudrasimha was not the sharpest arrow in the quiver. After all, he had admitted to killing Deva in front of everyone!

* * *

His father on the gleaming garuda-shaped throne, the rich and famous of the town occupying rows and rows of seats, the silver-clad columns in the room glinting in the morning sun – it was business as usual in the throne room as Chandra took his place next to Kritavarma.

The first topic of the day was the war prisoners. Kritavarma summed up what they had discussed earlier and then added, 'The Shaka king should pay us war expenses. I suggest that he mint gold coins with Prince Chandra's name and picture on them. Shakas, after all, are experts in coin minting. And, our prince here deserves recognition.'

Samudragupta nodded his acceptance. Chandra, to his embarrassment, blushed deeply when people applauded. A coin with his name? Once he'd recovered from the surprise, he got up to awkwardly bow to his father and then to the gathering. 'Thank you. I don't know if I deserve this honour but thank you! If I can make a request, can the coins be minted in my brother Rama's name too? He almost lost his life in the battle.'

* * *

Two weeks later, Rama headed to Atma's house with a handful of coins. He was quite pleased to see his face on the shiny new coins.

Atma, as usual, took his time before he spoke, 'So, you think this is an honour?' he asked Rama, looking at the coins in disgust.

Rama knitted his brows. 'No, I think it's an insult that there are gold coins in my honour!'

'Enough with the sarcasm, Prince. Don't you realize your brother has bestowed pity on you? He is growing in popularity at your expense. What does the world see here? First, Chandra rescues you from under Rudrasimha's feet. Now, with these coins, he shares his glory with you!'

Rama looked at Atma in disbelief. Was there truth in what he was saying? He felt deflated.

As if reading his mind, Atma said, 'I see things that you don't because I'm old and have seen a lot more of life. Go back to your room and think again with a clear head.'

Rama knew wine was not the answer to his questions but decided to head to the tavern anyway. Self-control was not one of his virtues.

32

'Father!' Rama bowed to Samudragupta slightly. The best time to talk to his father was when he was in the garden at night, waiting for Harisena.

'Rama, good to see you. Have a seat.' Samudragupta pointed to a chair opposite him. Rama wondered if his father had been drinking. He had never been that civil to him before!

Patting Kusha's head, Rama sat down. Kusha curled up under the chair and went to sleep.

'Father,' Rama stammered nervously, 'when will you name me the heir to the throne? Most kings who have sons my age have already done so. Including your good friend King Pushyavarma.'

Samudragupta studied him for a moment. 'Why is the throne important to you, Rama? Why do you want to be king?'

Rama's head started to pound. *That's a trick question*, he was sure. 'I can give you all the lofty answers: how I want to protect our people, expand the kingdom, bring more prosperity to the kingdom. But, at this point, I want to be named the heir because it is my right. I am the first-born son to your chief queen.' There! He'd said it. Even the cool breeze did nothing to soothe his nerves. What would his father say?

Samudragupta nodded. 'Being a king is not a luxury, Rama. It involves sacrifices, big and small. Your life does not remain yours. You have to start living for others.'

God, the same boring speech again, thought Rama. *Come to the point, Father. When will you name me the heir*? He wanted to scream but tried a saner response, 'I understand, Father. When you were away at war, I managed the kingdom. And I'm sure, when a situation demands, I'm capable of living for others and making sacrifices.'

'You managed the kingdom, yes, but then you also gave up. Now, let us test what you just claimed. Can you sacrifice Kusha?'

'What?' Rama almost fell off his chair. 'You want me to kill my dog?'

'Of course not. Just give up Kusha. Hand him over to the guard and never see him again. He will be well cared for.'

Rama felt outraged. 'He can't live without me! I have looked after him since he was born.'

After a few moments of uncomfortable silence, Rama asked bitterly, 'If I give up Kusha, will you name me the heir?'

'No. It isn't time to name the heir yet. But, you said you can make sacrifices. I'm asking you to do so.'

Rama's eyes welled up when Kusha got up with him to head out together. Summoning the guard who stood at a distance, Rama handed over Kusha's rein and walked away briskly. His tears flowed uncontrollably when he heard Kusha barking. As he neared the end of the path, his father called after him, 'Come back, Rama. Take Kusha with you.'

Rama turned back in surprise and saw the dog running towards him. Hugging him tightly, Rama looked at his father. Samudragupta said softly, 'Never abandon someone who depends on you and is helpless. Don't worry about the throne. I haven't chosen either Chandra or you yet.'

33

A few months later, when Samudragupta resumed the war campaign he'd cut short, Chandra accompanied him. He had to brave stiff opposition from his mother. Samudragupta was not convinced either that his young son should weather the tortures of a long war. But Chandra had begged, pleaded and argued, and eventually, he had his way.

Once his father left with his brother and Kritavarma, Rama sighed with relief. After allowing himself a few days of lethargy, he started following Atma's advice. Well, for the most part. He would still give in to his old vices every now and then. However, he became a regular at all assembly meetings. He made sure no private councils were held without him. He arranged for Harisena and Lakshmidhara to meet with him and his mother every other night. True that most of these things were Atma's ideas, but Rama was surprised at how well he executed them.

'Prince, the key is for you to be present in every meeting, every single day. Listen intently and make suggestions. Make your voice heard. Be the final decision-maker. Your mother's support will lend you credibility. Tell me everything that goes on in there, important or otherwise. I can't plan our next move without that information.'

Not all of Rama's suggestions were accepted in the assembly meetings. Some were turned down. But, as Atma had predicted, officials now waited for his opinion before passing any rule. Rama had wondered at first why Atma was insistent that his mother be a part of the council meetings, especially the private ones, but now he understood why. When she was with him, seniors like Harisena took him more seriously.

After about three months, Rama started to feel the strain of his rigorous life. The morning and evening public meetings lasted anywhere from four to five hours each. On many nights, there were private meetings. Rama often thought if that was the life of a king, then a peasant had a better one! He decided that he was going to endure everything only for the time being – until he'd firmly established himself. Beyond that, no matter what Atma said, Rama had decided to lead an easy life.

* * *

Rudrasimha looked at the rain that had been pelting down relentlessly for the past four days. It was a welcome change after almost four years of drought. *The crops are going to be abundant and profitable*, he thought, trying to cheer himself up. His happiness was short-lived when he remembered that Samudragupta would take away more than half of those profits. Samudragupta had let him go free after the war but had levied such heavy taxes that freedom felt like slavery. The defeat at Pataliputra haunted him even after two years. Chandra, that inexperienced youngster, had brought about his downfall. Rudrasimha vowed to bring about the destruction of the Guptas. As he boiled and seethed silently, he heard the door creak open. It was Kedara.

'Namaste, Maharaj.' Kedara settled into a chair after Rudrasimha signalled him to do so.

'We haven't set foot outside in four days,' said the minister as he picked up his wine and a hot pakoda. 'Thank God for the good cooks in the palace,' he tried to joke in an attempt to lighten his master's mood.

Rudrasimha continued to drink in silence. Then he asked abruptly, 'I'd asked you to send a scroll to the king of Kamarupa saying that I wish to marry his daughter. Has he responded yet?'

'Well, King, I didn't ...'

Rudrasimha knitted his brows and frowned.

Kedara continued in a barely audible voice, 'Princess Dhruvadevi is too young. I thought King Pushyavarma might not honour your proposal.'

'Since when did you start making your own decisions, Kedara? Write down what I dictate and send it out now. I'm telling you, Pushyavarma will jump at the offer.' Rudrasimha's raised voice made Kedara shrink into the chair.

The minister rubbed his hands nervously, his gaze downcast as he spoke, 'Also, the king of Kamarupa and Samudragupta are good friends, Maharaj. He may not want to align with us.'

'Do as I say, Minister.' Rudrasimha banged his fist on the table, almost shattering it. 'He is merely a subordinate of Samudragupta but is glorified as an ally. Siding with me will make him equal in strength to Samudragupta. So why will he reject my offer?'

* * *

'King Samudragupta is going to halt on the outskirts of our town for one night the day after tomorrow. I'll go and meet him,' Dhruva heard her father say to her mother.

'Where is he going?' Dhruva intervened.

Pushyavarma ruffled his daughter's hair affectionately. 'He is continuing his war in the far east. Do you want to go with me to see him?'

Rahula guffawed. 'Yes, Father. You must take her. She'll faint and be such a lot of help in a battle.'

Dhruva snorted derisively. 'Isn't there any brain inside your head? Do you think anybody battles at night? Father is going to simply meet the monarch, not to join his battle.' Before her brother could come up with a retort, Dhruva turned to her father and asked, 'But, Father, why didn't you join the monarch's war campaign? You said many other allies are fighting alongside him.'

Pushyavarma smiled. 'Because neither am I a great warrior, nor is my army big enough to serve the monarch. But I do keep a part of our forces ready in case he needs them.'

Dhruva nodded and smiled. She liked that her father was always straightforward and honest with her.

She stepped out, closing the door to her parents' room behind her. Rahula sped past her, calling her slower than a snail. Before she could respond, Dhruva heard her mother shriek, 'He wants to marry Dhruva? He is older than *you*!'

Wait a minute. Who wants to marry me? Instantly worried, Dhruva waited to hear the rest of the conversation. 'Rudrasimha is insane. Don't bother about his letter. In any case, Dhruva is too young to be married,' said her father.

'No, she's not. Seventeen is the right age to start looking for a groom. Who knows how long it'll take to find the right one?'

Dhruva rolled her eyes and muttered under her breath: *Ma! Listen to my wise father for once!*

34

'Will this rain ever let up? I am soaked to the bone,' King Angada's booming voice entered the tent before he did. He was the king of Ahichatra who'd fought alongside Samudragupta in most wars. Walking behind Angada was Pushyavarma.

'Pushya, you didn't have to brave this rain to see me. I'd have visited you on the way back,' said Samudragupta, looking visibly happy. Chandra smiled. His usually reserved father always got excited when he saw his old friends.

'You have to stop on the way back too. But with you this close, how could I not pay a visit?' asked Pushyavarma. Then he looked at Samudragupta and asked in alarm, 'King, why have you become so thin? Are you well?'

Samudragupta smiled at his friend. 'A stubborn cough, that is all. Nothing to worry about.' He broke into a coughing fit just as he said so. Chandra rushed to his father, offering him the medication kept by his bed.

'Do you recognize this young man here?' Angada drew Pushyavarma's attention to Chandra.

'Prince Chandra! How tall you have grown, Son!' Pushyavarma hugged Chandra. 'You were half this size when I saw you last. But you are still as thin as a reed. By the way, my son Samu hero-worships you!'

Angada replied for Chandra, 'He deserves to be admired. Prince Chandra is a commander now. He is one of our best attackers.'

'I'm mentored by the best.' Chandra smiled. Angada was the one who taught him how to fight on the frontlines.

'Chandra, I know you are a brave man. But how are you coping, Son?' asked Pushyavarma. 'Wars are harsh.'

Angada patted Chandra on the shoulder. 'He has survived it all – food that tastes like dung, roofs that leak, the death of hygiene.'

Chandra laughed. 'It has been rough but exciting. Now let me leave you three with your game of Chaturanga. Father, if you feel all right, I'll go now and see you in the morning.'

Samudragupta patted Chandra on the shoulder. 'Go on, Chandra. I am fine. I've a match to win against these two!'

As he walked out, Chandra thought about his harshest war experience. It had to be that nameless disease that had taken the lives of many soldiers a few months back. He worried that some such disease had afflicted his father, who was growing weaker by the day.

Going past rows and rows of sheds that housed the soldiers, Chandra reached his tent. Only the higher officers got individual tents. The rest of them bunked under the sheds with thatched roofs. Chandra felt sorry for these soldiers since the rain made their conditions utterly miserable.

By the time Chandra reached his room, Pranava was already there. He sat on a water drum, aiming small stones into a puddle in the middle of the room. Chandra looked at his friend, amused.

'You sure know how to keep yourself entertained,' Chandra remarked, claiming another upended drum for a chair. His living conditions were not luxurious either. Most nights, his tent leaked and on some especially fretful nights, it split open to the rains!

'Where is Vasanthi?' asked Pranava, continuing to throw stones into the puddle. 'You can grow some fish here, you know.'

The tent flap opened as a girl about the same age as them entered the room. 'One of you must have left the flap open. I'm sure it was Pranava. Now there is so much water inside.' She pointed at the puddle, flashing a look of disapproval.

'I did. Just so that you'll have something to complain about. Now that we're taking a break from the battle, you look too relaxed,' Pranava teased her. Vasanthi was a volunteer nurse who travelled with the battalion. She had treated Chandra and Pranava for their battle wounds, and the three had slowly forged a friendship.

'When do we resume the battle?' asked Vasanthi, standing by the tiny window, trying to close it.

'The king of Pushkarana is hiding behind the palace fort. We will start a siege once the rain lets up. This is our last conquest anyway. Then it's back home,' said Chandra but regretted his words when he saw Vasanthi's face fall. She only had the women's shelter to go back to, not a home. She was an orphan and lived in Bodh Gaya.

'Why don't you move to Pataliputra and work in a hospital there?' suggested Pranava.

Vasanthi lit up. 'I can do that! There are plenty of charitable dispensaries in Pataliputra, thanks to our king's kindness.' Then she flashed a wicked grin at Pranava. 'This means I'll have more time to make a decent man out of you.'

Pranava gave a look of exasperation. 'Why did I suggest that? It was my one chance to get rid of you, you cleanliness-freak!'

Chandra couldn't decide if Pranava and Vasanthi were just friends or on the verge of becoming something more. Pranava, of course, vehemently denied any special feelings for Vasanthi. But their bickering certainly provided entertainment for Chandra.

'Whoa! What is that? Looks like a flying flame!' Vasanthi said, looking out of the window.

Alarmed, Chandra and Pranava ran outside the tent. There they were! Hundreds of flying flames. Some of the sheds had caught fire despite the rain. The Pushkarana king had started a stealth attack on their camp with flaming arrows.

In the wet weather, the arrows were useless, but they still succeeded in hitting a few soldiers. Within minutes, the entire Gupta battalion was alerted, except Samudragupta, who slept on, sedated by the physician. Kritavarma, Angada, Chandra, Pranava and a few other commanders huddled inside a tent to plan a counter-attack. They were not geared for this stealthy ambush on a rainy night and helplessly watched enemy soldiers wreak havoc with their gleaming spears.

'Looks like an enemy suicide squad has infiltrated into our camp. They will destroy as many of us as they can before we can respond.' Kritavarma made a plan quickly. 'Let's spread out and counter them. Only a few would have gained entry inside. But we have to prevent more from coming in. Prince and Pranava, get a set of shooters and block the frontline of the encampment. We will fight the ones who are already here.' Chandra was no longer treated with kid gloves. He was one of their best commanders, and Kritavarma assigned him tasks befitting his expertise.

Before carrying out Kritavarma's orders, Chandra rushed into his father's tent, where only a dim oil lamp flickered. Even in the din of the battle, Samudragupta slept peacefully with Pushyavarma sitting beside him. After taking a long look at his father, Chandra touched his feet and then King Pushyavarma's. 'Wish us well and please take care of my father while this melee lasts.'

Pushyavarma's hand rested briefly on Chandra's

head. 'May victory be yours, Son. Take care of yourself and your people. I'll be right here with your father.'

35

Neither side gave up in the battle that raged all night. Chandra, with Pranava and a group of soldiers, held off the enemy at the entrance. They made sure not to let a single Pushkarana man enter the camp through the makeshift barricade.

'No more men trying to gain entry. Should we join those who are battling inside?' Pranava asked Chandra after a period of lull.

'That sounds good. We will leave these soldiers here just in case the enemy decides to act up again,' said Chandra, looking at the enemy soldiers strewn on the ground, dead or wounded.

Chandra and Pranava turned back, but the slushy mud made it impossible for them to go any faster than a slow trot. A few soldiers, Chandra's designated bodyguards, followed them. The rain still lashed them, with no light anywhere, except for occasional lightning. Even the moon had gone to rest behind the clouds. A few minutes later, they heard loud noises – thuds and screams. Then more thuds and screams. They looked back puzzled, and saw the enemy destroying their barricade.

Chandra stood frozen for a moment looking at the men pounding the wall with gigantic hammers. Behind those wreckers were horsemen, all set to rush in. It had always bothered Chandra that their barricade was not strong enough. But his father had said they didn't have the resources to make a temporary wall any stronger.

The barricade caved in, and the Pushkarana horsemen rushed inside like water gushing in through a broken dam. 'Ride on, Pranava. We have to inform the commander of this. I hope he's deployed enough soldiers to encounter this large pack of wolves!'

Chandra's horse, now used to the rain, picked up speed and so did Pranava's. At that rate, they would have plenty of time before the enemy riders reached the heart of the camp. Without waiting for his struggling bodyguards to keep up with him, Chandra raced on.

However, his horse couldn't navigate the slush. When its front legs descended into a mud pit, the horse stopped with an abrupt jerk. Chandra quickly got off the frightened horse and patted it reassuringly.

He could see Pranava trying to turn back to help him and shouted, 'I can manage this. You go! Tell the commander about the enemy.'

Luckily, two of Chandra's guards had caught up with him. Calming his horse, Chandra carefully led it out of the pit, with one of the guards helping him. Relieved that the enemy was still struggling with the rain and the slush, Chandra tried to remount his horse. That was when he felt an excruciating pain course through his body. Someone had stabbed him! He could feel blood oozing out of his burning back. For a moment, he couldn't fathom what had happened, and then he heard one of the guards whisper into his ear, 'Mount the horse.'

The man Chandra had thought to be his guard had him at knife-point! With a hand wrapped around Chandra's mouth, he dislodged his sword and threw it. Chandra knew he had precious few minutes before he could escape. Removing his dagger from his side pocket, Chandra ducked and kicked the man on his shins.

As the man doubled over in pain, the second man took charge and pinned Chandra to the ground. Chandra felt breathless and dizzy in the mud. He twisted around, grabbed the man's ankles and pulled him to the ground.

The man fell with an audible thud, but another man materialized out of nowhere and pounced on Chandra. *Where are my real bodyguards?* Chandra wondered, feeling helpless. *Pranava must be out of earshot too.* But there wasn't enough time to think. Chandra had to act, move, hit, whatever it took to escape the attackers. Before he could do anything, someone had covered his face with a hood over his head and tied his hands behind his back.

When the man tried to haul Chandra onto a horse, he resisted. 'Let me ride my horse. You ride yours. No need for an outing together!' Chandra mumbled through his mask.

The man grunted, 'I don't need your advice. Get on the horse.' Chandra winced when he heard the man slap his horse with the reins. Chandra's horse, already frightened, began to neigh uncontrollably in pain.

'Get on the horse, or I'll slit your—' The man's words were cut short, and his grip on Chandra's neck loosened. The dreadful hood came off Chandra's head.

Taking a deep breath, Chandra watched as Pranava plunged his sword into the enemy soldier. As the man screamed to his death, Pranava cut the ropes binding Chandra's hands.

Stretching his hands to get rid of the stiffness, Chandra sighed, 'How did they know who I was? Are they bats with night vision?'

Pranava chuckled and handed Chandra the reins to his horse. 'Thank God, your horse neighed. Or you would have been on a jolly ride with the man. It was funny to see him haul you onto the horse! Did he think you are so frail?'

Chandra began to laugh, but then he yelled to his friend, who was slightly ahead of him. 'Pranava, watch out!' A group of men now surrounded them both.

* * *

Chandra looked around the room he was in. It was a vast yet ordinary-looking space with nothing but an oversized chair and a thin carpet on the floor. The men who had attacked them had hauled him and Pranava to this place.

'Does it hurt?' Pranava asked, looking at the wound on Chandra's back. The Pushkarana men had been courteous enough to bandage Chandra's bleeding back.

'I am sure it was a butcher who bandaged me. It hurts when I move. And my legs are so numb sitting on this carpet. They seem to weigh a ton.' Chandra felt sick and nauseated.

'Footsteps. Someone is coming,' said Chandra, now alert.

'Must be the leader of the giant clan. Those who lugged us here were huge!' Pranava shook his head in dismay. 'Which breed of humans were they? I'm sure this chair will be a snug fit for their bottoms,' he said, pointing at the abnormally large chair.

A man entered the room and announced dramatically, 'King Varma of Pushkarana is on his way. Get to your feet.'

'How can we with our tied hands and feet?' Chandra snapped at the announcer.

The man who entered next stood before them sizing them up. Given the amount of silk and gold piled on him, he had to be the king. He stopped the royal entourage at the door. Pointing a finger at Chandra, he laughed. 'You look so pitiful! No need to stand up for me. Just stay where you are and grovel for mercy. That is humiliation enough for the Gupta prince.'

Chandra blurted out in anger, 'You coward! You ordered an ambush at night. Your men infiltrated our army. You had me kidnapped! Everything about you is unethical.'

The king did not seem offended by Chandra's words. Sitting on the chair pompously, he crossed his legs. 'What was I to do, Prince? Fight ethically to lose all my men and my throne in the process?'

'That is what a real king would do,' said Chandra.

The man laughed. 'That is what a fool would do. A smart man does whatever it takes to protect himself and his throne.'

'Even street dogs fight more honourably than you. What is your next plan?' Chandra scowled at the king.

'I don't need to plan anymore, Prince. Your father has declared a truce and retracted. I'll soon have my men take you back to your mother.'

Chandra turned red in rage. 'You blackmailed my father by keeping me here.'

'Smart boy.' King Varma got up and laughed at Chandra. 'Go home and sleep. Don't bother us ever again.'

Now, Chandra was not only angry but also remorseful. He had lost a significant battle for his father. They were supposed to return victorious, but he had caused his father's first debacle in the campaign.

36

'Get out ... get out of here,' Atma yelled at the girl who was dancing for Rama and Megha.

'What are you doing here?' Rama slurred from the chair he was sitting on. 'Why are you shooing the girl away?'

When the scared young dancer had disappeared, Atma glared at Rama. Vidura and Megha stood quietly and looked on.

'Who let the old man in?' a woman screamed outside the door in crude language. Heads looked into the room to see if there was a drama unfolding. Atma signalled to Vidura to shut the door.

'How can the prince of the Gupta clan be in a place like this?' Atma pointed at the run-down room. There were dirty clothes strewn around. Plates caked with food were piled in a corner. 'How can you sleep on those blankets? This is a filthy dungeon.'

'Look, Minister, you are helping me, and I'll reward you when that help is useful. Get out now,' Rama yelled at Atma.

'You worked hard for nearly two years. People had started respecting you. Now in two months, you've thrown it all away. That too when your father has returned.'

Rama guffawed. 'I am celebrating my brother's downfall. Didn't you hear how he single-handedly lost the Pushkarana battle?'

Atma snickered. 'Who is telling you these fantastic stories? Your father lost the battle because the enemy cheated. People now not only revere your brother, but they also sympathize with him. Did you see the grand welcome they are planning in the town square for him?'

At this, Rama seemed to sober down. After a pause, he said, 'Of course, Chandra will forever be a hero to people. What do you want me to do now?'

When Rama walked towards him, Atma stepped back and turned his head, unable to bear the smell of cheap wine and sweat. *What am I doing? Is this man worthy of ruling the glorious Magadha kingdom even for a short while?* Atma cringed at the thought, but only momentarily. His mission was to save Magadha from Samudragupta. If what he'd heard was true, Samudragupta was ailing. That meant he would select an heir to the throne soon. He had to make sure Rama became the next king. After that, it would be child's play to dethrone Rama and build a Magadha of his dreams.

'See me tomorrow at six,' said Atma and walked out of the dilapidated building as quickly as his bad leg permitted.

37

'If you are going on a trek to the Himalayas, you must take our guide,' said Chandra's uncle firmly. 'You have to go in a group. It's not safe to go alone.'

'We are not planning to climb the highest summit! Just a few miles up before we come back down and head to Kamarupa.'

'A few miles or a few hundred miles, Chandra, the rule stays. No guide, no trek.' Chandra had to agree when his uncle said it with an air of finality.

This trip was his dream come true. Samudragupta had approached him a month after the war to ask if he wanted to head to Kamarupa.

'Chandra, this is for the Ashwamedha Yagya. The province that ties up the white horse we've sent out will have to battle with us. Nobody east of us has braved it. So, our friend, King Pushyavarma, has tied it up in jest. He wants his people to know how talented our swordsmen are. Instead of a battle, there will be a match – one of our swordsmen will fight against four of theirs. Do you want to take up this challenge?'

Chandra had agreed instantly. He needed a diversion to forget the Pushkarana debacle that haunted him day and night.

'I'll go, Father. But I don't want an entourage. Only Pranava and me.'

Samudragupta had been reluctant to entertain the idea. 'Chandra, it isn't safe for you to travel alone. Take at least a few trusted guards with you.'

When Chandra had refused to budge, his father had given his consent half-heartedly. 'Then, let's not tell anyone about this. Not even your mother if you can avoid it.' But Chandra had told his mother anyway.

Instead of heading to Kamarupa directly, he and Pranava had travelled up north towards the Kathmandu valley. Samudragupta's relatives ruled this beautiful province bound by the Himalayan mountains.

Now, after three days of extreme pampering by his aunts, Chandra was all set to trek the Himalayas with Pranava and a guide on the insistence of his uncle. They joined a small group of yak herders who were familiar with the terrain. His uncle, as paranoid as his father, had kept Chandra's identity a secret even from the guide.

* * *

It was the third day of the trek. They'd passed pristine rivulets and the vibrant Himalayan woods to reach a higher altitude. The first two days were tiring, but everything, even the chill, was bearable. In the middle of the snow-covered mountains, all they could see were the mighty peaks of glistening snow. Walking in the snow on a steep track was strenuous. The altitude too was making them increasingly breathless.

Pranava panted, 'I am never climbing another mountain again.'

Chandra tried to reply, but he could not feel his mouth against the icy wind. They could hardly see anything in the mist that enveloped them. The yaks, however, seemed comfortable.

'The wind is picking up. Let's make a quick stop for lunch and then trek some more. There's a small settlement where we can halt for the night,' said the guide, who was as comfortable as the yaks.

* * *

That night, as soon as Chandra and Pranava stretched out on the tent floor, the ground rumbled.

'Is it my head making up things or did we just shake?' asked Pranava.

'Unless my head too is making up the same stories as yours, the ground shook.' Chandra sat up. The next moment, everything around them started to shake violently.

The guide, instantly on his feet, peeked outside and screamed, 'Oh no, dear God, no.' He then muttered a few curses in his native language. He spat out the words, 'Avalanche. Run outside and hug the tree. In case you get—'

Before the man could finish his sentence, the tent had become a kite. It flew away, exposing them to howling winds. Chandra stared in disbelief at the giant wall of snow hurtling towards them. They began to run to join the herders. Chandra had no idea where Pranava or the guide was, but he kept running with the herders. They must know how to handle the avalanche!

Then, to his dismay, something struck his leg, hard. He tripped, fell, and then tumbled like a stone. When he screamed for help, it only made his lungs freeze. Nobody heard him. When he kept sliding on the sleet with the giant wall of snow closing in on him, he knew he was a dead man.

38

As he sailed through the ice, Chandra tried to remember the lessons the guide had given them before the trek. *Make an air pocket with your hand for breathing. Grab something sturdy to stop the slide. Don't let the snow bury you.* Now it seemed like he needed at least five hands to carry out those instructions! As the avalanche swept over him, Chandra frantically tried to grab at something to stop his fall.

Then, his hands curled around something – probably the stump of a dead tree. God had heard him after all! Chandra held on to the stump with all his strength and fervently hoped that it would not come loose. Snow and small rocks, and God knows what else, pelted at him relentlessly. Soon, his right arm, holding on to the stump, began to tire. With his left hand, he was cupping his nose for breathing, which was proving more and more ineffective. Determined not to give up, Chandra dug a groove with his foot for a toehold. That seemed to ease the pressure off his arm a little. As he hung on to the tree stump, the pelting started to wane. Then, to Chandra's relief, it stopped!

His face was numb. His body was almost buried under the snow, but he was glad to be breathing again! Then he saw someone running towards him. Pranava and the herders!

They pulled him out of the snow. Chandra sat up, still unable to believe that he was alive. Except for a few bruises on his body, he was not hurt. He tried to stand up with Pranava's help but stumbled. His legs had turned into mashed potato.

'Are you sure you can stand?' asked Pranava, worry writ large on his face.

'I sure hope so!' Chandra smiled in relief when he managed to regain his balance. He felt better. 'Pranava, you sound serious. You must have been very worried.'

The herders bowed to Chandra. 'They know who you are. I needed their help to find you. Please reward them like a prince!'

'Where is the guide?' Chandra asked, scanning the faces around him.

Pranava said angrily, 'I'll strangle him if I ever find him. He abandoned us when we started to look for you. As though he didn't want us to find you at all.'

The head of the herders offered to escort Chandra and Pranava downhill. As they trekked down, Chandra remembered something. 'Pranava, I didn't trip and fall. I felt something hit my leg. I don't think I was hallucinating.'

Pranava stopped. 'The guide. I am sure the guide did it. As soon as we took shelter under a boulder, I knew you were missing. But, he said you were safe under a tree a little ahead of us. Even after the blizzard ended, he stopped us from finding you.'

'So, someone planted him to kill me. Did he have to choose an avalanche? Most of my body is still frozen.'

Pranava breathed deeply. 'Prince, shall we go back to Kathmandu and ask your uncle for the guide's whereabouts?'

Chandra shook his head. 'A waste of time. Someone is on to me. I'm sure there'll be more killers along the way. Let's focus on them.'

39

'Princess! We'd better head back. It's almost dusk, and there's nobody here except us.' Priya held her friend's arm anxiously. They had escaped from the royal guards since Dhruva found them unbearably stiff.

'Just a few more minutes for the deer to come for a drink.' Dhruva bent down to take a sip of the river water. 'Relax, Priya. Look around. It's so green everywhere. We've come out of the palace after months, thanks to the rains!'

'We can become prey to wild animals. We can be robbed or kidnapped, and nobody will even know. This was a crazy idea, Princess,' Priya howled. Dhruva smiled at her friend's distress. They were only a few miles from the palace, and she knew the way back to the city. Moreover, she knew the guards would find them soon.

'Nobody will rob us. Look at us! We look so poor.' Dhruva pointed at themselves. They did look downtrodden in the clothes they had borrowed from their maids. 'And we're so close to the city. The only wild animal you'll encounter here is a dog!'

'The deer!' Dhruva exclaimed, dragging Priya away from the river. 'Let's not scare them. Hide!'

Hiding behind a tree, they looked at the deer moving cautiously one by one towards the water.

'Oh, look at them! How pretty! Poor things are petrified of crocodiles, I guess,' whispered Dhruva.

'What! There are crocodiles in the river, and you are telling me now? We were there only minutes ago!' Priya almost screamed, making Dhruva laugh.

'Relax. I was only trying to scare you. There aren't any crocodiles in the river.'

A few minutes later, their thirst quenched, the herd went back into the forest. As the girls watched them, the deer suddenly broke into a nervous run. While all the others disappeared into the woods, a small fawn was left behind.

'What is happening, Priya? Is that a snake curled around the fawn?' Dhruva ran towards the animal that had now collapsed. She stared in horror at the python that was snuffing the life out of the baby deer. It was coiling itself tighter and tighter around the deer's tiny body.

'Help! Somebody help!' Dhruva screamed as loudly as she could and continued to scream even after her voice turned hoarse.

'Stop screaming, Princess. You are disturbing the snake! What if it wants us instead of the deer?' Priya tried to drag Dhruva back to safety, but Dhruva didn't budge. She had to save the baby deer.

Suddenly, an arrow lodged itself in the python. Dhruva and Priya gasped. They watched in awe as the snake started uncoiling slowly. The deer tottered to its feet, and the next moment, it had taken off.

Dhruva glanced around to see who the shooter was. Two men were walking towards them. One of them had a bow slung on his shoulder.

Priya nudged her friend and whispered, 'We don't know who they are. They could be dacoits for all we know. Let's run.'

'Can you run faster than his arrow? Let's talk to them.'

Chandra looked at the girl who'd been screaming her lungs out only a minute ago. Now she was eyeing them suspiciously. *She looks vaguely familiar*, he thought. He immediately dismissed the thought. There was no way he could have known a common girl in the far province of Kamarupa. What didn't escape him were her sparkling brown eyes and flushed cheeks. She looked almost as frail as the deer he'd just rescued.

'Step back. The python isn't dead. You don't want to be his next meal,' Chandra heard Pranava warn the girls. Chandra inched closer to the python. If he retrieved his arrow, the snake might even live.

Chandra then turned to the girls. 'Why are you here at this hour? Go home.'

Dhruva knitted her brows and challenged him, 'Why? You two can be here, but not us?

'We have weapons for protection. How about you?' Chandra asked her mockingly.

'My voice. Didn't you just hear how loudly I can scream?'

Chandra smiled. 'True. That's more powerful than any of our weapons.'

'Princess!' They all turned in unison towards the voice. A few men on horses were approaching them. One of them had already drawn his sword.

Dhruva rolled her eyes in exasperation when she saw that the guards had caught up with her. 'These two mean no harm.' She stopped the man with the sword.

'Princess ...' Chandra drawled as he looked closely at her. 'You are Princess Dhruva! I knew I'd seen you somewhere.'

'And who might you be?' Dhruva looked closely at Chandra. 'You look familiar too.'

'Chandra. Son of King Samudragupta.' He quite enjoyed the expression on Dhruva's face.

'Father did mention you would be here. But I expected a prince, not a hunter!'

'I didn't expect to see a princess in a pauper's garb either!'

The entourage soon headed towards the palace, with Chandra and Pranava on their own horses. Priya nudged Dhruva. 'He is quite a good-looking man, I must say! You never told me about him.'

Dhruva smiled. 'I was no more than a baby when I last met him. And he looked like a skeleton then! Let's hope he's a good swordsman because Father's arranged a duelling contest for him.'

40

Two days later, at the Kamarupa palace, Chandra and Pranava strolled lazily around the garden. Chandra sighed. 'Pranava, this rest is killing me. I want to get on with the fight and head back home. I'll ask the king to arrange for the duel tomorrow itself.' Pushyavarma had forced Chandra to rest for a week before the sword fight.

'I agree. What a sleepy little town! I went to their wrestling arena. It's like a children's play area. Not to mention the men who were practicing there. They were babies too!'

Chandra laughed. 'That's a bit harsh, my friend. But I do think that Kamarupa is better off being a peace-loving province!'

'Given their baby wrestlers?' Pranava smirked.

'Well, I hope they have baby swordsmen too! Then we can head back faster,' Chandra added. 'Pranava, look, that's our white horse. God, I want to take him back with me!'

A burly man tending to the horse at the stable smiled

at them. 'Prince, this is a great horse. Ride him on your way back home.'

* * *

'This is insane!' Chandra exclaimed, looking at the sea of people gathered around the arena the next day.

'All of them are here to see you, Prince. You better fight well.' Pranava patted Chandra on the shoulder.

'Thanks. That helps.' Facing them, in the front-row seats, was King Pushyavarma with his family. Dhruva sat with the friend they'd met at the riverside. Samu, her brother, approached Chandra.

'You know, I should wish for our swordsmen to win. But I want you to win!' Samu sounded earnest and almost dreamy-eyed about Chandra.

'So, will you cheer for me? In public?' Chandra cocked a brow at him teasingly.

'Even if I'm stoned for doing so!' Samu hugged Chandra and wished him well.

Pranava stared at the three men now warming up. 'One of them looks like a mountain! Watch out, Prince. What is with you and giants!'

'In a swordfight, a large body is a hindrance, my friend! So, don't worry and watch the show,' said Chandra, heading towards the fighting rink. It was a circular patch cleared for the fight. All around it was open space packed with people. There was a lot of noise. So much so that Chandra worried he might become deaf by the time the fight ended.

* * *

‘I still don’t see any point to such fights. Chivalry as a game is overrated,’ Dhruva bent down and whispered to her brother.

‘Shh ... just watch. You’ll never see such a display of swords again in your life.’

‘I have to be quiet too? How long will this be?’ Dhruva tried to sound nonchalant, but she felt nervous. *How can one man fight with three?* It seemed like an unfair contest. But Chandra had agreed to it. As he warmed up, he looked entirely unfazed.

‘What is he doing? Yoga or swords?’ Priya whispered to Dhruva and was again shushed by Samu.

‘The two of you should just leave. Don’t ruin the mood for us.’

‘Look at those muscles,’ Rahula said dreamily. ‘I want to become like Prince Chandra.’

‘Dream on, stick,’ Dhruva ran her hand on Rahula’s skinny arm. ‘Now, shh ... Don’t ruin the mood for Samu.’

* * *

‘Dear people,’ the referee began speaking into the bullhorn. ‘Prince Chandra—’ He stopped for a dramatic pause and then continued in a raised voice, ‘Prince Chandra of Magadha is here with us today.’

Most people roared and clapped, but some of them booed the referee. ‘Get on with the fight, old man. Enough talking.’

The referee then looked at Chandra. ‘Out of these three swordsmen from Kamarupa, who do you choose for the first fight, Prince Chandra?’

Though Chandra was irritated at the way the man kept repeating his name, he tried not to show it. Taking the bullhorn from the man, he announced, 'I've decided to fight all three of them at once.'

There was a murmur from the crowd. The referee stared blankly at Chandra. 'That is very unusual, Prince Chandra. I must seek permission from the king.'

After a few minutes of intense discussion, the referee was back. 'Prince Chandra—' *Stop saying that!* Chandra wanted to scream but managed to control himself.

The referee continued, 'We will honour your challenge. But, if at any point I sense danger, I hold the right to call off the game.' The man continued with the rules of the contest, undeterred by the heavy booing thrown his way. 'Only the swords and shields we've provided can be used. Weapons can clash with weapons but not the body parts of opponents. When a participant's sword falls to the ground, he will head out of the arena accepting defeat ...' The crowd's cheers and shouts drowned the rest of his words.

The contestants began the fight after a quick prayer and a bow to the king. Two of his opponents looked normal to Chandra, but the third resembled an elephant. And, oddly, familiar. Chandra felt an unease build in him when he met the bloodshot eyes of the beefy man.

41

No matter which way Chandra turned, one of the three men was staring him right in the eye, clumsily taking turns to clang at his sword. They were nowhere close to the exceptional swordsmen Chandra was used to in Pataliputra. These men were strong but neither quick nor talented.

'Prince, attack the one to your right,' Pranava screamed. 'Now, attack now!'

The man to Chandra's right had his shield down. Chandra deftly sliced at his sword. Bang! The sword fell, and the combatant was gone.

The burly man spat on the ground and shouted at the referee. 'He got help from outside. That is illegal.'

The crowd shouted. Chandra couldn't decide if they were booing or cheering. But it looked like they were supporting him. The referee shrugged. 'People will yell things when the game is on. I can't stop that. Get on with the fight.'

The man moved close to Chandra and grunted, 'Don't gloat. I'll get you.'

Pranava ran to the rink. Trying to push the man away from Chandra, Pranava yelled, 'Hey, if what the prince did is illegal, then you are illegal too. You are three people stuffed into one.'

The man looked murderous enough to throw both Pranava and Chandra out. But he only grunted and twirled his sword.

'Go back to your seat. You can't come here when the fight is on.' The referee sent Pranava away, signalling to the combatants to continue.

Chandra decided not to go on the offensive for a while, and only defend himself. *That should frustrate the men.* And it did. Much to the annoyance of his opponents, Chandra kept nimbly deflecting their blows. The harder they tried to dislodge his sword, the quicker he got. Chandra silently thanked his instructors for all those long and tedious hours of training.

Despite the guards yelling for silence, the crowd was chanting and roaring continuously. Chandra knew he had to end the contest soon, before he got tired. Besides, the pair of them were now fighting in tandem. They were bringing their swords down on his in unison. Though their action looked more like wood chopping than swordplay, Chandra had to be careful.

When the two of them came down hard on his sword again, Chandra swiftly withdrew it from underneath instead of thrusting upwards. He thrust his sword with all his might against the shield of the non-burly opponent. The push had the desired effect – it propelled the man backwards, making him lose his balance and hit the ground. Quickly spinning around, Chandra hit the hilt of his sword.

The good news: he was now down to the last opponent. The bad news: his remaining opponent could crush him with his bare hands.

Their swords pointed at each other, the two men began to circle the deck. The audience had gone deathly quiet. Then, out of the blue, the opponent kicked Chandra in the stomach. Even as he doubled over in pain, Chandra managed to keep the shield against his chest. He watched in horror as the man swiftly removed the cover of his sword, exposing a lethally sharp blade!

It all happened quickly. By the time the referee could intervene, the man had stabbed Chandra in the arm.

Chandra's vision blurred. His grip on the sword loosened and his legs refused to hold him upright. He registered Pranava running towards him. Soldiers were surrounding them, and his attacker was being pulled away. Then he fainted.

* * *

Chandra woke up in a room that smelt like a hospital – neem, camphor and white linen. Pranava was next to his bed, juggling oranges. Chandra tried to sit up, but his head spun.

'Rest,' said Pranava, stopping Chandra gently from getting up. Then he grinned. 'And, welcome back to life.'

'That is a nasty stab,' said Chandra inspecting his arm, which felt heavy and painful. 'Who was that man?'

'He was the one we met at the stable yesterday – the one who asked you to ride the white horse home. He apparently came in as a replacement swordsman last week. Now, someone has killed him in prison. So, nobody knows who he was. The king said he's investigating the man who recruited the killer. The recruiter is lazy and stupid. When he needed a replacement, he blindly hired this one.'

They remained silent for a while, watching the curtains flutter.

'Someone planted the trekking guide to kill me, then this swordsman. Wonder what else awaits me!'

'Your father was right. We shouldn't have travelled without bodyguards,' said Pranava.

Chandra shook his head. 'I am glad we took this

trip, Pranava. Surviving these vicious attacks makes me feel stronger.'

Suddenly, there was a flurry of activity outside the room. The guards at the door stood at attention. Some guards walked in stiffly towards Chandra's bed. Following them was King Pushyavarma.

Chandra tried to sit up straight to welcome the king, but his body refused to cooperate. Taking a seat next to Chandra, the king asked him to lie down and relax. His prolonged apologies about the mishap made Chandra extremely uncomfortable. He wanted to change the topic.

'Prince Chandra, there is a reason your father sent you here. It was not just to show how competent the Guptas are. It's something more personal.'

Chandra narrowed his eyes. What could it be? It'd better be something good! He was in no mood for more bad news.

The king added after a pause, 'A while back the Shaka king, Rudrasimha, had expressed his intent to marry my daughter Dhruva.'

'What?' Chandra almost choked. 'He is older than you! And if your daughter ever saw him, his evil face would make her faint!'

'Well, I declined the offer, of course. But by doing so, I've made an enemy out of him. An alliance with your kingdom will keep him away from us.'

Chandra was getting tired. He resisted the temptation to look at Pranava and roll his eyes. His back was aching. He wanted to lie down again.

'This will be a critical alliance for both the kingdoms. I get protection from the Shakas, and I'll guard the eastern provinces for your father. I'll have more authority to do so if I'm related to the king.'

Where is this going? Chandra wondered. *This man sure knows how to drag a story!*

Pushyavarma continued, 'It is your father and my wish that you marry my daughter, Dhruvadevi. But, only if you like each other. That's the reason you are here,' he concluded in a measured tone.

Chandra almost fell off the bed. His head would explode from the blood rush. He looked at Pranava, who looked more bemused than shocked!

'But I am not getting married anytime soon! Of course, your daughter is a fine young girl. But I am not ready. Not ready at all,' Chandra spoke emphatically. *Marriage was for ancient people!*

Pushyavarma laughed. 'My daughter said the same thing. But, you only need to get engaged. You can marry later when you both are ready. Here is a letter from your father.'

Chandra skimmed the short letter. His father had written what King Pushyavarma had just said.

The king stood up from the chair and turned to leave. 'Dhruva is coming here with her brothers to see you. Spend some time together and see if you like each other. If all goes well, we can arrange for the engagement ceremony in three days. The doctor says your arm will be a lot better by then.'

After the king and his entourage left, Pranava started making sounds of wedding trumpets. Chandra gave him murderous looks. 'No jokes. Or I'll wring your neck.'

Pranava touched Chandra's hurt arm. 'You can't! So you're going to marry the fine young girl!'

Chandra pretended not to hear Pranava and closed his eyes.

* * *

Three days later, Chandra was engaged to be married to Dhruva. And, surprisingly, he didn't mind it at all! Being with her was like being with a good friend – she was witty, intelligent, and matched his obsession for board games!

42

'Mother, why didn't you send word for me? I'd have cut short my journey and returned.' Chandra was shocked at his father's deterioration. He'd returned from Kamarupa that evening and gone to visit his father right away. He found that Samudragupta had shrunk significantly. He looked dwarfed by the large bed.

'Now that you are back, he'll get better,' said Dattadevi. Though she smiled, it was not a happy smile. Worry and pain were etched on her face.

'Your mother is right. With you around, I already feel strong enough for the next battle.' Samudragupta flexed his arm.

Dattadevi patted his arm down. 'You'll only help me take care of the garden with your arms. No more wars.'

‘What happened to you, Father? You were not half as sick when I left,’ asked Chandra worriedly.

Samudragupta managed a weak smile. ‘My cough has become worse. And the sore throat isn’t letting me eat. Enough about me. What happened to your arm? How did you get injured?’

Though he’d come to tell his father about the murder attempts, he decided not to. ‘Something got lodged in my arm while swimming in the rapids. Nothing to worry about. I was treated in Kamarupa.’

The queen asked, ‘Where did you swim? Was it in Kamarupa? How careless of the king to let you!’

Chandra thought her outburst about King Pushyavarma was unfounded. ‘It was on the way somewhere, Mother. Not in Kamarupa,’ he lied.

Samudragupta intervened. ‘We have been waiting to know about our future daughter-in-law. Tell us about her and the engagement.’ Though tired, the king’s eyes twinkled with happiness.

Dattadevi gave a taut smile. Was that disapproval he saw in her eyes? Chandra suddenly felt protective about Pushyavarma and Dhruva.

‘She’s very well-read. She studies the scriptures,’ Chandra said, sounding defensive even to himself. He waited to see his mother’s reaction, but she didn’t say anything.

A knock at the door interrupted their conversation. ‘I’d asked Minister Harisena to join us. I want our conquests to be inscribed on a stone pillar in Kaushambi. The minister has kept a log of all the older campaigns. You have to fill in the details of this last one, Chandra.’

Samudragupta looked at Chandra and smiled proudly. 'The next set of inscriptions on the pillar will be of your conquests, Son.'

'Why just his? What about Rama?' Dattadevi's voice was angry. 'You seem to forget you have an older son. We should have got him married before Chandra.'

She got up, adjusting the pleats of her heavy silk saree. Chandra held her arm. 'Of course, Ma. I promise you, I won't monopolize the pillar.'

Dattadevi smiled ruefully at Chandra. 'I know you won't.' She glared at Samudragupta. 'It's your father I'm worried about.'

* * *

As Chandra walked back to his quarters, his eyes were heavy, and he longed for sleep. The journey back from Kamarupa had been rough, with rising storms and heavy winds. The murder attempts on him and the whirlwind engagement had resulted in many sleepless nights.

Though exhausted, sleep eluded him for a long time. As he tossed around, the thoughts of Dhruva and his wedding started to invade him. He still couldn't imagine himself as a married man. He liked Dhruva. She was nice, witty, intelligent and kind.

On the evening of their engagement, her brother Samu had teased her: 'You can't hate weapons or warfare now. Prince Chandra is a famous warrior.'

She'd let that dig pass and had blushed a little. Later, while they played pachheesi, she'd given Chandra a note. 'I only hate weapons, not warriors.'

The day he'd started back, her father had said he could say goodbye to her in her scriptures class. When he'd found her, she was the only pupil sitting under a tree listening to an old man. Chandra had tried to focus on the lecture, but almost fell asleep on his feet. Spotting him, Dhruva had excused herself from the lesson and spoken to him.

He'd mumbled an apology for disturbing her in the class and asked why she was the only student there.

'All the others ran away,' she'd said ruefully. 'He is our substitute teacher.'

Chandra caught himself smiling. It may be nice having her around! He'd grown up without any girls around him.

Then, his mind drifted to his father's failing health. When he finally fell asleep, all he dreamt about was someone chasing him with a lasso rope. He thought it was Rama, but it turned out to be his mother.

When he woke up in the morning to the loud chirping of birds, he started thinking about his journey and the attempts on his life. What if the killers had abducted him and asked for ransom? What if the men, whoever they were, had other plans to usurp their kingdom? Chandra decided to talk to his father and tell him about the incidents on his trip.

* * *

'What is wrong, Minister? Why are you sitting in darkness?' Vidura adjusted the wick on the lamp and lit it.

'It was a golden opportunity to finish off Prince Chandra, but Rudrasimha ruined it. He's so useless.' As soon as Rama had told him that Chandra was taking a trip alone to Kamarupa, Atma had sent word to Rudrasimha. Queen Dattadevi was the weak link in the royal palace. She could never keep a secret from Rama.

Vidura's hands trembled slightly as he lit another lamp. 'Sir, do we want to kill Prince Chandra? He hasn't harmed anyone.'

Atma snickered. 'Vidura! He's his father. He'll inherit not only the throne but also his father's useless ideals. He'll wage wars that are more wasteful than the king's. War campaigns should bring wealth to a kingdom, not bankrupt the treasury. Samudragupta's Unite-Bharata theme will finish off Magadha.'

'How will Rudrasimha be any better, Sir? He is mad and power-hungry.'

'How many times have I told you that he will be a ruler only in name?' Atma snapped. 'I'll do the administration. Just leave all the thinking to me, will you? Summon Rama here tomorrow.'

Vidura murmured, 'You have to retire from all this, Minister. Time to rest and pray.'

'I'll do that after I lose my brain.' Atma buried his head back in a scroll.

* * *

Rama watched his father walking in the garden of his royal quarters. What a grand structure! The marble courtyard was lined with sculptures, a lush green garden, and a pond big enough to swim in.

Rama looked at his father's lounge chair, a massive wrought-iron one with soft cushions. He thought of all the times his father had sat in it and reprimanded him. Including that terrible evening when he'd asked Rama to abandon Kusha. Well, if he ever became the king, the first thing to go would be that chair. Better, he would melt it and leave it to the palace dogs to mark it.

'Rama, what brings you here?' Samudragupta's voice jolted him out of his quiet rage. His father was lowering himself in the chair with great difficulty. Rama thought of helping him but refrained. There was a nurse standing by.

'I came to ask you something,' said Rama looking at the nurse. Taking the hint, the woman covered Samudragupta with a warm shawl and walked away. The sun was about to set, and the birds returning to their nests were making an incredibly loud noise.

'Why didn't you send me to Kamarupa to marry Princess Dhruva? I too could have won that fake duel.' Rama had no patience for small talk that evening. Words, Atma's words, tumbled out of him. Though his father gestured for him to sit, he continued to stand. He felt better glaring down at his father.

Samudragupta looked surprised at first but recovered quickly. 'Because the king of Kamarupa invited Chandra. It was not a fake duel, and frankly, I don't think you could have won it.' Samudragupta's face was taut. Rama hated that grim face. His father's words cut him like a knife.

'What you think is not always the truth. You arranged for a sword duel because Chandra is better at it. Why not wrestling or lance throwing or hunting – things at which I am good? Let me guess why Pushyavarma invited Chandra. Because you told him that Chandra will be the next king.' Rama felt his face grow hot as he spoke. He hoped he didn't look flushed like a ripe tomato, which often was the case when he spoke to his father.

Samudragupta started coughing, which racked his body violently. When the nurse tried to attend to him, he stopped her with a shake of the head. Rama stood looking at him defiantly, waiting for a reply.

Samudragupta resumed talking once the cough had subsided. 'Pushyavarma has seen Chandra lead an army in a battle. He must have liked him enough to offer his daughter in marriage. You weren't there in the battleground wrestling or throwing lances, Son.'

He then bent down and picked up the glass of water. Taking a sip, he looked at Rama blankly. 'Chandra would have had the courtesy to offer me water when I coughed.'

'Chandra lost the battle of Pushkarana because he didn't wait for his bodyguards to go with him. He almost got killed twice on his way to Kamarupa because of his idiotic chivalry. He is the most impulsive nitwit I've known, and he's your favourite?' Rama screamed. He didn't care anymore what his father thought.

Samudragupta sighed and twirled the ring with the insignia of garuda on his finger. 'Chandra almost got killed, but he survived. He is impulsive, but mostly to help others. Stop listening to Atma and do something useful with your time. I have a feeling Chandra almost got killed on his way to Kamarupa because you told

Atma about his trip. You are naive, Rama. Don't trust anyone so blindly.'

Rama's head spun. *Father knows about my meetings with Atma!*

'Till now, I was only lazy and disobedient in your eyes. Now I'm naive too?' Rama stormed out. There was no point talking to his father. Not then, not at any other time. As he walked on, he recollected his father's accusations about Atma. *Did he plan to kill Chandra?* Rama quickly decided not to pursue that thought. Atma was the one man who cared about him.

* * *

Six months later ...

Rama fidgeted on the podium. He and Chandra stood flanking their parents. He hated having to pose with them like a happy family! The bright smile his mother was flashing would make everyone think they were one.

It was the concluding day of the Ashwamedha Yagya Samudragupta had performed over the last seven days. The smoke from the altar still hung in the air. Everything was grand and festive – vermilion, turmeric, heaps of flowers, strings of mango leaves tied all around. But Rama didn't feel grand. He wanted to be anywhere but there with his father and Chandra.

Rama glanced at the audience, who seemed eager for their king to begin speaking. That day's attendees were not ordinary people. They were high-ranked officials of the Gupta kingdom, as well as kings from all over

Bharata. Sighing, Rama focused his attention on his father. It would be another thank-you note, he was sure.

Samudragupta began, 'My dear people and beloved kings, I truly wish I could convey this message fully. But, my voice, as you can make out, does not seem to obey my orders.' He smiled and paused for the mild chuckle from the audience to subside. 'So I've requested my dear friend, Minister Harisena, to read out my message.' The cough had reduced his voice to a hoarse whisper.

Rama was alert. This could be more than a thank-you note! Clearing his throat, Harisena read from the palm-leaf scroll he held, 'I welcome all of you distinguished people here to a momentous occasion. As you know, the Gupta kingdom has two able heirs – my sons, Ramagupta and Chandragupta. I request the gathering to cast their votes for one of them as the next king of the Gupta dynasty.'

Was this a joke? Who does this sort of thing? Rama began to feel nervous. *Who would vote for him?* There were murmurs in the court. Rama saw that his mother looked as shocked as everyone else.

Harisena continued, 'I, the king, will refrain from voting, so that I don't influence your decision. You'll need to choose right away based on your current judgement of the princes. So, those in favour of Prince Ramagupta, please raise your hands.'

Rama looked on, dumbfounded. People were talking, but no hands went up. He wanted to die of humiliation. This was his father's intention – a public embarrassment for him. Then he saw his mother's hand go up – royally, determinedly. The crowd continued to murmur, but no other hands were going up. Rama looked at Chandra, who stood stoically. His hand, of course, did not go up.

His gaze swept over Kritavarma, Harisena, Guna – all kept their hands to themselves. Rama then decided to act in his own favour and raised his hand. If he didn't pick himself, who would? After a few minutes, a few hands began to go up – a few ministers, probably those who hated Samudragupta; a few vassal kings who craved freedom and thought he would make a weak ruler; a few guild-heads, who probably needed favours from his mother.

The hands were counted and written down. Harisena retook the stage. 'Now those in favour of Prince Chandra ...'

Rama's head throbbed when Chandra was declared a clear winner. He was too exhausted to feel anything – to be ashamed or angry.

43

Chandra couldn't decide how he felt when he saw his mother waiting for him in his quarters. Let down that she preferred Rama over him? Angry? Sad?

'Chandra, you know why I chose Rama. It was the right thing to do. The first-born gets the throne,' she said almost immediately when she saw him. So she did feel guilty for what she'd done.

'It's all right, Mother,' Chandra sighed, sitting down on his chair. 'I was not hankering to be a king like Rama was.'

'I know you were not. I am also glad people chose you because you'll make a better ruler. You are more disciplined, hardworking, and compassionate.' The queen rolled the juggling balls on Chandra's table as if she were trying to occupy her hands.

Then you should have chosen me! Chandra wanted to shout, but he also understood where his mother was coming from. 'How is Brother feeling? Not too depressed, I hope?' Chandra asked, changing the topic.

Dattadevi didn't answer for a while. Then she mumbled, 'Your father never really liked him. The people don't like him either. How do you think he feels?'

She got up to leave. Chandra could see the tears in her eyes. 'That is not true, Ma. Brother is—' Chandra tried to console his mother. Then he stopped abruptly, sensing his own anger rise. *Why can't she be happy for me today*?

'Ma, I have to meet Father in an hour. I'll come to see you later,' said Chandra and watched her leave. He tried to relax, but couldn't. The events of the morning hadn't sunk in yet. He, the king? It was a surprise to him since his father had never even hinted at it.

The light of the evening lamps shone through his window. The wind had become chilly. There was a knock on the door – probably someone to light the fires in his room. Chandra got up and grabbed his coat. He might as well go riding for an hour. When he opened the door and stepped out, something felt wrong. Where were the guards? Then a hand covered his mouth from behind, dragged him back inside the room, and shut the door.

Chandra found himself gagged and bound. Pinned to the door, with his captor's feet planted on his, Chandra was immobile. The man was tall and wearing a mask. Chandra tried to talk through the gag but could only manage to babble.

'Shut up,' the man whispered. He wrapped his large hands around Chandra's throat and began to squeeze. Chandra struggled against the grip. He tried to move to escape the increasing pressure, but the man held him in a vice-like grip. If Chandra didn't die from being strangled, he would certainly die of a broken neck.

Even as pain numbed him, Chandra tried to kick at the man's shin. But the attacker was sturdy. It was like thrashing against a tree. Chandra, mustering all his strength, pulled his feet from under the man's boots and drove his knee into his gut. That, fortunately, seemed to work. The grip on Chandra's neck loosened as the man held his stomach in pain. Seizing the opportunity, Chandra kicked the door open and ran out.

The instant Chandra was outside, the man rushed out too and disappeared into the darkness. Chandra's guards, who were ambling towards his quarters sharing a joke, ran to him when they saw him gagged and bound.

Once they'd untied him, Chandra sank to the ground. He touched his throbbing neck. What had just happened? That was when he saw a palm-leaf note fluttering in the wind. The attacker must have dropped it.

'If you are still alive, think of this as a small sample of what we can do. If you want to live, if you want your parents to live, then step down. The throne belongs to your brother.'

'Where were you both?' Chandra asked the guards, who looked bewildered. His neck still hurt, and his lungs burnt. 'Did you see a man running out of the room?'

'We saw a snake. A cobra. We wanted to make sure it slithered away from here,' the guards confessed sheepishly.

'Good, you drove away a cobra while I almost died here,' Chandra muttered to himself. *Who could have staged this? Brother? Has he hired assassins now?*

Chandra changed his mind about riding and headed towards his father's quarters. The night air was filled with the strong fragrance of champak flowers. It aggravated his headache. He had forgotten to wear his winter coat, but he couldn't even feel the chill. He felt drained climbing up the stairs to his father's room. The note hadn't scared him as much as it had angered him. Someone attacking and threatening him right in his own house was shameful.

In the chair next to his father's bed was Kritavarma, going over a scroll. The king was asleep while a nurse sat in a corner. Kritavarma looked up, hearing the footsteps, and smiled when he saw Chandra.

'Prince, you are early for a change.'

Chandra disliked jokes about his tardiness. But he usually let them go with the commander.

'Someone attacked me in my own room to deliver this.' Chandra handed the note to the commander.

As Kritavarma read it, Samudragupta woke up. He sat up with the nurse's help and took the note from Kritavarma. Chandra dismissed the nurse.

Samudragupta spoke after a pause, 'Well, someone is desperate for your brother to become the next king.'

'The only person who is desperate for my brother to become the king is my brother,' Chandra replied wryly, adjusting the pillow for his father so that he could sit up comfortably. He told them about the attack.

'Your brother didn't do this. He is not capable of it. Not yet, at least.' Samudragupta shook his head. 'I suspect Atma. The old bat is capable of anything.'

After his return from Kamarupa, Samudragupta had discussed the matter of Rama visiting Atma with Chandra. He was aghast, but Samudragupta had been unfazed.

'Why don't we arrest Atma? He is a troublemaker.' Chandra looked at his father with concern. 'Brother should not be friendly with him.'

Kritavarma continued to be quiet but crumpled the note into a ball, betraying his anxiety.

'We have no proof of Atma's treachery. For now, let us observe them. He seems to be helping another kingdom to uproot us. My guess is, Rudrasimha.'

'How can you be calm about it, Father?' Chandra's voice rose a notch.

'Son, when you are a king, more people want you dead than alive.' Samudragupta smiled wryly. 'You have to learn to survive dangers and threats. You already have! Multiple times in the past few months!'

'Father, the letter warns of harm to you and Mother,' Chandra said hesitatingly. 'I can step down.' Chandra's worry was evident in his voice. 'Being the king is not important to me.'

Samudragupta pursed his lips. He took the letter from Kritavarma and tore it into pieces. 'Don't let anybody become your weakness, Chandra. Your mother has survived these threats for decades. Forget that this ever happened.'

Kritavarma spoke finally, 'I agree with you that Atma should die in a dungeon. I agree with the king too that you should not step down because of threats.'

* * *

Two nights later, Samudragupta died in his sleep.

44

Chandra gazed at the funeral pyre by the bank of the river Ganga. His mind was switching between grief, worry and anger. How could his father be dead?

The river flowed as calmly as ever, undisturbed by the fact that his father was dead. Chandra's eyes welled up. He missed his father. A sea of men in white waited for the pyre to burn out. Pranava had stayed by Chandra's side all day. Kritavarma, Harisena, Guna and Lakshmidhara looked tired and suddenly older. They hadn't lost just their king but a dear friend.

A hand on his shoulder jolted Chandra out of his thoughts. It was Kritavarma. 'Let's get back. You need to be with your mother.'

The cremation ground felt eerie to Chandra as he walked back. His father had died precisely two days after that threatening note. What if someone had murdered him?

As they walked, Kritavarma said softly, 'Now that the final rites are over, we have to plan for your coronation.'

Chandra's heart lurched at Kritavarma's words. How could he take his father's place just yet? First, he had to figure out how his father had died. 'That can wait, Commander. I want to talk to the doctor who treated my father. Now.'

Kritavarma didn't argue. He and Pranava went with Chandra instead. The doctor, an old friend of Samudragupta's, seemed to be in shock.

'He was recovering. He was responding well to the new medicines I had started.' He added after a pause, 'What bothers me is that he died struggling to breathe. He didn't show any indications of a troubled lung when I checked on him that night.'

The trio's next stop was at the nurse's quarters. But questioning her proved futile. She trembled in fear and mumbled gibberish. From what they could gather, the king had passed away after she had fallen asleep.

'Let's question the guards posted outside Father's room.' But Chandra had started to give up hope. Whoever it was, was a clever man.

Both the guards swore nobody had come near the room, though Chandra doubted their story. They were hiding something. After a few threats by Kritavarma, they confessed to having accepted a drink from another guard. They'd been out like a light until the nurse had screamed.

'Where does this leave us?' Chandra kicked the ground hard in frustration. 'Someone kills the king of Magadha, and we have no clue who it was.'

Kritavarma guided Chandra to his room. 'Relax for some time, Prince. We will solve this. I promise.'

* * *

After the funeral, Rama rushed to his mother's quarters, barely escaping a brewing storm. Atma had insisted that he do so that very evening. Rama felt nervous like never before. If the old man's plan failed, he would kill him with his bare hands.

Dattadevi was sitting by the window, staring outside. She looked so lifeless; it almost scared him. He felt guilty burdening her with his request, but he had no choice.

'Ma, you have to help me.' Dattadevi stared into Rama's distraught eyes as he pleaded with her. She listened to him at first in a daze, then with alarm. The help he was asking for was both impractical and impossible!

'Who will listen to me, Rama? My voice can't rise above your father's.' Dattadevi was genuinely surprised that Rama had even considered it.

'It can, over my *dead* father's.' Rama sounded desperate, but he didn't care. He wasn't going to leave until she agreed. 'Ma, Father never gave me a chance. You can try giving me a chance. Even if you fail, I'll be happy that my mother supported me. At least she doesn't think me a worthless man.'

When his mother's eyes softened, he knew he was winning. He shushed the tiny voice of guilt that rose in him. He was manipulating the affection she had for him, but he was doing it only because his father had been unfair to him.

Dattadevi sighed wearily. 'I'll try, Son. But I don't think it'll work. Don't get your hopes up.'

Rama petted his dog, who had followed him. 'I know this is as impossible as Kusha turning into a cat. But thank you for doing this for me, Ma.' And he meant it. He was happy that his mother had agreed to help him.

45

Chandra paced up and down in the windowless room that had started to suffocate him. With a bed in a corner and a plush settee, it was a comfortable space. He had spent enough years exploring their palace fort, officially and unofficially, to know that he was under room arrest. That was where his father kept officials under investigation or high-profile spies. What was my crime? *Having an idiot for a brother*, Chandra thought bitterly. As he sat staring at the blank walls, his mind went back to the events that had landed him here.

* * *

A day after his father's death, his mother urgently convened a meeting with all the ministers and commanders. The small council room was packed, but there was an eerie silence in the air.

The queen's no-preamble, jump-straight-to-the-matter announcement, shocked everyone. 'I, the queen of the Gupta kingdom, declare my elder son, Prince Rama, the king of the Gupta dynasty. Are there any objections?'

After a few moments of shocked silence, Minister Harisena spoke. His tone, usually mild and soft, was borderline stern. 'Queen, our beloved late king had already chosen Prince Chandra as his successor.'

'I am aware of that, Minister. But now with the king's demise,' his mother had choked back her tears, 'I intend to change that. From what I understand, only Prince Chandra can oppose this. What is your decision, Son?' Her eyes bore into his.

Chandra was dumbfounded. He still hadn't digested the loss of his father, and his mother had sprung this on him.

'Prince, ask for time until tomorrow morning. We will discuss this issue,' Kritavarma, who sat next to him, advised urgently. 'You can't be impulsive tonight.'

Chandra looked long and hard at his mother. The look of utter helplessness on her face, coupled with the guilt that his father might have been murdered because of him, made him decide quickly. *What if Mother gets killed too if I become the king? If she chooses Rama to be the king, then so be it.*

'I abide by the queen's wish and don't wish to challenge her decision,' he declared to the assembly.

The gathering was deathly quiet for a few moments. Then the whole room broke into a panicked chatter. People talked over each other as they directed their concerns at Chandra.

'The kingdom is unsafe in Rama's hands.'

'You have to abide by your father's decree.'

'It was not your decision alone. You should have talked it through with us.'

'Your brother doesn't even know the boundaries of our kingdom. How will he rule?'

Chandra wanted to scream, asking everyone to shut up, but kept his calm. He managed to say the right things, 'A ruler is only as good as his advisors. Whether it's my reign or my brother's, we will anyway act on your guidance.'

That night, there was a note waiting for him in the room. *'Good decision. Remain a prince, and you and your mother will get to live a fuller life.'*

He crumpled the note and threw it into the bin. *Who are these people?*

A week after the coronation, Chandra was planning to go on a journey to collect levies from the vassals south of Pataliputra. He couldn't wait to be away from home. Chandra was angry with his mother for springing that coup. He was fed up of people telling him what a grave mistake he'd made.

* * *

However, he never took that trip. Something mixed in his breakfast on the day of his journey knocked him out cold. When he woke up, all groggy and aching, he found himself in the investigation room.

Why am I under arrest when I've given up the throne? What threat could I pose to anyone now? How long is it before someone realizes I never made the journey down south? He needed to get out of that room to find answers to those questions.

'Why doesn't this place have a window?' he muttered to himself, stretching on the bed out of sheer boredom.

Then his thoughts switched to Dhruva. In the last six months, their only communication was through a few letters they'd exchanged. Would it matter to her that he had renounced the kingship? She didn't seem that shallow. He hoped she was not.

* * *

It was at Atma's insistence that Rama had considered marriage to the princess of Kamarupa. As always, the old minister had been highly logical in his argument. 'The entire country covets the woman. If you marry her, it'll add to your prestige. If you don't, King Pushyavarma *will* marry her off to another king. It's highly unlikely that he still respects his daughter's betrothal to Prince Chandra, who is no longer going to be the king.' Atma had continued after a pause, 'But until your wedding to Princess Dhruva has been conducted, we have to keep Chandra under house arrest.'

Rama was appalled. 'I can ask Mother to talk to Chandra instead of arresting him.'

'House arrest is not like prison, King.' Atma had started addressing Rama as 'King', which pleased him immensely. 'Chandra will still be unhappy about renouncing the kingship to you. Now if you express a desire to marry the woman he's betrothed to, he might turn against you. Remember, your brother still has the support and sympathy of all the senior ministers and the influential vassals and officials. He can oust you easily and keep his woman and the kingdom. But all of that will change once you're married. Nobody will support Chandra in stealing your wife.'

* * *

Dhruva didn't know what to feel anymore. Her dreams of a happy life were shattered within minutes by the news. She was not going to marry Chandra but his brother!

'If we deny your hand in marriage to King Rama, we will be severing our friendly ties with the Gupta kingdom, Dhruva. A small province like ours needs their protection,' her mother said.

'I won't marry anyone but Prince Chandra. You may change your mind for practical reasons, but I won't, Mother.' Dhruva was furious with her mother and then desperate. 'Please understand, Ma. I've spent the last six months thinking of being married to Prince Chandra. I can't even imagine marrying anyone else.'

'Our mind is the only thing we can control in our lives, Dhruva. Being a student of the scriptures, you should know that better than me. Start thinking of King Rama as your husband and Prince Chandra as your brother-in-law until your mind accepts it. You're better off marrying a king than his brother any day.'

Dhruva's last hope was her father. But he too concurred with her mother. 'Dhruva, I don't want anything more than your happiness, child. But I am helpless. I can't tell King Rama, who has sent the marriage proposal, that you wish to marry his brother and not him.'

'Life has its highs and lows, especially the life of a royal, Dhruva.' Her mother stroked her hair when she collapsed, crying. 'You've only seen the highs so far – a prosperous life in a lavish palace, people who worship the ground you walk on, every wish and desire of yours fulfilled. But now you have to put your land and your people above yourself. If you refuse to marry King Rama, Kamarupa might face war. That will be the end of us.'

And the wedding was in a week!

46

Dhruva waited for a miracle to happen on her wedding day. She kept hoping for Chandra to come and whisk her away. But all that happened only in the books she read and the plays she watched. In reality, Rama had replaced Chandra. She hadn't even looked at him through the wedding ceremony.

After only two days in Kamarupa, they started for Pataliputra, with Priya accompanying her. *New life, new place, new marriage, at least one old friend.* Dhruva sighed as the chariot raced on the well-paved roads with lush farmland on either side. Her eyes threatened to well up when they left Kamarupa and the provinces they passed through started to look unfamiliar. But she held back her tears. She had cried enough.

* * *

Three months later, Chandra watched his brother walk on the carpeted passageway that led to the throne. The loud chanting of the priests, the hails for the king, flowers on the ground he was walking on – everything was the same as when his father was around. But Rama did not look even half as convincing as a king. The praises sung for him sounded like mockery, because they were all Samudragupta's accomplishments.

Chandra's eyes fell on Dhruva, who accompanied Rama. It had been three months since she had started living in their palace. But they hadn't met even once outside the assembly. He saw her in the throne room every morning when she lit the lamps and left soon after.

Chandra was livid when he heard of Rama and Dhruva's wedding. He'd just been released from house arrest. Harisena asked him not to confront her. 'Nothing good will come out of it, Prince. She's a married woman now. Let her be,' he'd said. 'She married under dire circumstances, and she's trying to cope.'

Two months later, he lost his mother. Dattadevi never recovered from Samudragupta's death. Chandra felt lost. He was grateful to Pranava, Harisena and Kritavarma, who never left him alone.

Trying to ward off the sad memories, Chandra watched Dhruva depart from the side door. He liked seeing her, even if briefly, in the throne room every morning. He felt dull once she left – as though she'd taken the light with her when she left the room! Then the assembly began.

'The first issue for the day,' the announcer started the list. 'The vassal provinces to the south of us request alms to tide over the summer.'

Lakshmidhara agreed to send help. These provinces had helped them during Samudragupta's campaign in southern Bharata.

The next issue: the farmers' guild requested reduced taxes due to severe summer.

Chandra objected, 'They have had a good crop despite the heat. We should have their records investigated.'

The final issue was left for the next day: Pushkarana was demanding tributes from Magadha for having defeated them in battle.

Chandra rolled his eyes. 'They didn't defeat us. They just hoodwinked us.'

Rama instantly took a dig at Chandra, 'They hoodwinked *you*. Father withdrew the army because of that.'

* * *

Lately, Rama had begun to feel restless after every assembly. The thought that he was a mere puppet on the throne haunted him day and night. He had nothing to say because he knew nothing! The ministers and Chandra handled most of the questions. He had once enjoyed being a contributor to those discussions, especially when his father and Chandra were on a war campaign, but now all he felt was reluctance. That had to change.

Rama took a deep puff of ganja from the pot and stretched on his bed. He was in his old room – the same place where he had grown from a sad boy into an angry man. A high started to kick in from smoking and made him think about Dhruva. He was still clueless when it came to conversing with her or spending time with her. Dhruva's idea of a good time was to play a prolonged board game of some sort or watch a performance. Despite the differences, he liked her. She was pleasant and warm. She never talked about the circumstances under which they had been married, or about her engagement to Chandra.

Rama's thoughts drifted from Dhruva to his mother, whom he missed sorely. He suffered pangs of guilt for putting her through the ordeal of making him the king. People who'd once loved her dearly detested her after that. Rama sighed. His life had seemed vacant and meaningless after her death, but Atma had guided him out of it: 'Focus on what you have, not on what you've lost. Spend time with your wife, and enjoy being the king.'

Just as he was about to fall asleep, Megha entered the room with Atma and Vidura. Vidura started fanning away the smoke furiously. Atma looked visibly disgusted.

'It's like a chimney in here! Make it quick before I faint from all this smoke.' Atma sat on a chair as far away from Rama as he could. 'Who lets a dog on the bed?' he mumbled disapprovingly.

It took Rama a few minutes to even remember why he had summoned Atma to his room. Kusha, sensing Atma's dislike for him, moved closer to Rama on the bed, and fell asleep. Propping himself up on a pillow, Rama said, 'It's been three months since I was crowned king.

All I've done so far is warm the throne twice a day.' The words tumbled out of Rama's mouth. 'Minister, you were supposed to help me.'

Atma sighed. 'When have you asked for my help in the last two months? Anyway, you need to share with me the topics that are discussed in court. Let's begin with today. Tell me what happened.' The man wasted no time.

Rama stopped smoking and thought. The ganja had indeed scrambled his brain. Then he began to remember slowly. 'Most topics were simple. The only open item is about Pushkarana. They are demanding a tribute claiming that they've defeated us.'

Atma's eyes narrowed. 'That's it. This will be your first decision. Tell your brother to subdue Pushkarana and occupy it. Allot him only half the army he asks for. Get Kritavarma to go with him so that we can make some changes here while they're gone.'

Megha looked aghast. 'But, why would you send Prince Chandra with half the army? If the commander goes too, who will protect the city?'

Rama shushed him with a look. In his compromised state, Atma's plan sounded right. He could never take control of the kingdom with Chandra and Kritavarma breathing down his neck. 'Minister, why can't you be a part of the council? Why are you still hiding behind me?' Rama asked.

'There's a time for everything. Now is not it,' replied Atma grimly.

* * *

The next night, after the evening assembly, Chandra sat gazing intently at his hands in Harisena's house. Kritavarma paced, Lakshmidhara poured over a script, while Guna and Harisena engaged in a hushed private conversation. The one common factor was the worry on their faces.

'Dinner is served, Sir,' announced an attendant in a low voice. Nobody moved.

'This is a coup against Prince Chandra. What was wrong with King Rama today?' Kritavarma exploded.

Chandra took a deep breath. 'It is obvious that he wants me dead. I am to conquer Pushkarana with ten thousand footmen, two thousand cavalry, and fifty elephants? He might as well send me directly to the execution chamber!'

Kritavarma stopped pacing to speak. 'It's as impossible as a toddler wanting to climb a rock. Don't go on this campaign. Let's reason with the king.'

'No, Commander,' Chandra said determinedly. 'I am going on this campaign. I am not going to beg for mercy from my brother. We will find a way to win. I don't feel obligated to fight fairly with the Pushkarana king, given how unfairly he fought with us.' He turned to Kritavarma. 'But I want you to stay back. Even though our king orders that you accompany me!'

Kritavarma disagreed vehemently. 'If you're going, I'm going with you. We'll win this battle together.'

As he rode out of Harisena's house, a plan was forming in Chandra's head. He needed an insider in the palace. Someone who held sway with Rama.

47

Dhruva walked towards her chariot after visiting the hospital for orphans. She was there to supervise the conditions and determine if they needed more financial aid.

'Queen,' someone whispered into her ear, startling her. Dhruva was in plain clothes and was riding in a commoner's chariot since the children would have been intimidated by a queen with her entourage. Who could have recognized her despite that?

The woman who had startled her was around her own age, and a nurse. She said to Dhruva hurriedly, 'I am Prince Chandra's friend, Vasanthi. He wants to talk to you today in the evening.'

Dhruva was aghast. She knew the right thing to do would be to climb into her chariot and ride away. But Vasanthi looked friendly and non-threatening. Dhruva remembered Chandra mentioning Vasanthi. Why did Chandra want to meet her now?

'Where and when?' Dhruva asked after a pause.

'Today, at dusk. I'll take you if you can manage to come out in disguise and meet me at the palace temple.'

In the hours that followed, Dhruva felt restless. For a few months into her marriage, she was angry with Chandra that he had given her up so quickly to his brother. But Harisena, who was now her scriptures teacher and a mentor, had soothed her. 'You don't know his circumstances. Please don't judge him harshly. My advice? Don't try to analyze things from the past. Go along with your life with the king.'

She was trying to do just that. But she and Rama had very different personalities. He rarely got her humour and dozed off in the plays she liked. In turn, the wrestling matches and animal fights he loved repulsed her. It was a challenge to make her marriage work.

* * *

Dhruva waited impatiently for the chime to indicate dusk. She was too jittery to do anything. Kusha followed her like a shadow as she moved about her room aimlessly. She sat down and hugged him. Knowing her love for Kusha, Rama left the dog with her. She'd heard from the staff that her husband shared his dog only with her, no one else! Dhruva sighed. Rama was making efforts, just like her, to make their marriage better. He had even sat through a classical music concert the week before, trying his best not to yawn.

It was sunset, finally! Dhruva managed to get ready despite Kusha jumping around and climbing on her. The dog had sensed that something about that evening was not ordinary. Dhruva wore a plain saree and tried her best to dress like a palace help. They aroused the least suspicion going about their work. Letting out a breath of relief once out of the quarters, Dhruva hurried towards the temple. Vasanthi approached her from a corner and began to walk beside her.

'It feels good not to be recognized as the queen! I would go about in disguise all the time in Kamarupa,' Dhruva was excited.

'But one look at your gorgeous face and anyone will know you are not the ordinary maiden you are pretending to be!' Vasanthi teased Dhruva.

'I don't believe what you are saying, but still, let me remedy your concern!' Dhruva drew the loose end of the saree around her head, hiding most of her face.

Vasanthi burst into a giggle. 'Now you look like someone practicing to walk blindfolded!'

Dhruva joined in the laughter. She liked Vasanthi and her sense of humour. She was not the least bit conscious that she was with the queen of Magadha. Dhruva secretly hoped they could be friends one day.

As they walked, Vasanthi asked softly, 'Are you nervous about meeting Prince Chandra?'

'Not nervous,' Dhruva drew a deep breath. 'But a little unsure if it's right to meet him stealthily. The last time I talked to him was more than a year ago when he was in Kamarupa. So, I do feel a little awkward.'

They walked past the fort gates towards the river. Dhruva knew that the far end of the palace had a natural river fort, but she had never been there. Finding herself walking on a narrow path that wound through prickly shrubbery, Dhruva stopped to look at a marble gazebo at a distance. The scene was breathtaking – the river, the greenery and the cliffs that rose to the sky.

When they neared the gazebo, Dhruva could see Chandra. She felt her pulse quicken. Her heart was pounding erratically.

'What does he want to talk about?' she asked Vasanthi, trying to even her quivering voice.

'He'll tell you himself! He's only a few steps away.' Vasanthi held Dhruva's hand lightly. 'I'll wait here and keep an eye out for intruders.'

Dhruva approached Chandra unsurely. When she looked at his familiar smiling face, the awkwardness in her began to melt.

'Queen,' Chandra bowed as she entered the beautifully carved marble gazebo.

'Prince,' Dhruva bowed back, smiling cheerfully. 'You look different from what I remember. Have you grown taller?'

'A foot or two maybe.' Chandra laughed. Though he joked and laughed, he looked different – far more mature, reserved and worried than the man she'd met before.

'Take a seat, please.' Chandra pointed to the ornate granite stone bench that faced the river.

Dhruva sat on the edge of the bench but not before stopping to admire the carvings on it. 'This is Dashavathara carved in stone!' she remarked excitedly, all traces of the initial strangeness evaporating completely. 'How sad that I've never been here before!'

'A few sculptors from Mathura carved it for us. They chose Dashavathara for the guaranteed hefty reward from Father! You know he was a devotee of Vishnu.'

Dhruva chuckled. 'Clever sculptors. You should employ them as your financial advisors.'

After a few moments of scrutinizing the place, Dhruva asked Chandra, 'Is it safe here? It looks deserted!'

Chandra smiled and sat on the adjacent bench. 'Many believe that the tamarind tree over there is haunted. Hope that doesn't scare you.'

Dhruva knitted her brows and looked at Chandra intently. 'Are you Prince Chandra or his ghost from the tree?'

Chandra replied equally gravely, 'The ghost, of course.'

Dhruva smiled. It was nice to continue the banter, but she knew Chandra had something important to discuss. However, nothing had prepared her for what he said.

* * *

It was well past midnight when Rama finally walked into the quarters – just when the wait had started to make Dhruva sleepy. He entered the room noiselessly, but Kusha was already at the door, barking. Rama always took care not to disturb her sleep. Hurrying to her desk, Dhruva picked up a scroll, pretending to read. She couldn't look like she'd been waiting for him.

He looked surprised. 'That must be one interesting book if you are still awake at this late hour. Why have you kept this rascal in the room?' Rama rubbed Kusha on his neck.

Dhruva smiled back at him and yawned. 'The book is not that great. I was too bored to fall asleep. But Kusha kept himself and me entertained by chasing his own tail. How was your day?'

He was in plain clothes, which made her wonder where he had left all the royal jewellery. 'Another general evening assembly. Then I went out in disguise with Megha to interact with people.'

Dhruva knew that was a lie since his breath was reeking of wine. Maybe he'd been interacting with a tavern owner! Trying not to react to the strong smell of ganja and wine, Dhruva helped Rama out of his coat and shoes. He flashed her a look of gratitude when she handed him a glass of water.

'King—' she started to ask him after a moment of hesitation. *Would this work?* Worry gnawed at her. He raised his brows in question, fighting to keep his eyes open.

'Can I sit through the assembly sessions? I've nothing much to do around the palace, so I thought that might keep me occupied.' She was careful in her choice of words. Chandra had warned her not to offend Rama in any way.

To her surprise, Rama laughed. 'If your life is boring, our assembly meetings are excruciatingly so! Why do you want to punish yourself?'

Then, watching her face fall, he said softly, 'If you so badly want to, you're welcome to join in.'

Letting Kusha out of the room, Dhruva watched Rama doze off within a minute of hitting the bed. But she could hardly sleep. That was only the first step. Chandra wanted her to become Rama's close confidante, and eventually a part of his private council. As she tossed and turned in bed, her mind went over the conversation she had had with Chandra earlier.

He'd explained how Rama was sending him and Kritavarma to Pushkarana with only a small army. He'd also told her how he suspected Atma's influence on Rama. She had listened intently. All that was news to her.

'I want you to tell me what is going on around Rama. I suspect something bad is brewing. While I'm at Pushkarana, if you find anything alarming happening here, please send me a scroll. You can give it to Vasanthi. She will give it to my friend Sura. He knows how to reach me.'

At first, Dhruva had been hesitant. 'You are asking me to spy on my husband for you! It doesn't feel right. It's the case of the fence eating the crop.'

'If the crop turns out to be a poisonous weed, then the fence has to eat it! I'm asking you to help us keep Magadha and the Gupta kingdom safe. You are the queen of the kingdom now. You must protect it, even if it's from the king himself.'

At the end, he had looked at her with concern. 'You look lonely. Hire Vasanthi as your aide. You both will have a good time together.'

It was almost dawn by the time Dhruva fell asleep.

48

'I want to lead this campaign, Commander. If you stay back at the capital, it'll give me a lot of peace of mind,' said Chandra.

Kritavarma shook his head. 'The forces assigned to you are not even a quarter of what we need for this battle. I'd rather be with you than here. Also, the king has asked me explicitly to accompany you.'

Chandra had to agree. He announced his plan to Kritavarma and Pranava. 'We will attack only with infantry and cavalry. We won't take any chariots or elephants. It has to be a stealth operation.' He took a sizeable palm-leaf sheet. 'Here's how we go about it. The army will split into ten groups. Each group will arrive in exactly a week in Pushkarana ...'

After Chandra had explained his scheme, Kritavarma sighed. 'This is a little too ambitious, Prince. But you seem to have thought it through. Given the joke of an army we have, this is as good a plan as any.'

Chandra, secretly glad that Kritavarma hadn't turned the plan down, said to Pranava, 'Get some fast riders to head towards Pushkarana to spread the news that we will be laying siege to their fort in three days. But we will attack in fifteen days.'

Pranava grinned. 'Exasperate the enemy! This is exciting. Thank your brother for me!'

Chandra couldn't help laughing at Pranava's enthusiasm. 'We will thank him if we come back alive.'

* * *

The next three days, Chandra travelled non-stop with Pranava and a group of twenty trustworthy soldiers handpicked from their elite wing. The last thing he needed in the campaign were traitors. His whole operation depended on people he could trust. Dhruva and Sura were going to be his informants in Pataliputra.

Soma was going to join him in Pushkarana with a troupe of catapult experts. Chandra felt confident of his operation.

'We'll reach Pushkarana by tomorrow evening. Let's split up and meet at the riverside of the fort by midnight,' said Chandra as they had their dinner. Because he had camped in Pushkarana before, he knew the lay of the land.

'I heard at the diner that the Pushkarana king is getting ready for our siege,' said Pranava, wiping his mouth after dinner. 'Our messengers have done a good job spreading the news!' A smile played on his lips.

Chandra found it amusing that his friend looked forward to the battle!

The next night, as planned, Chandra swam till the fort wall with his five soldiers. 'Start,' he ordered the men. They started digging the ground beneath the fence wall. The moonless night was a great blessing. They had to be done in ten days to escape the full moon!

'Is it going to be a tunnel?' one of the men asked, panting. The hot night and the physical exertion were making them sweat buckets. Monsoon was just over, and a second wave of heat for the year consumed the country.

Chandra stopped to wipe sweat off his forehead. 'What else can it be? A temple? Of course, it's a tunnel.'

The others chuckled. The man who'd asked the question muttered, 'I thought the plan was to collapse this gigantic wall.'

Chandra patted him on the back. 'You are right. The original plan was to weaken the wall and smash through it, but the soil is looser than I imagined. So a tunnel is easier than collapsing walls.'

They swam back after three hours of digging. Pranava took over the task with his small group of men. A big group would mean more noise and waking up the sleeping guards of Pushkarana.

* * *

By the eighth day, they were done. They had dug a tunnel that led them into the palace complex! The next morning, in the wee hours, Chandra used the tunnel to sneak inside the palace complex. He went alone, in the garb of a commoner. Pranava insisted on going with him, but Chandra asked him to stay with their soldiers. The men were not traitors, but he couldn't take any chances by leaving them alone. Quickly closing the open end of the tunnel with dry leaves, he waited in a corner until the palace awoke. The passage was just about enough for a single man to squeeze through.

King Varma lived a lavish life. Though Chandra had seen the inside of the fort briefly, he was struck by how vast it was. As massive as their own, almost. He walked the length of the fort. Acres of land that produced enough grains and vegetables for months, abundant cattle, poultry and gardens. The king could withstand months of siege and stay inside his fort.

A large group of troopers marched in front of the palace, equipped with crossbows and swords. Chandra was sure that was because of the siege rumour he'd spread. He was curious to see the rest of their army, but it was too dangerous. Most kings stationed their forces in the far corner of the fort. An ordinary man walking in that direction would be inviting trouble for himself.

Chandra could spot a sea of chariots in the distance, and hear elephants trumpeting and horses neighing. That was where the preparation for the battle was going on. He walked towards the main gate that was shut. So, the king had chosen to wait out the siege and not attack!

He stopped an old man carrying two large sacks of vegetables. 'Let me help you,' Chandra offered. The man, though surprised, gladly transferred the load to him.

The man then offered the information Chandra was looking for. 'The Guptas are going to attack is what the king heard. But so far, the only attack we've seen is by the mosquitoes in the moat!' he rambled. 'The palace gate is closed shut, which means no help enters inside. People like me are made to work like donkeys.'

Chandra responded, 'We can open the gate and attack once they approach. Why shut it even before the Gupta retinue is here! We'll certainly know when they are near us.'

The old man sighed. Luckily, like most people his age, he was more interested in talking than knowing anything about Chandra. 'The king has heard that the Gupta prince is going to be here. Without chariots and elephants. Only with infantry and horses.'

Chandra's heart stopped for a moment. *Who'd given away that piece of news?* They hadn't disclosed it even to the soldiers. Everyone was under the impression the chariots and the elephants would follow.

Who knew? Who knew? Chandra racked his brain. Except for Kritavarma and Pranava, only Rama knew. Had he turned traitor to his own land? That was foolish. Surely, he wouldn't tell the enemy king how to defeat his brother! Atma! It had to be that old crook. Chandra felt as though his head would explode with anger.

49

On the tenth day, Kritavarma waited with the army in the battleground outside the city. If they approached the palace gate, they would have to hurt the citizens. King Varma was banking on the fact that no decent army would do so. But Kritavarma was going to approach the gate by scaring away the citizens, not by killing them. He only had to wait for Chandra's signal.

Pranava and Chandra, along with fifty soldiers, went into the tunnel, one by one. It was difficult to swim and then squeeze through the narrow space in wet clothes. 'Now I know how wet dogs feel,' muttered Pranava under his breath.

'We've been doing this wet-dog act for ten days now. What's new?' Chandra replied, hoping the tunnel would not cave in on them! They had reinforced it, but nothing in that tunnel was strong or sturdy.

They wiggled out of the other end with a feeling of triumph. Pranava and Chandra had been there multiple times in the last two days to assess the situation. But that day, with the soldiers, it felt different. With Kritavarma camping outside, the entire fort was on full alert. But nobody cared about that corner, thinking that the river guarded it well.

They had to be careful. Chandra and his men, in the same green uniforms as the Pushkarana soldiers, dispersed. Chandra and Pranava walked towards the heavily guarded large fort gate. If they managed to unlock the gate, Kritavarma would be able to march inside with the army.

From close observation in the past few days, Chandra had understood how the security at the gate worked. The guards changed every six hours. The challenge now was to infiltrate with the new platoon, which would relieve the existing ones. When they heard the soldiers marching, Chandra signalled to Pranava. They joined the troop seamlessly! Chandra hoped some of the soldiers had done so too, as they'd been instructed. There was no way to check. Chandra's heart thudded with anxiety as he marched with the Pushkarana soldiers towards the gate. The platoon would now split into three segments. One would remain on the ground going in a circle. The other two would climb the left and the right ramparts to guard the fort.

Pranava joined the Pushkarana soldiers who climbed the steps to the left rampart. Chandra joined those who marched at the gate. After a few minutes, Chandra took a deep breath. It was time for action. When he neared the entrance, he stopped and quickly slashed at the middle latch. One of Chandra's soldiers cut the bottom lock, and Pranava tackled the lock on the top. Before the shocked Pushkarana guards could react, Chandra and his men threw open the gate to let Kritavarma race inside with the cavalry.

* * *

Moving through the melee, Chandra reached the back of the palace. A few designated soldiers followed him. He had seen a dilapidated set of stairs that led to an even more rickety balcony. Perhaps a servants' entrance once, but now abandoned.

Chandra started to climb the shaky wooden steps, half expecting to crash-land on the ground any moment. The stairs creaked and wobbled, but Chandra continued to clamber up. As he neared a window, he hoped to see an empty room. The balcony was only a few steps from there.

To Chandra's utter shock, the window opened into a room – a room full of maids! The minute they saw him, the women shrieked. He hurried to the balcony and kicked open the door. His men followed him.

But the women had done the damage. On the other side of the room, facing Chandra, were Pushkarana soldiers with their swords drawn. Remembering that he was in their uniform, Chandra shouted, 'Our king is under attack. Save him!'

The men, probably second-tier soldiers, were at first taken aback. Chandra almost made his way out through them, but the rest of his soldiers storming into the room through the balcony didn't help. The Pushkarana men knew something was wrong. One of them threw a lance at Chandra. The lance hit him on the hand and he almost lost his grip on the sword. Chandra held the sword in front of him with his bleeding hand and started backing up.

But his ill luck didn't end there. When he saw the look of terror on the faces of his men, now held off by the Pushkarana soldiers, he felt something was wrong. Suddenly, someone stabbed him in the small of his back.

50

'Drop the sword, Prince,' a voice spoke from behind him. Feeling dizzy with pain, Chandra tried to turn, but the man spoke again, 'Try to be smart, and I'll stab you to death this time.'

Then, just as suddenly, the man who held Chandra at sword-tip screamed and collapsed. He was bleeding from his temple. The Pushkarana men were getting pelted with a shower of stones. Soma! Chandra couldn't believe his friend's skills. Soma was standing on one of the wobbly steps and throwing stones at the enemy soldiers.

The women screamed even more loudly now, but a Gupta soldier scared them into silence with his sword. Quickly closing the door behind them, Chandra ordered his soldiers, 'Hit the men with the hilt of your swords. We don't want them waking up anytime soon.' Then he bolted towards the corridor that stretched outside the room.

Soma caught up with him. 'This is the servants' quarters. The next building is the main palace. There is a way to jump from here to there. But wait a minute.' He rummaged through his waist pouch, took out some herbs and a long piece of cloth. 'Let me dress your wounds.'

Chandra couldn't be more thankful for Soma's twin skills of catapulting and nursing that day! He felt much better.

'Soma,' Chandra said as something suddenly occurred to him, 'how did you manage to hit only the Pushkarana men when we wore the same uniform as them?'

'Slightly different shades of green!' Soma grinned.

Chandra laughed. 'Thank God, the Pushkarana men don't have your skills! Or we would have been long dead by now.'

Soma led Chandra and the troops to the terrace from where they could see the main palace. While the soldiers waited for their orders, Chandra assessed the distance they had to jump. It didn't look too bad, probably five feet or so. But the ground below did look very far away!

Smiling wryly, Chandra muttered, 'If we jump right, we reach the palace. If not, we'll crack our heads and reach heaven!'

Soma laughed. 'Simple as that! Let me go first. Don't overthink it. Just jump.'

Before Chandra could say anything, Soma had leapt to the next building and landed nimbly on a small balcony. Taking a deep breath, Chandra took the leap. He almost missed! Coming to a clumsy, faltering halt next to Soma, who steadied him, Chandra shook his head in dismay. 'I'm never going to be good at these death-defying stunts!'

Composing himself, Chandra looked at the door next to them. After levelling a couple of soft kicks at it, he gave up. It was a solid wooden door. There was no way they could break it open without making a significantly loud noise. Also, what if there were people inside that room? There might even be more screeching maids. He shuddered at the thought.

He stood for a moment scrutinizing what lay ahead of him – a series of other balconies at their own level. He saw a man step into one of those and lean against it leisurely.

'Hit him!' Chandra whispered to Soma urgently. 'He is our ticket to get inside.'

Three stones from Soma's catapult had the man crouching down until his body hit the ground. The back-to-back hits had him out cold, without as much as even a scream of pain. Jumping across the balconies quickly, Chandra and Soma reached him.

Signalling the soldiers to follow him, Chandra entered the room. They made sure not to trip over the man Soma had felled.

The room was small, with a bed that occupied most of it. A mid-sized window at the other end of the room was closed shut. Prying it open carefully, Chandra looked outside. For the first time that day, he felt hopeful. There was a staircase at the end of a wide-pillared corridor, with rooms on either side. They could see guards sporting lethal swords pacing the corridor.

Soma whispered, 'There are more guards near the stairs. Wonder what or who they are protecting!'

'The king's chamber,' Chandra whispered back. 'I'm sure the stairs will lead to the king's room.'

If he was right, their victory depended on vanquishing those guards. Chandra turned to face his men. 'We will infiltrate two at a time by posing as Pushkarana guards, and then attack. Don't wander too far away from the stairs.'

After half their men had trickled out and paced alongside the Pushkarana soldiers, Chandra decided to take the risk. He was going to attack the guards at the stairs, and then rush up. Nodding to Soma, he turned to the rest of the soldiers. 'Follow me.'

Chandra charged out of the room, with his sword out. Stabbing three guards on his way, he reached the stairs. By now, his soldiers were engaged in a swordfight with the king's guards, who still looked confused. Chandra ran up the stairs, lined with a plush carpet.

Kicking the door open, Chandra found his prize of the day – the king of Pushkarana, looking old, frail and scared. The man was not a fighter. The moment Chandra held out his sword, the king surrendered.

The battle was over. Pushkarana had been won. But, unfortunately, only for now.

51

It had been four days since the campaign had ended in Pushkarana. King Varma was kept imprisoned in his quarters. All his people, from the palace help and the officials to the army, were sent out of the fort. Now all they needed were additional troops from Pataliputra to consolidate their position in Pushkarana.

Strolling in the sprawling palace gardens, Pranava quipped, 'This king has good taste. I'm sure he has great cooks too. We should have kept them and sent out our pathetic ones.' He grumbled, 'Ages since I ate anything that doesn't taste like tree bark.'

'We sure should have kept the Pushkarana cooks. They could cook us food and season it with poison!' Chandra patted Pranava's stomach. 'Don't always think with your stomach.'

Kritavarma inspected every closed gate of the fort diligently, giving a little yank here and a kick there.

'Our scroll must have reached King Rama two days ago. So, the cavalry should be here in four days if they have been dispatched immediately,' said the commander as they climbed up the lookout tower. Flags bearing the Gupta emblem of the Garuda flag were flying high at the main gate and at different points in the city. The Pushkarana army had now camped in the battleground.

'Our army has to be bigger than theirs if we're to claim the throne,' said Pranava, looking at the enemy forces.

'We have asked for fifty thousand infantry and twenty thousand cavalry. That should do it,' replied Chandra.

He was determined to win Pushkarana to avenge his humiliating abduction the last time.

That night, a few scouts came in with news. The Pushkarana army was getting restless, not knowing why they were sitting idly. Most citizens of Pushkarana were excited to have the Guptas, the most powerful kingdom in Bharata, rule them. The city had gone back to being peaceful.

'Could you spot our cavalry coming from Pataliputra?' asked Chandra.

'We went as far as a hundred miles, but we didn't see any.'

Dismissing the scouts, Chandra looked at Kritavarma quizzically. 'What do you think is taking our army so long? Are they lost?'

Kritavarma knitted his brows. 'Maybe it's the adverse conditions. We've sent two commanders to lead the army. They won't get lost. Relax.'

Another day passed without any information from Pataliputra or any trace of the army. That night, Chandra and Pranava decided to dress up as Pushkarana soldiers and venture out – to learn firsthand what the enemy commanders were planning. They decided to leave once Kritavarma went to bed. The commander would never allow them to leave the fort.

Slipping out along with two of their scouts, Chandra and Pranava strolled around the streets for a while. It was deserted, except for a small tavern. They went inside and bought two bottles of wine.

'Why are the Guptas hiding in the fort?' Chandra asked a man sitting next to him.

'They must be sleeping!' The man and a few others laughed. 'You are the soldiers. You tell us,' said the man. Chandra remembered that they were dressed as soldiers.

'We are low-level workers. Who tells us anything?' Pranava drawled. He loved these charades but usually overacted, much to Chandra's chagrin.

'The Guptas don't have a large enough army. That is why they are hiding. We should lay siege and get inside the fort,' said another old man.

'Then the Guptas will kill our king,' Chandra tried to sound concerned.

'Not all our generals are loyal to the king. If the king is killed, it'll be easier for them to usurp the throne. It's only a matter of time before our commanders barge inside the fort.' The old man's words confirmed Chandra's worst fears. After that, he was in no mood to go around the city. He'd heard enough.

They were far from safe. Holding the enemy king hostage didn't mean they had won the kingdom. The Pushkarana army was so large that they could squish the minuscule Gupta contingent like ants!

They had to get their army soon. If the Pushkarana commanders rebelled, they should have enough of their own to quell the uprising.

But there was no sign of their army the next day or the day after. That night, Chandra walked into Kritavarma's room. 'Commander, I don't want to sound panicky, but something is wrong.'

Kritavarma too sounded worried. 'I don't know how long we can wait here. Do you want me to ride to the capital and check?'

'No ... let's send one of the commanders. It's not safe for you to be here alone. If the Pushkarana men barge inside, we're good as dead with our joke of an army.'

The next day, there was still no army, but there was a scroll from the king.

Chandra read it hurriedly, '*King Rama orders that Prince Chandra remain in Pushkarana until he establishes Gupta rule. The king has determined that there is no need for additional forces from Pataliputra.*'

Chandra couldn't decide whether to laugh or cry or wring Rama's neck with his bare hands.

He went to meet Kritavarma. 'The enemy army is ten times our size! How are we supposed to consolidate the Gupta rule here? Whose ridiculous idea is this? Why did Harisena consent to this?' Kritavarma's fury rose with each question.

After a pause, Chandra said, 'It's Atma at the helm of things. Of course, my brother wants me gone too but Atma wants me dead. No less. He was the one who disclosed our attack strategy to King Varma.'

Just then, another soldier approached them with a new scroll. 'From the prince's friend, Sura.'

Chandra grabbed the scroll. It was from Dhruva. What did *she* have to say? As he read it, his face turned red. His breathing quickened. He gave it to Kritavarma to read.

The scroll was long and literary, typical of Dhruva. But, it conveyed terrible news. The king had released Vijaya and Shashi, the traitors they'd arrested for scheming to kill Samudragupta. If releasing them from prison was not bad enough, Rama had reinstated them in his cabinet! Vijaya was the chief assistant to Nakula, the commander-in-chief in Kritavarma's absence. Shashi was Lakshmidhara's deputy in the finance department.

'Prince, there is a bigger coup brewing back home. Go back to Pataliputra. I'll stay here for you. I've no intentions of returning to have Vijaya-the-worm for my subordinate,' declared Kritavarma gravely.

Chandra shook his head. 'We will station the army here and vacate tonight. Not a very heroic deed but we don't have a choice. Let's see if we can together convince our brilliant king to send an army with us.'

Kritavarma refused to leave. 'We have captured it, and we will rule it. Go back and get an army. I'll hold the fort until you come back.'

* * *

Atma had put together a new council for Rama. With Chandra and Kritavarma gone, making those changes was a lot easier. At Atma's insistence, Rama had reinstated Shashi and Vijaya into his ministry, although he was himself very unsure of the move.

Atma had persuaded him, as he always did. 'Vijaya is an able commander, and Shashi, an intelligent finance expert. Harisena and Kritavarma pushed them into the dungeon because they were insecure.'

'But they were traitors! They sided with the Shakas to murder our king,' Megha had opposed vehemently.

'What's the proof? Was there a public interrogation? Their twin crimes were that they were good and that they were my friends,' Atma had said, convincingly enough for Rama to fall for it.

When it came to the private council, Rama wanted two ministers – Guru and Chandana. Almost his age, they had been junior ministers during Samudragupta's reign, but they had been very supportive when Rama had taken over. Megha had refused to take up the position of minister but had finally agreed to become the king's advisor. He was part of the private council too.

Atma held the position of senior advisor to the king, while Harisena continued to be the prime minister. Rama was surprised that Atma didn't want to be prime minister.

'I want the best for Magadha and Harisena is doing his job well.'

Chandra, who was currently the defence minister, was left in that position, but he was not in Rama's private council. Nor was anyone else who had been a confidante of Samudragupta's.

* * *

The first thing Chandra did after reaching Pataliputra was meet Dhruva. It was late evening when they met at the same place as before.

'What is happening around here, Queen?' Chandra asked grimly. They never had time for exchanging pleasantries.

'Well, a lot of things are happening. None too good.' Dhruva sounded worried. 'The king is planning to increase the tax on goods and services to ten per cent.'

'That is double of what it is now! There will be riots by the guilds. How did Minister Lakshmidhara agree to this?'

'Nobody knows yet. It was decided only yesterday in the private council meeting. A bit of good news is that I'm now part of the private council.'

Chandra smiled. 'Good that my brother trusts at least one honest person! Was this tax increase Atma's brilliant idea?'

Dhruva nodded. 'Yes. And another of Atma's bright ideas was to make you stay back in Pushkarana. How did that campaign go?'

'I've run like a coward from there, leaving Commander Kritavarma behind.' Chandra smiled weakly. 'God seems to have created Pushkarana to humiliate me!'

A strong wind blew, and Dhruva tried unsuccessfully to tame her hair. She was silent for a while. 'God is only humbling you, child,' said Dhruva in a mock matronly tone to lighten the mood.

Chandra laughed. 'Really, Grandma? Now I feel so much better.'

Dhruva got up giggling. 'Go home and sleep. I'll see you tomorrow at the assembly.'

Chandra got up and stretched. His bones creaked like an old chair. 'I'll do as the queen bids. Go back to the palace safely. I hope nobody recognized you when you came here.'

Dhruva pointed to her attire. 'People have no interest in a maid walking around! Don't worry about me.'

52

Rama's brows furrowed when he saw Chandra in the morning assembly. *Wasn't he supposed to be in Pushkarana?* He looked at Atma, who was sitting in the first row. Atma gave a small nod signalling Rama to stay calm. Rama's head began to pound. Chandra was the last person he needed when he was about to make an important announcement.

Also, didn't they have an elaborate plan for Chandra? He was not supposed to win that battle of Pushkarana at all. Now, he was supposed to stay back and get kicked out by the Pushkarana soldiers. How can that happen if he's sitting here?

What was that thing Atma said often? '*We have to make Chandra a loser in people's eyes. Only then will they give you a fair chance.*'

Rama looked at Dhruva sitting next to him. She seemed to be as uncomfortable as him in all the heavy silk and jewellery. But it was hard to read her stoic expression. *Has she even seen Chandra?* He was almost tempted to whisper to her, but he controlled himself. It was a crowded assembly, and he had to look his dignified best even when he felt like a beetle dying on its back.

But it was nice to have Dhruva with him in these sessions. She had an elephantine memory and registered every detail of what transpired in the assembly. Atma had seemed less than thrilled (evident from his grim face) when Rama proposed that Dhruva be a part of their private meetings. But the old man hadn't said anything.

Dhruva's discreet tap on his hand jolted him out of his thoughts. Rama tried to focus on the issues being discussed. Nothing was new – one or the other needed something or the other.

But one issue seemed to be exciting: a dispute between two vassal provinces. Rama was fully awake when both kings started sparring with words. God, he liked a good fight! But he watched with a mild look of disapproval, as was expected of him.

'Your foolish soldiers have trampled our crops,' one accused the other.

The other was quick to respond, 'That's because your bright men have grown crops on the road!' Everyone laughed.

The other king turned red with anger. The argument quickly escalated to a fistfight before the guards took them away. As more and more people started talking, Rama became impatient. Some of them spoke in long monologues. Why couldn't people speak briefly? He had a proposal to make. *Shouldn't the king be the first to speak? Why had Father run the court in this manner?* Just when Rama was dangerously close to falling asleep out of boredom, it was his turn to talk.

'The king has a proposal. Attention everyone!' the royal announcer's voice through the bullhorn was loud enough to wake up even the dead.

Rama felt nervous. How would people take the new change? He stood up, adjusting his silk shawl. He was not a good public speaker. But he had come prepared after rehearsing his words multiple times. Also, the first issue he was going to talk about was dear to him. 'We are going to procure a fleet of Arabian horses and elephants. What we have are very ordinary.'

Atma had tutored him to embellish his proposal with a preamble, but Rama had decided to present the issue quickly. However, now that he had spoken, it sounded terse to his own ears. *A preamble would probably have been better*, Rama thought. Since he didn't use shouters or a bullhorn, he had to speak slowly and wait for the information to spread through the audience. He preferred it that way since it bought him time to gather his thoughts.

The first to respond was Lakshmidhara, who looked quite astonished. 'How many are you planning to buy, King?'

Rama felt at ease. He knew the numbers. 'Ten thousand horses and two thousand elephants,' he answered proudly. Shekhara, their new finance minister, had said their budget could accommodate that. Besides, they now had a plan for increasing their revenue too.

Lakshmidhara shook his head disapprovingly. 'That will be very costly, King. I don't think we have the resources for that.'

Rama, surprised, yet relieved that his brother had kept his mouth shut, tried to speak as authoritatively as he could, 'That's why we have formulated a new financial plan. For decades, the tax on both goods and services has been five per cent. I propose we increase it to ten.'

Atma had advised him that if he proposed ten per cent, the guilds would agree to at least eight.

A commotion started as his word spread through the crowd. Rama sat back on the throne, feeling almost ill. He hadn't expected this at all. Well, he hadn't given much thought to the tax part since the idea of new Arabian horses had excited him so much.

A burly middle-aged man stood up and walked closer to the throne. He was the head of the gold guild. Snatching the bullhorn from the announcer, he almost barked out his words angrily. Rama's palms began to sweat. The man's gruff voice echoed through the hall. 'We are helping the royal treasury only because King Samudragupta kept the taxes low. We lend money to people.' He added arrogantly, 'On the king's behalf, if you didn't know.'

Rama fumed inside, turning a beet red. *So, people think I don't know even the basics.*

Next to shout at him was the head of the farmer's guild. 'And we're building hospitals and charitable institutions.' He mimicked the previous guild-head, 'On the king's behalf.'

Before more people could take a dig at him, Rama dismissed the assembly and headed out of the hall. The short walk from the throne room to his quarters seemed unending with every eye on him.

* * *

Dhruva watched with concern as Rama collapsed into a chair and ordered wine. The chamberlain duly removed Rama's crown, the heavy coat and the elaborate neckpiece. Rama dismissed him and picked up the large silver cup of wine. *Does he want to get drunk rather than address the problem at hand?* Dhruva wondered.

As Chandra had predicted, the proposal to increase taxes had met with a disastrous response.

She busied herself around the room, putting away the gold jewellery that Rama had taken off. She hoped he would open up to her. After he'd spent a few minutes scowling and shaking his head, Rama sighed. 'I blindly proposed what Atma and Shashi suggested.'

Dhruva continued to be silent. She knew he only needed to vent and didn't need a solution at that point. 'I don't know anything about our finances, the military, or even the general running of the state. I feel so helpless. I tried at one point but had to give up because my father saw no merit in my hard work.'

Dhruva felt genuinely sorry for Rama. She offered hesitatingly, 'If it's all right, I can help you with this. We can go over the historical and the current documents together.'

To her relief, Rama didn't scowl. Instead, he nodded with a sad smile. 'That would be great, Dhruva. You have a lot more stamina for mental work than I do.'

Dhruva, knowing Rama's tendency to procrastinate, proposed, 'We can start from today itself. We can ask Minister Lakshmidhara to send five years of financial records.'

They decided to start soon after lunch, and asked Megha to join them. While they waited in the parlour for Megha, Rama said, 'Chandra was supposed to consolidate the Pushkarana province for me. I don't know why he's come back. I didn't want to insult him by asking in the assembly.'

Dhruva was tempted to ask Rama why he had put Chandra's life at risk. But she was aware that talking in Chandra's favour would only trigger Rama's temper. She had seen it every time Megha supported Chandra.

So, she said instead, 'Well, it doesn't matter, does it?'

Rama's face relaxed a little. 'That's true. But he will only cause trouble for me if he's here. Now with the change in taxation that I'm introducing, I don't want rebels from within.'

Dhruva weighed her words carefully before saying, 'What trouble can a prince cause a king? You are wasting your energy thinking about him.'

Rama smiled. 'You are right. Atma keeps saying that Chandra might overshadow me.'

She had to be tactful in undoing the damage Atma was causing. 'Atma does not know what you are capable of. He needs to have more confidence in you. He still thinks of you as his disciple!'

Before Rama could respond, Megha walked in. Dhruva pointed to a small pile of the scripts they needed to go over and grinned. 'Welcome, Meghanad.'

Rama yawned. 'Just looking at these documents is making me sleepy!'

Dhruva laughed. 'There are three of us here. It won't be that difficult. Let's start from the most current details and work backwards. What do you both say?'

Megha bowed. 'You're at least ten times smarter than me. So I'll agree with whatever you say, Queen.'

Rama chuckled. 'That she is, and, ten times more diligent than me! Bring it on, Queen.'

After four hours, gallons of herbal tea and tons of snacks, they had finished one year.

'So, what's the verdict?' asked Rama, getting up and stretching. 'It's almost time for the evening assembly. I missed my nap.'

Dhruva scowled for a few minutes and then read aloud from her summary. 'We haven't had a good year at all. Not even ten per cent of the taxes collected have gone into the treasury. About fifty per cent has been spent on infrastructure and welfare projects, thirty per cent on the war campaign, and the rest on the Ashwamedha Yagya. We have saved nothing this year.'

'Great! My father's hunger to be famous has left us bankrupt!' Rama cried in exasperation. 'So, we do need higher taxes to make up for the losses.'

Megha spoke, 'Well, not really. If we refrain from waging wars, then we can save a lot. Why anger the guild-heads if there is a way to keep them happy?'

Dhruva pursed her lips in thought. 'It may not be that simple. Even if we don't initiate war, someone might attack us. But, I do agree with Megha. If there is a lot of opposition, then you might want to defer the tax increase.'

Rama took a deep breath. 'Let me talk to Atma before I decide.'

'If we work the next five afternoons, we will know how we fared in the previous years.' Dhruva felt excitement building in her.

'We'll see about that. I may go hunting tomorrow. Megha refuses to come along. He can help you. Give me a summary when I'm back,' concluded Rama.

A hunting trip at a time of crisis like this? Does he plan to increase the taxes and immediately take off? Dhruva's excitement came down a notch. She hadn't expected her husband to palm off work on her completely!

53

The next morning, when Rama entered the morning assembly hall, he felt good. Working with Dhruva the previous day had boosted his confidence. He'd consulted Atma, and they had decided that they would increase the taxes by seven per cent, and stick to it, no matter how bad the opposition. However, before announcing his decision, he asked the courtiers if there were any issues to be settled. The first to speak was Chandra, making Rama instantly angry.

'King.' As soon as Chandra began to speak, some attendees cheered loudly, sinking Rama's mood further. 'What is the plan for Pushkarana? Commander Kritavarma is going to run out of supplies soon. We have to go back to Pushkarana with a sizeable army and capture the city.' Chandra's words sounded like a challenge to Rama. 'This will be a good win for Magadha.'

Leaning forward, Rama looked at Chandra as dismissively as he could. 'We won't send any more army. We sent word to you to occupy the throne and make their army listen to us.'

Chandra let out derisive laughter. 'What are you saying? Seizing the fort means nothing. The Pushkarana army laying siege outside the fort is easily five times bigger than ours.'

Rama's head throbbed as the murmurs in the court became increasingly louder. More and more chieftains began to support Chandra. 'We have to send in the forces, King. Otherwise, the commander will have to relinquish the province and return. It isn't wise to lose a battle we have won!' summarized one of the commanders.

'Stop, all of you!' Rama's voice grew shrill. 'I'm the king and I make the decisions. The assembly is dismissed for today.'

Then, before getting off the throne, he announced into the bullhorn, 'I've decided to increase the taxes by seven per cent. If there are any objections, keep them to yourself.' Between anger and humiliation, his self-control had taken a holiday.

* * *

That afternoon, after Rama had unceremoniously dismissed the assembly, Chandra headed to Harisena's house with Pranava. He had to find a way to capture Pushkarana and keep Kritavarma safe. *How can Rama be this unreasonable? Even birds have more brains than him,* thought Chandra, staring at the pigeons pecking at grains. Soon, an idea came to him. After a few moments of pondering, he was convinced that it was a great idea. Now he had to convince the others!

He saw Harisena and Lakshmidhara huddled in a corner, talking. Chandra spoke, 'I want to wage a war against Pushkarana. I'll build my own army with the hunters and tribal men. But—' He added after a moment, 'I need money to do so.'

Pranava interrupted, 'Why don't we take the army and go? You are a commander anyway. Everyone listens to you.'

Harisena pursed his lips. 'No such hasty decisions. Let's think of a way. Rebelling against the king causes undue unrest in the kingdom.'

'If we have a sound plan, we can use the emergency treasure King Samudragupta had set aside,' said Lakshmidhara softly. He then added with a catch in his throat, 'We have to get Kritavarma back.'

By late afternoon, they had a plan. Harisena would convince the chief of the gold guild, Ravi, to accept the king's proposal for tax increase, but only for a year. However, Lakshmidhara would reimburse Ravi the increased part of the taxes he had to pay. In return, all Ravi had to do was convince the king to send an army with Chandra to Pushkarana.

'Prince, Ravi will help us but even then, I'm not sure the king will send a sizeable army with you. I suggest you borrow from the emergency treasury and gather the army you need. You'll need the money to buy the cooperation of the Pushkarana commanders too,' Lakshmidhara concluded.

Pranava, who had been mostly silent till then, asked curiously, 'But why would Ravi do this for us? Why would the king agree for only a year of increased taxes?'

'Ravi has always been a good friend to all of us. He will do this for Kritavarma. The king, or in other words, Atma, will lap up this opportunity because if the gold guild accepts their terms, then the others will follow. Gold merchants and spice traders wield a lot of influence and goodwill among other guilds,' Lakshmidhara explained.

Pranava glared at Chandra. 'None of these problems would have arisen if you hadn't donated the kingdom to your brother.'

'Thanks, that helps a lot,' Chandra muttered.

Harisena intervened, 'The past can't be changed, but the future should be planned based on the follies of the past. Prince Chandra, your lesson from these events is to pause for a moment or two or, better, for a night before you act.'

'Pause for a year before you act.' Pranava chuckled.

'This coming from a patient saint like you! If I'm impulsive, you are the mother of impulsive!' Chandra slapped his friend on the shoulder in jest.

Harisena concluded smilingly, 'The two of you are good together. But you can also be very volatile! So be patient in whatever you do. We will see you both at night in the secret room.'

* * *

That night, Chandra and Pranava entered an office complex that housed twelve identical meeting rooms. Except for a select few, nobody knew that one of these ordinary-looking rooms had a secret door that opened into a secret passage, leading to a flight of stairs to an underground room packed with vaults. Harisena and Lakshmidhara joined them.

Locking the main door to the office complex shut, Chandra looked at the ministers and spoke urgently, 'Pranava and I will enter first. Since we haven't been there in six months, there's sure to be a battle with creepy crawlies in the passageway.'

Chandra and Pranava moved the door camouflaged in the wall, to enter the dark space. Chandra jumped back in horror when he was instantly covered in cobwebs. Swatting them away, he murmured, 'Spiders have made themselves at home!'

Right behind Chandra was Pranava. 'I should have gone first. Why did you enter before me?'

Slowly adjusting to the darkness around him, Chandra quipped, 'Why? Do you have an anti-spider venom on you?'

Carefully walking down the narrow steps, Chandra wondered how Harisena would manoeuvre those steps given his frail state. Lakshmidhara, though almost as old as Harisena, was in better physical shape.

Once they entered the room, Pranava sighed. 'It smells muggy in here.'

Chandra replied. 'That is good news because it means nobody has been here.'

Deftly lighting the lamps kept in the corner, Chandra picked up a broom and showed it to Pranava. 'No servants here.'

Pranava stood in stunned silence for a moment before snatching the broom from Chandra. 'You are not cleaning. You are the future king of Magadha.' Then, he turned around, mumbling, 'Besides, I don't think you'll do as good a job as me.'

Chandra laughed. 'I've done this a hundred times before, for your information!' Even as he said so, a sadness enveloped him. He remembered the days when he used to come here often – the days when his father and Kritavarma would laugh and banter.

Chandra gave himself a mental shake. He didn't want to get sucked into the whirlpool of emotions and tried to disengage from his melancholia. He had already lost his father. He would not lose Kritavarma too, who was no less than a father to him. He would fight till his last breath for the safe return of the commander.

When they heard footsteps, Chandra rushed to the stairs. 'Let me help you down the stairs, Ministers.'

'Too late. We are already here,' said Lakshmidhara.

Before the ministers entered the room, they heard Harisena sneezing. Chandra looked at the old man with concern. 'Are you all right? Have you brought any medication with you?'

Harisena spoke in a voice that had gone hoarse from inhaling the dust, 'I'll be fine. We've never let this room grow dusty.'

Is that remorse in Harisena's voice? Chandra wondered. But there was no time for small talk.

Lakshmidhara patted Chandra on the shoulder. Instead of heading to the vaults, the minister led Chandra to a wall that he'd always thought was an ornate stone-engraved wall.

Chandra watched in surprise as Lakshmidhara tapped on a series of figurines. To his astonishment, the minister then slid open the wall to display a long shelf filled neatly with brass pots.

'In the name of Vishnu! When was this even built?' Chandra lightly touched a pot in awe. 'What do these contain?'

Lakshmidhara patted Chandra on the back. 'Enough wealth to tide over our kingdom for at least a decade. Your father had it built a year before he passed away. He wanted me to show this to you at the right time.' He continued wistfully after a pause, 'His wish was for this money to be used for the welfare of the kingdom.'

Soon, Chandra and Pranava were carrying two separate stashes of gold. The idea was for Pranava to start that night towards Pushkarana and Chandra to join him after the morning assembly. Going through the town at night would attract undue attention.

'How many more secrets does this room hide?' Pranava exclaimed, looking at the small door hidden behind a table in a corner.

Laughing, Chandra gently pushed Pranava towards the passage. 'Ministers, you can go home. I'll go with Pranava, since he may get scared in the dark. Once we're outside, I'll come back to the palace and Pranava can proceed towards Pushkarana. He can buy a horse in the next town.'

Pranava laughed. 'You are coming because you don't want me to have all the fun!'

Harisena hesitated. 'Prince, let Pranava go by himself. Just give him instructions. It is not wise for you to come back through the town with all the gold.'

Chandra had to agree, though he felt a strong urge to go with Pranava. He didn't want to disobey the ministers when they'd consented to his proposal.

Handing Pranava a small lantern and a key, Chandra explained, 'When you reach the end of the passageway, there is an iron door on top. Unlock it and push it open. Haul yourself up, and you'll be outside. Afterwards, close the door, lock it from outside, and keep the key with you. Make sure to cover the entrance with shrubbery so that a cowherd doesn't accidentally stumble upon the entrance!'

They dispersed for the night, but nobody saw the pair of eyes that was watching them closely.

54

Nightmares plagued Chandra all night. So much so that he woke up before the sun came up. That was new to him. He was someone who seldom saw the sun rise. There were no sounds except for some overzealous workers sweeping the grounds.

Soon his restlessness turned into anxiety with the news Sura had brought. The royal police had arrested Pranava on the outskirts of Pataliputra. Chandra rushed to the prison where the police had kept Pranava. But the guards refused to let him in. It was at the king's orders, they said. The same guards, who'd seemed to adore him once, shooed him away like a stray dog.

Harisena was the next person Chandra visited. He needed to talk to somebody calm. 'Prince, it means that someone followed us last night. You must speak to the king. But do so in the privacy of his quarters.' The minister placed his frail hand on Chandra's shoulder. 'Stay calm with your brother. No matter how much he provokes you.'

Chandra walked towards Rama's quarters, the king's quarters – a place he loved visiting when his parents had been alive. He hadn't gone anywhere near it since Rama had moved in. Chandra sent word to Rama and waited in the parlour.

It was an hour before Rama sauntered in, sporting a look of irritation. 'What?'

Rama's rudeness wasn't lost on Chandra, but he stayed calm. 'Why is Pranava in prison?'

Sprawling himself on the large chair, Rama spoke slowly, 'Because' – Rama seemed to take pleasure in uttering the words – 'he is a thief. He stole gold from the royal treasury.'

Chandra pulled another chair towards him and put his foot on it defiantly. 'No, he didn't. I gave him that gold. Gold that Father had left for me.' Chandra added, 'Just like he'd left the throne for me.'

Rama's face turned red with anger. 'Shut up, Chandra. I know the truth – the secret room with its hidden treasure and the tunnel through which you smuggled the royal gold.'

Chandra froze in shock. *Who'd given away the information?*

Rama got up from the chair and walked towards Chandra. 'I can match the gold Pranava had on him to the gold in the secret room. I can have him executed for stealing from the royal treasury.'

Chandra pushed Rama away and walked towards the window, feeling as helpless as a trapped mouse.

'If you want your dear friend alive, stop interfering in the affairs of state. Don't side with the guilds. There will be other changes too. I want your silence when they are proposed.'

'A king who blackmails! You should be ashamed of yourself. Set Pranava free, get Commander Kritavarma back. Then you can go back to ruining Magadha.'

Chandra stormed out and didn't show up for the morning assembly or the evening assembly. He was in no mood to know what was happening in the court anymore. All he wanted was Pranava by his side, and Kritavarma back in Pataliputra. Capturing Pushkarana, the tax increase – these things no longer seemed important.

That night, Harisena came looking for him. Sitting opposite Harisena in the visitor room, Chandra stayed quiet.

'What did the king say?' Harisena asked softly.

Chandra realized he hadn't informed the minister about his conversation with Rama. 'I'm sorry I didn't fill you in earlier.' Chandra tried to sound calm, but his heart seemed to break as he began to explain Rama's threat that morning.

'Because of my ill-conceived plan, we've lost the emergency treasure. And, Pranava's life is in danger along with the commander's.'

Harisena sighed deeply. 'It's not your fault. We were all part of that plan. Someone followed you around and reported to Atma. I don't think they've found the stash that Lakshmidhara showed you. They have only seen the gold in the vaults kept in the basement room. As for Pranava, we have to offer something to the king to make him release Pranava.'

Chandra looked away dejectedly. 'What can we possibly offer him when he's calling for my blood?'

'The same thing we had discussed before. Let's ask the head of the gold guild, Ravi, to accept the increased tax, but in turn, the king has to release Pranava, and send word to Kritavarma to head back.'

Chandra didn't reply. He hated playing into Rama's hands, but there was no other way.

'For the time being, it's best if you stay out of Pataliputra,' said Harisena. 'You can visit the vassal provinces, and resume the levy collection that you did while your father was alive. Take Pranava along.'

Chandra suddenly felt sad and empty. So even Harisena wanted him out of sight now! As if reading his mind, Harisena put a hand on Chandra's shoulder. 'It's for your safety and sanity, Prince. You can't stay here and remain a mute spectator in the court. We will handle the king and his men, and keep you updated.'

Chandra nodded. The minister was right. It was wise to be out of Pataliputra for a while. Before that, he had to meet Dhruva and tell her what had happened. Rama would certainly have fed her the story that he'd been caught smuggling gold from the treasury.

* * *

Everything went according to plan for the next few days. After Ravi spoke to Rama, Pranava was a free man. A scroll went to Kritavarma asking him to head home. Chandra got ready to start his journey with Pranava. A day before leaving town, he met Dhruva at Vasanthi's house.

Dhruva had dressed like an elderly woman instead of a maid that evening – an old silk saree, large bindi, hair in a tight bun. She completed the look with a shawl around her shoulders. When she met Chandra, Dhruva burst into laughter at the look of horror on his face.

'Sorry. I came here to meet a young queen,' Chandra muttered.

'She's sent me on her behalf,' Dhruva smiled. 'I didn't want to dress the same way every time I met you.'

After a moment of silence, Dhruva asked Chandra softly, 'I heard Pranava was caught carrying gold. What's the story here?'

The word 'caught' in her question irked Chandra. It implied that she thought Pranava was a criminal.

'Which version of the story do you know?' Chandra asked grimly.

'That Pranava had on him gold from the treasury and—' she stopped.

Chandra sighed and asked her if she knew about the secret room. She didn't. He told her the truth. Except for the vaults hidden in the wall. It was not safe for her to know that information.

'God, this is stranger than fiction!' Dhruva mumbled in disbelief.

'I hope you don't think we're a bunch of thieves.' Chandra didn't understand why he felt compelled to make Dhruva believe him.

Dhruva pursed her lips. 'I never thought that! You did what you did to save Commander Kritavarma. Unfortunately, you are being blackmailed into leaving Pataliputra.' Dhruva's voice grew weak. 'I don't think you should go.'

Chandra sighed. 'Only for the time being. It's good for everyone. I'll meet you whenever I'm in Pataliputra.'

After Dhruva left, Chandra walked to his horse, feeling a sense of loss. Meeting Dhruva had become a routine he looked forward to.

55

In the next few months, Rama finally began to understand how their kingdom ran and how the offices operated. But it hadn't come easily. He had pored over every dossier and document with Dhruva and Megha, listened to Atma's boring explanations, and paid attention to the matters discussed in the assembly. Moving about town in disguise was bittersweet, but mostly bitter. People still seemed to pine for his father.

But Rama now made efforts to help the citizens. He got more canals dug for irrigation, employed skilled youth in the palace, built more hospitals and increased the salary of the army personnel. He wished his mother were alive to see his hard work.

That evening, Rama waited for others to join him in the private council chamber. It still seemed unreal to him that the hall where his father had wielded power once was his now.

There was a knock at the door. Megha walked in. Megha had been looking so grave lately that Rama wondered if he was the same man who'd lounged for hours on the riverbank with him.

'I wanted to talk to you before the others join us.' Megha politely refused a glass of wine. Rama sipped his drink. They waited for the servant to leave the room.

'Why aren't you drinking? Is it because of what happened the other day? Get over it, friend!' Rama was irritated. Megha had been refusing wine for weeks now, after an unfortunate incident one evening.

A scuffle had broken out in the tavern they'd visited. Rama, in spite of being in disguise, had almost been recognized. A drunk man had kept shouting, 'Th-ha-at is our k-k-king. Th-ha-at is our k-k-king, R-R-Rama.' Thanks to the fact that the man was really drunk, as was everyone else in the tavern, they had been able to escape. But the incident had left Megha devastated.

'You are a king now. You can't be found drinking cheap wine in a tavern.'

Rama too had been rattled, but not for long. When Megha had steadfastly refused to go out with him after that evening, Rama had roped in Guru and Chandana for company.

Rama decided to drop the matter. If Megha didn't want to go out with him, it was his loss. He spoke instead about why he'd wanted to meet him that evening. 'Megha, I've been talking to Minister Shashi all week. Increasing taxes on revenue hasn't helped much.'

Megha pondered over this. 'Is it because the guilds are refusing to help us?'

'Yes.' Rama paused. He knew Megha would oppose what he was going to say. So would Dhruva. So he hadn't invited her that night. 'The guilds are acting like stubborn children after the tax increase. We're considering introducing import and export duties. We might have to increase transportation charges too.'

Megha looked alarmed. 'We mustn't antagonize the guilds further. You must talk to Minister Lakshmidhara and Prime Minister Harisena.'

Rama's face turned grave. 'They can review it when I present it in the assembly. I'm struggling to break away from the system they've created. I won't consult them anymore.'

Megha nodded, but the disapproval on his face irritated Rama. 'Tell me, what's on your mind.'

'What was wrong with the system your father had, King? The kingdom was prosperous, and the people were happy. I feel Minister Atma is influencing your decisions too much.'

Megha's remark made Rama furious. 'You, of all people, should know how hard I'm working to make these changes. Atma is merely helping me.'

Harisena, who'd met him a few days earlier, had conveyed the same sentiment. 'Atma is a vengeful man. He will be good to you only as long as you continue to concur with all his ideas. Be careful, King.'

He was going to adopt Atma's new scheme of taxation, but he was going to change the perception that he was Atma's puppet.

56

Atma sat on his bed in the dark. Sleep eluded him. Unpredictable was the only word that could describe Rama lately. He'd shot down Atma's suggestion to add a fleet of elephants. 'We will add more cavalry. Elephants are harder to train, expensive to buy, and too slow on the battlefield.'

His suggestion that they ask the southern kings for tributes had been turned down. 'If they form a clique, and attack us, it'll be near impossible to counter them.'

That particular night, Rama had taken back the proposal to tax the ally provinces of the north. 'I thought about it, and I don't want to do it.' Rama had then gone on to add, 'The allies guard our borders, and they provide passageways for our merchants and army. We cannot antagonize them.' Even though he'd agreed to it only a week ago!

These acts of defiance couldn't have been Rama's decisions alone. He had a much better understanding of the kingdom now, but still, Atma didn't believe that Rama was smart enough to think this deeply. It was probably Queen Dhruva who was influencing Rama's decisions. But then, who was guiding her?

'Do you want me to light a lamp for you, Sir?' Vidura's words brought him out of his thoughts.

'No, Vidura. I'm going back to sleep. Starting tomorrow, follow Queen Dhruva until you find out everything about her and her routine.'

The news Vidura delivered after a week was not at all what Atma had expected. Dhruva met Harisena, yes, but she also met Prince Chandra, that too in disguise! Atma almost felt dizzy with this piece of information. He knew how to use it to his advantage. Blinded by rage and revenge unbecoming of an old man, Atma didn't stop to think if the gossip could ruin young Dhruva.

The next night, Shashi and Vijaya met Atma in his house. Though Rama had insisted that Atma live inside the palace fort, he had refused. The privacy that his small house provided was priceless.

'King Rama seems very different lately,' Shashi began, as they sat around in Atma's dimly lit house.

Atma scoffed, 'He is insecure and ignorant. He needs to be removed, but carefully.'

'Minister! You were the one who made him king! Are you regretting your decision already?' Vijaya sounded puzzled.

'Regret?' Atma laughed. 'When everything is going as planned? That reminds me, I have to write to the Shaka king soon.' Silence spread through the room like a thick fog.

Vijaya finally said, 'You have what you wanted – the power to rule and a king who follows your orders. Why are you still siding with the Shaka king?'

'I'm not siding with the Shaka king. We are.' Atma pointed at the two of them with his shaky hands. 'Do you think both of you are safe? Rama's kingship is a bubble waiting to burst. When it does, Chandra will be the king. Rama will be back to his old, wild ways, and you both will be back in the dungeon.'

Growing white and ashen with fear, Vijaya and Shashi sat still. Finally, Shashi spoke, 'So we're going to help the Shaka king oust Rama?' Atma didn't have to answer the question. His self-satisfied smirk said it all.

* * *

Rudrasimha was having his dinner and ignored Minister Kedara, who was waiting to talk to him. The minister sat waiting as the king chewed upon a piece of meat in the lamb curry. There was deathly silence all around, given the late hour of the night. The ones who served dinner to the king came and left the room with noiseless steps. Just the previous day, Rudrasimha had thrown a bowl of hot soup at a servant in rage.

'I want to strangle that old goat Atma with my bare hands.' Rudrasimha spat out some food on the plate. 'That idiot Rama has been on the throne for a year now, and we still haven't captured Pataliputra. Now, he wants us to wait longer! He does not want us to wage war but defeat the Guptas in stealth. As if he's capable of orchestrating such a coup.' His tirade against Atma continued, 'Everything that loser has suggested so far has been a failure. Attack on Samudragupta, flop. War against the Guptas, an utterly humiliating defeat.' Rudrasimha's anger turned to what he considered a matter of great personal shame. 'Pushyavarma, king of that tiny province Kamarupa, declined my proposal and gave his daughter in marriage to Rama. I could have destroyed him, but you stopped me saying the Guptas might back him. I'm fed up of this, Kedara. I need my revenge on the Guptas and Pushyavarma. I can't rest in peace till then.'

Kedara listened, nodding occasionally to show his support. He'd never liked Atma, but he agreed with him that they should not wage another war on the Guptas. Rama might not be a worthy king, but the kingdom still had stalwarts like Kritavarma, Harisena and Prince Chandra. However, saying that would make Rudrasimha go blind with rage, so Kedara had to choose his words carefully. 'I understand, King, and I want no less. Let's give Atma exactly another six months. Then we will have a plan of our own to exact revenge on the Guptas.'

57

Rama hated visiting Atma's cramped house – the thick ugly drapes that cut out the light, the smell of medicines. Moreover, the old man was always the bearer of bad news.

'Why can't you at least light a few more lamps? The darkness is depressing,' Rama muttered in disgust as he lowered himself into one of the creaking chairs. Atma had not got up to welcome him, which irked Rama further.

Then he stared at Vijaya and asked, 'Why is he here?'

Before Atma could reply, Rama snapped at him. 'It is cumbersome for me to come here in disguise. I cannot be at your beck and call all the time. I have plenty of other things to do.

'I won't keep you long, King. You asked me for ways to improve our finances. Here is another plan.' He gestured to Vijaya to explain.

Vijaya moved his chair closer to Rama's and placed a palm-leaf scroll on the table in front of them. 'Minister Atma and I have drawn up a list of allies who are not useful to us but are eating away at our resources.'

'I told you we're not taxing the allies,' Rama replied sharply.

'Vijaya, I want to have a word with the king. Can we have the room, please?' Vijaya got up and left.

'King, let me be straight with you.' Atma looked stern and disapproving, like a teacher reprimanding a wayward student. Rama had the urge to pick up Atma's frail body and throw him out of the door.

'I advise you not to discuss political matters with Queen Dhruva. Women are emotional and scare easily.'

Rama clenched the armrest of the chair. 'It's none of your business what I discuss with my wife. But let me clarify. If you think my wife is influencing my decisions, then you are out of your mind.'

'I'm happy to hear that. Forgive my words, but please don't shoot down this plan.'

'All right. Make it quick.' Settling back into the chair, Rama watched Atma summon Vijaya.

By the time the meeting was over, it was past midnight. Rama felt drained. Still, he was in no mood to retire for the night. He dismissed his guards and sent word to Megha to meet him by the river.

Rama's head buzzed with thoughts. *People think I'm Atma's puppet. Atma thinks I'm my wife's. What sort of a puppet king am I?* He laughed deliriously.

A rustling behind him indicated Megha's arrival. 'This feels like old times! You, me and the river when the world sleeps!' said Megha cheerily as he sat next to Rama, letting his feet dangle in the shallow water. Tiny fish chased each other in circles.

'But it's nothing like those times, Megha.' Rama's voice was rueful.

'At this moment, it is.' Megha threw a stone into the water.

'Did you bring any wine or bhang with you?' Rama smiled, punching Megha on the shoulder playfully. 'Only then will it feel like old times.'

Megha was silent. He was not going to supply any more of that self-destructive intoxication to the king of the Guptas. The river glinted and sparkled in the moonlight. All they could hear were the bhajans being sung by villagers nearby.

Rama broke the silence finally, 'Today, Atma and Vijaya listed the allies we can ask for contributions. I am considering it.' He decided not to share what Atma had said about Dhruva. It was too sore an issue.

Megha looked surprised. 'We talked about it the other day, and you decided against it! It sounds like a sure way to turn more friends into foes!'

'It's a good plan. We are targeting the weak provinces, where there is no threat of attack. They are not very helpful to us either.' Rama hated that his voice sounded unconvincing to his own ears.

Megha became serious. 'I hope you'll discuss this with Commander Kritavarma and the others before you make a decision.'

Rama blurted out in anger, 'How long should I keep consulting those ministers? Till my hair turns grey and my teeth fall out? I don't think so. I want to be a real king who makes decisions on his own.' He got up, signalling the end of the discussion.

He went to his old quarters that night. He didn't want to talk to Dhruva. This place had been his sanctuary since childhood. As he tossed and turned in bed, Rama's thoughts revolved around Megha. Something had changed between them. Megha, who'd never opposed him, now did so openly and frequently.

Talking and discussing things with Dhruva was good but Atma wasn't wrong. Most often, he did do what she suggested. He was growing too dependent on her.

Whom do I talk to now? Megha doesn't approve of my ways. Dhruva influences my decisions. Atma and his ilk are untrustworthy. The new ministers are still too new. Rama felt as lonely as the kitten that sat on the windowsill purring for its mother.

58

In the next few months, Rama made changes that ranged from highly disastrous to marginally useful. He introduced the new taxes at Atma's behest – irrigation tax (Use the river? Pay the charge.) and road tax (Use the road? Pay the fee.). To teach the arrogant gold guild a lesson, he set the levies on imports and exports at twenty per cent. The gold guild that routinely exported spices to Rome to import gold was livid at this news.

As if that wasn't enough, Rama followed through with the idea of demanding tributes from ally kingdoms. The task of collecting money from friends was assigned to Chandra.

Rama made a few functional changes here and there – a few new hospitals and schools, a salary increase for military personnel and the palace staff. But still, people snickered that he was only throwing a bone at them.

Every ally who had treated Chandra like a son earlier now rebuked him. That day, the backlash had come from the king of Samatata. 'We fought by your father's side, Prince. We not only lent our armies but also fought with him, putting our own lives in danger. Is this the reward we get?'

In the evening, Pranava pitched a tent, while Chandra went for a walk around the woods. The king of Samatata hadn't invited him to stay at the palace as before. Why would he? Chandra was now an enemy, not a friend. He could no longer bear the shame of begging for tributes and getting berated in return.

He saw a herd of deer and thought of hunting them, but quickly decided against it. The poor deer had enough predators to worry about. Why add another to the list? He looked at the river and thought of swimming, but decided against that too. Get wet on a cold rainy night? His answer at any other time would have been to just dive into the water, but not that day. Nothing seemed to appeal to him. He hadn't had the zeal to do anything for months now. He needed to come out of that state of despair.

Chandra took out his dagger, Ajeya, and cut off a low-hanging bunch of bananas for dinner. A group of monkeys swiped away the bunch as soon as he set it down! *My rotten luck never seems to end!* Chandra cursed softly. The monkeys flashed cute grins at him!

It started to drizzle. Chandra took shelter under a large banyan tree.

He was thinking. He met Dhruva every fortnight when he was in Pataliputra. It was nice to listen to her narrate at length (though he chided her for her long stories) the happenings in the court and the king's new ideas. They discussed the pros and cons of the king's plans, but those discussions had been useless lately. Rama had begun to ignore most of Dhruva's suggestions. Most of the news Dhruva brought to him showed that the kingdom was on its way to doom.

One bright moment in his otherwise dull life was meeting Dhruva. Whenever he met her at Vasanthi's house, they battled over a game of chaduranga or pachheesi. She was as insanely competitive as he was. Chandra smiled involuntarily at the thought.

By the time it stopped drizzling, Chandra had made up his mind. He was going to change his life and not sit around and mope any longer. 'Let's head back to Pataliputra, Pranava. I am done being a nomad! No more of this begging for alms.'

'Am I hearing you right? Did you eat a mystic berry that made you sane?' Pranava smiled. Then he grew sombre. 'I've only seen you struggle, first in the war campaigns with your father, and now with this. Demand a few provinces for yourself to rule.'

Chandra shook his head. 'My father's dream was to unite Bharata under our rule. I can't divide our own kingdom!' He threw a stone with all his might into the river and watched the ripples. 'But, from now on, I will be a part of the court. I'll claim what is rightfully mine, the rank of a prince.'

'And I'll claim the rank of the prince's friend. What does that entail?' Pranava asked mock seriously, biting into roasted corn.

'Nothing much! But we can annoy the king jointly.' Chandra laughed, sprawled on the ground watching the stars. He felt good after a long time.

* * *

Dhruva sat through the assembly analyzing that day's gathering. Ministers, commanders, chieftains, noblemen, guild-heads – attendees of all ranks and cadres – had one thing in common. They *all* disagreed with Rama. Then her eyes took in the decor of the throne room. Her husband had spent an obscene amount on renovating it. His throne was now bigger and grander. His new diamond-encrusted crown sparkled like a star. The throne room had a fresh coat of gold paint. There were absurd statues staring at her from all corners. The once classy throne room was now a gaudy theatre.

Rama had bought new fleets of Arabian horses and imported gold and diamonds from all over the world. He'd added a new wing to their personal quarters. Everyone had noticed these extravagances. They were not blind. They resented Rama more than ever.

What has brought about this change in him? How long will people tolerate this highhandedness? Who was guiding Rama now? Somehow, they seemed like his own ideas to her. He was the instigator of all that was happening.

59

It had been a month since Chandra had returned to the capital. No words had been exchanged between the brothers, but Chandra knew that Rama was furious that he had returned. Chandra had assigned himself the task of assisting Kritavarma. He diligently attended the assembly both in the morning and in the evening. He went riding, trained the soldiers and met his old friends. Somehow, life seemed a lot less dreadful now than before.

In the assembly, he was tempted many times to stand up and protest. But Harisena had warned him not to anger Rama. 'It is important that you stay in Pataliputra. If you raise your voice, your brother will find another reason to send you away.' Those were Harisena's stern words.

That morning, when the session began, the first to speak was the head of the blacksmith's guild. A guild-head speaking in the assembly lately meant disaster.

'We believe that the king is God. Raja pratyaksha devata?' The wiry man, as always, was highly dramatic. 'We heard the gold and the silk merchants are paying only half the taxes we're paying. Is that true?'

News spread fast! Rama had proposed a compromise with the gold and silk guilds only two days earlier. For a change, it was a decent plan, and both Harisena and Lakshmidhara had agreed to it. The guild-heads had agreed to the proposal that they would continue as moneylenders and help in the upkeep of orphanages and hospitals. In turn, their taxes would be reduced by half.

Minister Guru responded to the accusation, 'The king's court has valid reasons for its actions. We can't explain them to the public.'

'So, it is true!' The next to scream at Rama was the head of the farmers' guild, who banged his fist on the chair for added effect. 'Are you taxing us more because you consider us less important? Because we're not as rich as the gold and silk merchants? We want the king to explain this.'

'Whatever my ministers are saying are my words.' Chandra winced at Rama's reply. That would not go down well with the already angry men.

Murmurs of disapproval coursed through the audience. Chandra could sense his brother's anger rise. He was sure Rama was going to be angry. But Rama took him by surprise when he declared calmly, 'I wish I didn't have to tax you at all. I wish I could give you more resources. But my hands are tied because we are just not rich enough.'

After a moment of silence, another guild-head spoke, 'What do you plan to do about it other than taxing us?'

Chandra watched Rama's face begin to contort again in anger, his momentary calm all but gone. Then Dhruva said something to Rama.

'We will disclose our plans when the time is right.' Rama regained his composure quickly. Dhruva was a miracle worker, indeed!

During the next hour, the pattern of discussion was the same. Each guild-head started with a demand and ended spewing venom for the tax benefit given to the wealthy merchants.

Chandra sighed. *How long will this unrest continue?* He wished he could talk sense into Rama. At least Dhruva understood the need of the hour was to placate the guilds by reducing taxes overall, but she was helpless.

* * *

The turmoil continued for weeks. As if to rub salt on the already injured treasury, Chandra heard dreadful news from the scouts. The Nagas, their archenemy, were planning an attack on Pataliputra. Chandra was sure many of the Gupta vassals and allies were supporting them.

The next morning, he announced the news at the assembly. First, there was silence. Rama's face was taut. Then, without even looking at Chandra, Rama spoke nonchalantly, 'We'll think about it when they're near.'

Chandra was aghast. Harisena patted his hand gently, signalling him to calm down. But there was only so much restraint he could exercise. 'Sure. Great plan. Once they are close, we can throw open the fort gates and welcome them in.'

'Stop being sarcastic!' Rama lost his temper. 'Are you the king, or am I? My mistake was not pushing you into the dungeon when you stole from the treasury.'

'You are the one robbing people, and you accuse me of stealing? Do as you please.' Chandra too had lost control. The assembly went eerily quiet at this open spat between the brothers.

'If you think the Nagas are attacking, then go wage war. You are good at losing battles for us anyway,' Rama blurted out sarcastically.

Chandra hit back, 'A king is the chief commander of the army. Why don't you go to war as a first?'

Before the squabble could escalate, Chandra left the assembly. Kritavarma offered to quell the uprising of the Nagas, which Rama accepted after a subtle nod from Atma.

* * *

'I want to send him to prison. I will, soon,' Rama fumed in his nightly meeting with Atma.

'We have enough to worry about. Ignore him.' Atma waved his hand. 'He does not matter. He's a frustrated man.'

'I can't believe how rude Chandra was to me. I should push him into the dungeon for his insolence,' Rama complained to Dhruva that night.

'Let it go. There are bigger issues to deal with,' Dhruva soothed Rama.

Later, when he was with Megha, Rama brought it up again. 'He thinks he can say anything to me and get away with it? He should be exiled from the kingdom.'

'He should not have been rude, but he may have a point,' Megha tried reasoning with Rama. He was duly reproached.

Eventually, Rama cooled down. They were all right. Chandra was a nuisance, but he should learn to ignore him.

Little did he know then how fate would make it impossible for him to ignore Chandra.

60

The Naga threat was contained for now, but the revolt from the people continued. Dhruva feared for Rama's safety whenever there were angry eruptions in the court. Her fears soon came true at Rama's next address at the town square. As soon as he started to speak, a group of agitators took over the scene with deafening shouts.

At first, they were shouts of protest, but these soon turned into insults at Rama's incompetence as king and his misspent youth. They demanded that Chandra be made king. Within minutes, the protesters swelled in numbers. Someone threw a stone at Rama. The security guards acted swiftly and whisked Rama and Dhruva out of there.

Rama, without saying a word to Dhruva, slept all morning and afternoon. In the evening, he left the bed and sat on a chair staring out of the window. He had neither eaten nor spoken. Dhruva looked at Rama and sighed. It must have been harrowing to be the target of an angry mob.

She touched Rama's shoulder gently. 'Don't take it to heart. These are the hazards every ruler faces.'

Rama laughed bitterly. 'In the history of mankind, I must be the first king to be pelted with stones, I'm sure!' He rubbed his temples. 'If I try to please one, I end up displeasing ten others.'

'Why don't we go on a holiday for some days? The mountains in Kamarupa will be ideal. I can ask my father to get a palace ready for us,' Dhruva proposed.

'Now, I'm only a tyrant. If I go away, I'll be a tyrant and a coward!' He got up. 'I'm going out for some air.'

Though her plan had been shot down, Dhruva recovered quickly. She debated whether to tell Rama what she thought. It was a tricky issue, but she had to try. 'Can you relax the taxes a little to win back the guilds? You have to give a little to get a little.'

Rama didn't reply. She was glad he hadn't shot down the suggestion.

* * *

That night, before heading out, Rama called for a quick meeting with Atma. Dhruva had voiced his own thoughts. People needed to be calmed down.

He got to the point quickly when Atma arrived at the council chamber. The old man's response came as no surprise to Rama. Taxation was Atma's obsession. He often quoted Chanakya and other scriptures, at annoying lengths to convince Rama to increase taxes, introduce more levies, and of course, to ask the allies for tributes.

So, when Rama told him that night that he had decided to retract the tax increase, Atma was livid. 'Reduce the taxes now? You will look weak. Our treasury will be empty again.' Atma leaned forward and wagged a finger. 'Send the protesters to the dungeons. Arrest a few guild-heads too. Show them your strength.'

'Looking weak is better than being dead! My decision to lower the taxes is final.' Rama got up to leave.

'King.' Atma narrowed his eyes. 'What is the reason for this sudden change of mind? Did our queen panic after today's agitation?'

'Did my wife suggest that I do this? Yes, she did. I discussed the issue with her because she was nearly killed too this morning. If you haven't noticed, she's an intelligent woman who cares about our kingdom and me.' Rama stared at Atma defiantly.

Atma, his face an expressionless mask, uttered inaudibly, 'As you wish, King.'

* * *

What the old minister felt after Rama left was not calm but rage. He summoned Vidura as soon as he reached home. 'Follow the queen again. Report to me as soon as she meets Prince Chandra. She will want to share the good news that they have succeeded in making Rama lower the levies.'

Atma wasn't wrong. The very next day, Vidura brought him the news he was waiting for. 'Minister, I just saw them by the edge of the fort.' He gasped for breath, having run all the way back to Atma's house.

'Vidura, get the chariot ready. We have to talk to the king.'

'I hope you are not going to tell the king about Queen Dhruva. That could be bad for both of them.' Vidura's voice quivered with fright.

Atma narrowed his eyes. 'Is she doing the right thing by meeting Prince Chandra behind her husband's back?'

Vidura was silent and left to get the chariot ready.

* * *

Unaware of what awaited her, Dhruva hurried back to her chambers. 'I'm late for the evening prayers.' Quickly changing into her royal attire in Vasanthi's room, Dhruva almost sprinted towards the palace. She entered the room in such a hurry that she bumped into Rama.

'King!' she exclaimed with a smile. 'You said you were going to be late.' But her smile dried up when she saw Rama's face. He stopped the maids trailing Dhruva. Then he gently shooed out Kusha, who was whimpering at his feet. He closed the heavy door with such a thud that Dhruva jumped.

'Why are you so late?' Rama asked. He looked furious – knitted brows, pursed lips and flared nostrils.

Dhruva's mouth was dry. In a panic, she blurted out, 'I got delayed walking with Vasanthi.'

'Stop lying! I know you were with Chandra.' Rama's breath was hot like furnace smoke. 'I never expected treachery from you!'

Dhruva froze in shock. She was not making any treacherous plans with Chandra! Before she could open her mouth, Rama flung a terracotta statue against the wall, smashing it into pieces. Dhruva watched in horror as he upturned a table. There were frenzied knocks on the door, but Dhruva did not have the courage to walk past Rama to open the door.

'What were you doing with that scoundrel? Planning to dethrone me?' Rama flung a brass vase against the wall. 'Are you conspiring to put me in the dungeon and marry him?' He followed it with another vase, another statue, and finally a massive bronze idol of Vishnu.

The knocks on the door became louder. Dhruva tried to move towards the door, but Rama gripped her arm. 'Why did you deceive me?' Her fear doubled as she smelt cheap wine on Rama's breath. *Was he going to break her arm?*

Rama shook her violently. 'Do you know what people are saying about you? That you are barren. That you are incapable of giving us a successor. But I shushed them all. I made sure nobody said a word against you. What do I get in return? Betrayal!' His bloodshot eyes threatened to pop out of their sockets.

Rama's words crushed her. Was that what he thought of her? A backstabber? Stung with humiliation, Dhruva found her voice, 'I've done nothing wrong. I met Prince Chandra to discuss matters of state. I can explain if you listen to me.'

'Matters of state?' Rama laughed derisively. 'I made you part of the council. What did you know before – other than to act self-important because you've read the scriptures?'

Rama pushed her aside and collapsed on the bed. His voice was now menacingly low. 'Maybe, according to all the books you read, it's all right for a woman to be a wife to brothers. You want to be Draupadi with two husbands, don't you?'

Dhruva felt an urge to slap him. Before she could say another word, Rama got up and started towards the door. 'I shared every thought with you. And you used it against me.' His eyes welled up. 'I trusted you like I trusted my mother.'

Dhruva ran to stop him. Tears rolled down her cheeks. 'Please listen to me—'

But Rama was gone. She stared at his retreating figure with tears rolling down her eyes. That night altered the course of the Gupta kingdom.

61

Rama opened his eyes, feeling groggy. Even a slight movement caused excruciating pain in his body. His mouth was dry, and his throat was parched. Water ... he was thirsty ... he needed water. Rama looked around. The hard floor on which he was sleeping was cold, and the air around him stale.

He tried to sit up, wincing in pain. Where was he? Filled with fear, Rama tried to stand up but found his legs chained. Scared and tense, he moved as far as the heavy chains permitted. He could reach a closed iron door. He banged on it until his hands were sore. But, the deathly silence continued. Exhausted, he collapsed on the floor and curled into a ball. *Help ... somebody help me ...* He was too weak to even say the words out aloud.

Rama forced himself to remember what had landed him in that situation.

* * *

After his showdown with Dhruva, Rama had a brief meeting with Atma. 'I will go away for a while, Minister. Towards Vidisha. I will take Megha and Guru with me. I'll be travelling in disguise.'

However, Atma insisted that he take Vijaya with him. 'That is dangerous territory, King. If you move any further west, you'll fall right into the Shaka provinces of Malwa. If you move north, you'll face the Nagas. It's not easy to travel as a commoner. Take Vijaya with you. He knows these regions well.' Rama agreed, and Atma assured him that he would take care of the administration in his absence.

They rode on ordinary horses and camped at public inns. It was an arduous journey towards Vidisha, but Rama felt free. He was finally himself. He was not a king, and nobody demanded anything from him. However, Dhruva's betrayal haunted him. He stayed intoxicated almost all the time. His excuse was that he was trying to forget her.

When they neared Vidisha, Vijaya picked a clearing amidst the thick forest to camp. Rama was glad to have

Vijaya, who stayed sober and made all the decisions. He was also thankful to Guru and Megha, who never left his side.

Little did he know then that his dream escape would turn into a nightmare. One fateful night, a sharp pain in his head woke him up. Before he could be fully conscious, he was bound, gagged and loaded on a horse, like luggage.

Half a dozen men stood nearby. They looked like gardeners or woodcutters. He noticed that Megha and Guru too were bound. Where was Vijaya?

* * *

He recalled the bang on his head that had made everything around him go dark.

The room, a cell in a dungeon, suffocated him. He was going mad with hunger and thirst. He kicked at the chains that bound his legs but only managed to injure his ankle in the process. *Where am I? How long have I been here? Who captured me?*

Then the right question struck him: *Who knew that I had gone hunting?* He tried to think logically. Only Atma knew where he was going. However, Atma held his power only as long as Rama was king. So there was no reason for him to kill Rama.

Chandra ... How about Chandra? Rama thought frantically. The more he thought, the more he was convinced that it was his brother's doing, with Dhruva's help. *If I'm kept prisoner, Chandra will get my throne and my wife. Why wouldn't he do it?* He felt sick. *What a fool I was to trust Dhruva!*

Megha had almost made him believe during the journey that Dhruva was blameless. 'You must talk to the queen when we go back. There might be a good reason she met your brother. I don't believe for a moment that she's conspiring against you. Don't trust Atma so much.' *How wrong Megha is! Dhruva and Chandra, under a facade of goodness, can fool anyone.*

Mired in misery, Rama went off to sleep.

* * *

'It has been ten days since the king left town. There's no news about him. Something is wrong.' Dhruva's voice choked with emotion.

Chandra had sent scouts out in every direction to find Rama, but they had all returned without any news. 'We will send out more people to look for him. I have a feeling Atma knows more than he's telling us. The old owl claims that all he knows is that Rama left on a hunting trip. And he waves around a letter from the king that appoints him regent.'

'Send better scouts. Ask them to look for clues. I'm sure the king went hunting, and something unfortunate happened,' Dhruva urged Chandra.

'I've sent the best. I'll go too if you prefer that. It's all my fault. If I hadn't asked you to meet me, none of this would have happened,' said Chandra. Guilt tore at him. He'd brought only trouble and hardship to her.

Dhruva replied firmly, 'No. We were trying to protect the kingdom. Once the king calms down, I'll explain everything to him. For now, I just want him to be safe.' Dhruva's voice choked again. 'Don't go anywhere out of Pataliputra. Who knows what kind of conspiracy is brewing here? Keep a watch on that evil old man.'

Chandra nodded. He hadn't had a proper meal since Rama had disappeared. Megha, Guru and Vijaya were missing too. Chandra was worried about Vijaya's plans. The man was a devil.

62

In the first few days, Rama tried to stay alert, listening to the sounds around him and hatching a plan to escape. With each passing day, he knew it was futile. He was never going to get out of here. A tray of inedible food came to him once a day. At first, Rama had left the food untouched, but eventually, he started waiting for it. Hunger had killed his taste buds.

A guard led him out blindfolded, once in the morning and once after sunset. Rama had tried talking to the guard, but the man had glared at him. Lately, Rama was barely able to move. His bones felt like porridge. He had broken into a rash that made it impossible for him to sleep. *Why don't my captors kill me? Death is better than this life.*

When the door creaked open that day, Rama didn't bother to move. Must be food, he thought groggily. However, the door opened wider and the light from a lamp hit Rama's eyes. He tried to focus. A large man stood before him.

'Stand up for the king, you arrogant fool.' The guard came near him and pulled him up roughly, making Rama wince in pain. But the word 'king' caught his attention. *Which king?*

Rama stared at the man before him. He looked vaguely familiar. Cold fear ran up his spine as it dawned on him who the man was. Rudrasimha! Rama felt numb. Why hadn't he thought of him? Who else could be capable of such cruelty?

'Clean him up and bring him to me in an hour. I can't bear to stand here a moment longer,' Rudrasimha barked out the words and left.

Rama howled in pain when the hot water touched his wounded body, and bawled when a doctor applied salve on his rashes, but it made him feel human again. They gave him a decent meal to eat. Then, a man blindfolded him and led him out.

After a short walk, when the blindfold came off, Rama squinted and looked around. The room looked like a meeting area in a ruined palace. Rudrasimha, looking as vicious as Rama remembered, was sitting on a large chair that was painted gold but not made of gold. He was wearing a gaudy, long, red silk shirt with a white silk dhoti.

He was constantly picking his teeth. It disgusted Rama, but he knew better than to show it. A mousy-looking man, probably Rudrasimha's minister, sat on a smaller chair looking through a scroll. The Shaka king got up from his chair to pace. The minister automatically stood up too.

'I wanted your father here, you know? Cowering before me like this,' said Rudrasimha, wagging a finger at Rama. Even in his state of distress, Rama wondered why his teeth were so black.

Walking closer, Rudrasimha poked a finger into Rama's stomach. 'You are not man enough for me to even consider a fight. Maybe that brother of yours is. Not an equal but close.'

Then why didn't you abduct my brother, you moron? Rama swallowed his anger. Fear lurked in a corner of his mind. *What is in store for me?*

'Why do you think I captured you?' asked Rudrasimha, making Rama almost dizzy with his stinky breath. 'Because your worthless old friend said that I can get Pataliputra in exchange for you.' The Shaka started to guffaw like a maniac.

He continued to laugh maniacally. His mousy minister joined in squeakily. *My worthless old friend? Who could that be? Atma? Should I ask this brute if it was Atma?*

Rudrasimha stopped talking and walked towards his chair. Rama took a deep breath. Heaving himself into the chair, Rudrasimha spoke in a strangely calm voice, 'My wise minister Kedara says your kingdom will do no such thing. They will let you die but not give me the Gupta empire. You are worthless to them, Kedara tells me. So ...' the king drawled, making Rama more uneasy with every word and pause.

'I have a new plan for revenge. But this wise man says that won't work either.' Rudrasimha patted the minister on the back, making him almost fall out of his chair. 'But I'll take my chances. Abducting you and your friends should not go waste.'

Rama stared on blankly. 'Do as I say, or I'll push you back into the dungeon.' Rudrasimha looked more like a mad dog than a human being. 'Forever.'

Rama's heart sank with fear. *What does this mad man want me to do?*

63

Kritavarma, looking grave, handed Chandra a palm-leaf scroll. 'I got this from a Shaka messenger an hour back.'

The commander had called for an urgent meeting at Harisena's house, though it was late in the night. As Chandra read the letter, his face reddened with anger. 'Would even an ordinary man write a letter of this sort, leave alone a king? Doesn't my brother have any honour, shame or decency left in him?' Chandra crumpled the letter and threw it away. Harisena sat, his head low. He looked pained, more pained than the day Samudragupta had died.

The letter was short. *'Shaka King Rudrasimha holds me captive. He demands that we give Queen Dhruva to him in return for my release. He assures me that he will keep the queen safe for a month, during which time he challenges us to wage war against him in Saurashtra and win her back. If Queen Dhruva is not sent to Malwa next week, he has vowed to kill me.'* The letter concluded with the location where the exchange of the queen for the king was to happen!

'How can you sell your wife for your freedom? Disgusting!' Chandra seethed with anger. 'It's better to die than write such an abominable letter.'

'The king must have given in to the Shakas' torture. They are notorious for it,' said Kritavarma in a hollow voice, looking distraught.

'And my brother is not the one to bear torture, is he? Even if it means destroying the honour of the woman he married.' Chandra was still seething with anger, but he forced himself to think about the issue logically. 'What if this letter is fake?' He looked at Kritavarma and Harisena quizzically.

Harisena answered, 'I analyzed the scroll, comparing it with the other letters by the king. It's your brother's handwriting and his signature. It's not forged.'

Chandra nodded. How had he forgotten that Harisena was, among other things, an expert handwriting analyst?

Harisena continued in a quiet voice, 'I agree with the commander. Rudrasimha must have put the king through unbearable misery. Only a man as low as that Shaka can think of something this vile.'

For a while, silence prevailed. Everyone was immersed in their own thoughts. The quiet of the night was broken only by the occasional screech of an owl. Then conversation resumed.

'Let's take the army and attack them,' said Kritavarma, but Chandra turned down the idea. 'Rudrasimha will sooner kill Rama and escape than fight us.'

Chandra suggested that he could lead a highly trained group of soldiers, stage a night attack, locate Rama and bring him back. Both the elders vetoed it. 'We can't gamble with both your lives. The Gupta throne will be bereft of a king if we agree to this.'

Harisena suggested that they take the help of a neutral kingdom to reason with Rudrasimha. Both Kritavarma and Chandra opposed it. 'We will only waste precious time and turn this filthy family drama into a public one. Also, Rudrasimha is too arrogant to listen to reasoning.'

The chiming bell indicated that it was three in the morning. They still hadn't decided on a course of action. Kritavarma concluded the meeting. 'Prince, let us get some sleep now. Let's meet tomorrow morning.'

An idea was forming in Chandra's head that he didn't voice. He had to talk to the queen before proposing it to the others.

* * *

As if extending a courtesy for writing that vile letter, Rudrasimha allowed a short meeting between Rama and Megha. 'Make it short. Don't forget that my people will be listening in.'

Rama leaned against the wall and closed his eyes as he waited for Megha. Rudrasimha had moved him from the prison cell to this small room with no chair, no bed, not even proper windows. But it was clean, and Rama was no longer being treated like a rabid dog.

The door creaked open. Megha entered. His eyes opened wide in shock. 'King, what happened to you?'

Rama, visibly weak, still had rashes all over him. His upper body was bare, and only a thin cloth covered the lower half. His eyes had sunk deep into their sockets and his head, now shaved, had the same rashes.

'Been through hell, Megha. A living hell where no human should ever be.' Rama's voice quivered.

Megha and Guru too had been abducted that night, and they were being kept in separate cells. 'I'm kept with other spies and prisoners of war. I don't know where Guru is,' Megha finished quickly. 'Now tell me what happened to you.'

Megha's eyes welled up as Rama narrated the events of the past few days. 'I so wished someone would kill me, Megha. I would have willingly died than go through that torture.'

'Oh, King.' Megha wiped his tears and sat next to Rama. 'How did the Shaka king know where we were?'

Megha was anything but shocked when Rama told him that the traitor was Atma. 'I asked the Shaka king who had tipped him off,' said Rama ruefully and stood up. Sitting cross-legged on the floor hurt his back and knees. He felt like an old man. 'He said it was Vijaya. As you suspected all along, that old rogue has always been the enemy. He was the one who helped Rudrasimha plot the battle against us when Father was away.' Rama shuddered at the thought. 'Megha, I'm such a fool to have trusted him. I thought his motive was to wield power. I never thought his sinister plan was to oust the Guptas.'

'Hang that treacherous old man and his men when we reach the capital,' Megha's voice was angry and full of hate. Then he asked Rama worriedly, 'What next, King?'

Rama hesitated. Should he tell Megha about the letter he had been made to send? He felt terribly guilty, so guilty that he hardly slept at night. He had had no choice but to write that letter. Would his friend understand him? He certainly hoped so.

When Rama finished narrating the sordid revenge the Shaka king was seeking, Megha's expression turned from shock to vehement disapproval. 'No, King, no. Why did you write such a letter? The queen is innocent. You can't put her life in danger.'

Rama took deep breaths, trying to stay calm. 'Megha, the Shaka king said I'd be sent back to the same dungeon if I didn't write that letter. I can't even imagine going back in there. I still tremble when I remember the time I spent in that hell.'

'But if *you* couldn't tolerate the torture of the Shaka king, how can the queen? How can you push her into the hands of Rudrasimha, knowing how cruel he can be? You've made a grave mistake. I hope someone in Pataliputra has the sense not to go through with this plan.'

What sort of a friend is he? Rama snapped at Megha, 'What do you know about torture? You've always been under the protection of the king, leading a life of luxury you haven't earned.'

Megha stood up. 'I'm grateful to you and your father for the life I have. But that doesn't change the fact that writing that letter was a crime. That evil old bag Atma might arrange to send the queen here, given he's the regent now!'

Rama's face contorted in rage. 'You know what? I want him to send her! Why should I die for her? She's the reason I'm suffering this torture.' Then, realizing the cruelty of his words, Rama softened. He placed a trembling hand on Megha's shoulder. 'I blurted that out in anger. Don't give up on me, Megha. I do feel terrible about the letter I sent. I promise you, I'll bring the army and fight Rudrasimha. I'll get the queen back safely. Whatever my problems with her, I don't want her life in danger.'

Rama's emotional appeal did nothing to soften Megha's stance. 'Can you believe a word of what that Shaka says? He is the scum of the land. Forget a month, he won't even wait for a day to ruin Queen Dhruva's life.' As Megha walked towards the door to leave, his shoulders slumped. 'I'll stay back and protect the queen. I'll die before she's harmed.'

Rama felt sick as he watched Megha leave. He was not proud of what he'd done. This act would always haunt him. But, in his defence, he hadn't given in to Rudrasimha easily at all. He had begged and pleaded, throwing away his self-respect. 'Why my wife? Ask for freedom from being a vassal. Ask for wealth. What you are asking does not befit a king.'

But Rudrasimha had baulked at him, 'Do you think I'm a beggar to ask for money? I'm giving you a month to take back your wife. Send that brave brother of yours to battle with us. I don't want to battle against a wimp like you.'

Rama, despite Rudrasimha's humiliating words, had felt oddly hopeful. *We can defeat this rogue and take Dhruva back,* he had convinced himself as he'd written the letter.

64

Dhruva stared at Chandra in disbelief. He'd just explained to her his strange plan to rescue the king. The more it sunk in, the more desperate she felt.

'So, what do you think?' His words jolted her out of her miserable thoughts.

'I feel like a sacrificial goat!'

'I promise to keep you safe, and I'll be with you through it all. I've worked out a solution for every little thing that can go wrong. If you agree to this, we'll talk to the elders.'

'If the plan fails, I become Rudrasimha's captive!' Dhruva shuddered. 'You were the one who once said he's a monster disguised as a human!'

Chandra pursed his lips and responded, 'That he is. But I'll be with you. I've defeated him once. This time, I'll kill him.'

Dhruva's eyes began to well up despite her valiant efforts. She was scared. More scared than when Rama was throwing statues and vases at the wall.

Chandra turned pale. 'We won't do this. Not if it distresses you. We will defeat the Shakas and bring my brother back.'

Dhruva stopped crying. She sat still for what seemed like ages. She had to think it through calmly. Maybe she should sleep on it. But she didn't want to prolong the agony. She had to quickly decide one way or the other.

Both Chandra and Kritavarma are brave warriors who will protect me at the cost of their own lives. What is the alternative? If we attack the Shakas, irrespective of a win or loss, Rudrasimha will butcher Rama. She couldn't live with that guilt for the rest of her life.

'I can't believe I'm saying this – I, who was nicknamed Princess Cautious at the age of five. Let's do it. Walk me through the plan again.'

'You never told me that nickname!' Chandra smiled at her. 'I'm sure Minister Harisena will fall out of his chair and hit me with the chair when he hears of the plan. But let's give it a try.'

Dhruva broke into laughter imagining the frail minister hitting the muscular Chandra with a chair.

As expected, all those who heard Chandra's scheme gave him shocked looks. They disapproved vehemently. They said it was reckless. But finally, Chandra and Dhruva succeeded in convincing everyone to go along with them.

* * *

As the horses raced ahead, Dhruva glanced at Vasanthi, who had dozed off. She'd been a blessing on the journey. She'd listened patiently when Dhruva ranted anxiously. She'd made the right sort of soothing sounds, advised her, and even made her laugh. Dhruva went over the plan again and again, both with Vasanthi and in her head. When she wasn't planning, she was praying hard to every god she knew.

To add to this mental stress was the physical duress of the journey. The wooden wagon she was in was not what she was used to. It didn't have comfortable cushions. It was drawn by ordinary horses. But it served its purpose in not drawing attention. Four additional such wagons carried Dhruva's female escorts, who posed as maids but were actually trained fighters. The same was true of the men following the wagons on horseback – the best warriors of the Gupta kingdom posing as merchants on the go. The group included Chandra and Kritavarma. Pranava had insisted on going with them. But Chandra had insisted he stay back to protect the capital.

If it had been another time, Dhruva would have loved that journey. Now, all her attempts to focus on the verdant paddy and cornfields were failing miserably. Her imagination was running wild with images of the Shaka king torturing her. Their journey was going to end soon. They were going to face Rudrasimha only in the dim light of dusk, as Chandra had planned.

Every now and then, Chandra caught up with her wagon. He would point to a fort or a temple and explain its history, show her a wild boar or a herd of elephants. She would smile politely and feign interest in his efforts to distract her. Kritavarma followed them without saying a word.

When the wagons slowed down and finally stopped, Dhruva nudged her friend. 'Vasanthi, wake up. You don't want to sleep through the drama that is going to unfold.'

Vasanthi, now fully awake, smiled sheepishly. 'I'm so sorry. I fell asleep.'

'It's okay. I was conversing with the Shaka king in my head.' Dhruva made a desperate attempt to joke. Her head seemed to weigh a ton since that dreadful showdown with Rama.

Holding on to the hand of a helper, she jumped off the wagon. Her legs felt wooden from the long journey. When she looked around, for a moment, she forgot the trouble she was in – massive trees, emerald green shrubbery and a shallow stream flowing in the distance to her left. On her right was the same forest but much thicker and more formidable. The entire region was filled with sounds from the forest – piercing screeches from insects, birds and occasional unnerving grunts.

As she walked a little further, she could spot an open glade surrounded by trees. Her heart sank at the sight. It looked like the spot Chandra had described. Hearing footsteps Dhruva turned to see Chandra. Breathing in the damp air of the forest, she asked, 'So, is this where I'm going to be handed over?'

Chandra looked away. After a pause, he said, 'You can freshen up at the stream. The men have carved a path.' He didn't answer her question.

Dhruva joined the women waiting for her. *My last few minutes of freedom*, she thought ruefully as she splashed her face with the cold water of the stream. A sense of doom descended on Dhruva when an escort asked her to head back to the wagon.

Sighing, she forced her legs to move. As she neared her wagon, she caught sight of Chandra, and, despite everything, she broke into a giggle. 'Now! Aren't you a pretty one, Prince?'

'Please, don't say it,' Chandra murmured self-consciously.

65

'Rest for a while,' said Chandra, pointing at her wagon, 'before the drama begins.'

The horrible feeling of dread was back. 'I just hope Rudrasimha finds me revolting and runs.'

Chandra shook his head. 'I wouldn't count on that unless you throw up on him or give him an eloquent speech.'

Dhruva smiled. 'I'll try and do both then.'

Then began the wait. Dhruva settled under a tree with Vasanthi. The soldiers walked about. It was odd to see the look of helplessness on the faces of the Gupta warriors, the best in the land. *All because of Rama who'd invited trouble for himself and others,* she thought bitterly.

They didn't have to wait long. The sound of hooves and the sight of the dust they kicked up made everyone rise to their feet. The soldiers positioned themselves in front of the women. Soon, a dozen sturdy horses slowed to a stop a good thirty yards away from them. Tall and bulky Shaka men, in their bright red and yellow uniforms, descended quickly. Kritavarma walked towards them.

Dhruva peeked through the line of men in front of her. *Was that Rama?* She couldn't believe her eyes. He looked pale, pitiful and shrunk. Strangely, she felt no sympathy for him. *He's saving himself by sacrificing me!*

One of the Shaka commanders spoke to Rudrasimha briefly and walked towards the Gupta retinue, chest puffed up and a long sword drawn in front. Kritavarma walked next to him. Dhruva's heart started to pound. Vasanthi squeezed her hand tightly, but it didn't help.

'King Rudrasimha, the Lord of the Shakas, demands that you present Queen Dhruva to him,' Dhruva heard the man declare. 'Once you hand over the queen, you can take back the king.'

She felt numb. She had known what was going to transpire but hadn't expected the exchange to be this quick. Even livestock were sold more cautiously than this!

Kritavarma nodded to her to walk with him. He looked expressionless. Vasanthi squeezed her hand even more tightly. Dhruva moved forward reluctantly without looking at her friend. The soldiers parted down in the middle to allow her to walk.

Dhruva, with the veil of her saree drawn around her head, looked down as she walked. She could feel everyone's eyes on her. She kept her spine erect out of practice, but her legs wobbled, and her throat was dry. She was thankful for Kritavarma's towering figure walking next to her. Then he stopped. She stopped too. All she could see were a pair of large, dusty leather boots.

She was startled when Kritavarma shouted, 'This is shameful for a king, Rudrasimha. You'll go down in history as the most cowardly king who lived on earth.'

She heard the man with the dirty boots laugh deliriously. 'That would be your great king Rama! Take this wimp and get out, you Gupta dog.'

From the corner of her eye, she could see hands roughly pulling Rama forward. She continued to stare at the ground.

'For one month, the queen stays at your palace with her maids. You treat her with respect if you want to live.' Kritavarma's voice held all his fury.

The man laughed again. 'Let me see what miracles you'll accomplish in a month.' Rudrasimha spat out red beetle leaf juice on the ground, nauseating Dhruva. *Why did I agree to this horrible plan? I could have simply moved back to my parents' house.*

'The great Guptas who sold their queen! Now let me take a look at your queen before you take back this joker of a king with you.'

Dhruva's fears doubled and then tripled when she heard Rudrasimha's words and saw his booted feet approach her. Mustering up courage, she looked up. Her stomach lurched as she looked into the cruellest eyes she'd ever seen. He was gaping at her open-mouthed.

'Good Lord, aren't you a beauty!' Rudrasimha's eyes wandered over her, making her want to slap the grin off his face. 'You belong to a real man like me. Not to the coward you are married to.'

Bile rose in her throat when the Shaka king's bearded face, with tobacco-stained teeth and foul breath, loomed before her. Controlling her revulsion, Dhruva stepped back to put more distance between them. As she braced herself to speak, she heard Kritavarma scream, 'You vile creature! Step away from the queen.'

Alarmed, Dhruva looked at Kritavarma and spoke with a calmness she didn't feel. They couldn't anger Rudrasimha now. 'Commander, please let me have a word with the king of the Shakas.'

She bowed to Rudrasimha courteously before she began to speak, 'I'm aware of the contract between you and the Gupta kingdom, and I'm willing to abide by it.' Then she lowered her voice, 'But I have a request, King.'

Rudrasimha grinned from ear to ear, as if unable to hide his glee. 'And courteous too! Unlike the foolish men of your land. Anything for you, my Queen. Anything for you.'

Forcing herself to look pleasant, Dhruva continued to speak in a hushed tone, as if she were sharing a secret with him, 'King, I need to talk to you in private tonight before I travel with you to your land tomorrow.' This seemed to please Rudrasimha.

He beamed with delight. 'Do you call that a request, beautiful? That is my pleasure!' he whispered back, chuckling idiotically. 'You can meet me in my tent once it's pitched. I'll be waiting, my Queen.'

Dhruva continued to stay calm. 'Now, with your permission, I'd like to freshen up. If you hand over the Gupta king, we can proceed.'

Rudrasimha shoved Rama towards Kritavarma. 'Get going. Take one last look at your beautiful wife. She will no longer be yours.'

Dhruva felt Rama's gaze on her, but she steadfastly refused to look in his direction. She was as disgusted with her husband as she was with Rudrasimha. She looked up at Kritavarma and nodded when he said to her, 'Take care of yourself, Queen. We will get you back as soon as possible. Your maids will join you now.'

* * *

Rudrasimha had ordered his guards to let Queen Dhruva into his tent and stay out of earshot while she was inside. He had ordered his men to decorate the tent as much as they could. When there was no sign of Dhruva even after midnight, Rudrasimha sent word to her. Dhruva walked from her tent towards his with five of her warrior maids, through a path only dimly lit by oil lanterns.

Attired in her royal clothes of glittering silk and gold, the loose end of the saree drawn over the head covering her face, Dhruva stepped into Rudrasimha's tent. His guards at the entrance retreated, as did her maids. Dhruva was barely inside Rudrasimha's tent and was about to close its flap when she heard one of the maids talking to the guards. 'So, you are the mighty Shaka soldiers. Show us your strength ...' The banter was to distract the guards.

Inside the tent, Dhruva glanced at Rudrasimha reclined on the bed in the far corner of the large tent. Even the wildflowers couldn't ward off the smell of wine that hung inside that almost airtight room. Dhruva walked with a slow gait towards him and then stopped midway. Leaning against a table, she lowered her head and fiddled with her bangles.

'Shy, are you? Suits a woman. I like shy women,' Rudrasimha shuffled out of his bed. 'Come near me, Queen. How can I hear you or see you if you stand there?' Rudrasimha slurred.

When Dhruva continued to stand where she was, he got to his feet and walked to her on unsteady legs. 'Then, let me come near you. A beauty like you can command me all you want.'

When Rudrasimha's hand touched Dhruva's chin in an attempt to lift her face to him, a large hand pressed down on his mouth. Another hand sprang out of the saree and thrust a dagger into his back repeatedly. Rudrasimha's body went limp, but the hand remained on his mouth. Rudrasimha's eyes widened in shock when he saw the face in front of him. She was not the woman he had seen earlier! The face staring down at him with cold, vacant eyes, waiting for him to die, was Chandra's.

Chandra heaved a sigh of relief when Rudrasimha's hefty body stopped convulsing. He took a long look at his archenemy, who now lay dead before him. Chandra plucked his Ajeya from Rudrasimha's back, wiped it clean on his robe and pushed the body aside. Then, he looked at himself. His saree was dishevelled and covered in blood. Chandra contemplated stripping out of it but decided not to. If the guards outside were not yet dead at the hands of their female fighters, he might have to carry on the pretence of being Dhruva a while longer.

66

But Chandra didn't have to worry about the Shaka guards posted outside the tent. When he cautiously walked out of the tent, he found all of them slumped on the ground like felled trees. The warrior women had done their job! One of the women hurried towards Chandra with Dhruva. She swiftly handed him a sword, a bow and a quiver full of arrows she had confiscated from the guards. As Dhruva watched, a little dazed at the overwhelming smell of blood all around her, Chandra shook himself out of his saree and blouse.

'Are you hurt?' Dhruva whispered, noticing the blood on his clothes.

'No,' Chandra's reply was hurried as he tugged at his neck chains and the bangles. He handed them to the woman who waited for his instructions. 'All of you share these and escape out of here safely. I'll take the queen with me.'

The woman said in a low voice, 'Hurry, Prince. Don't worry about us.'

Dhruva looked worried. 'Vasanthi—'

'We will take care of your friend,' the woman said, before Dhruva could finish. She put a hand reassuringly on Dhruva's shoulder before Chandra almost dragged her away. The danger was increasing with each passing minute. After a few minutes of walking swiftly in the dark, Dhruva stopped.

Panting, she clutched her side. 'My lungs are on fire. I can't take another step.'

Chandra said, 'We can't stop here because of the wild animals, and we aren't that far from the Shaka camp yet. From this point on, the forest will get thicker, and we're only safe as long as we're quiet and keep moving.'

Before Chandra could complete his sentence, a spear whizzed past them. 'Where did that come from?' he cursed. 'That's all we need, after all the excitement we've just had!'

Before he could hide behind a tall tree with Dhruva, a group of tribal men had surrounded them. Thrusting their spears out, the men started slowly circling Dhruva and Chandra. One of them, who carried an oil lamp in one hand and a spear in the other, came forward, dangled it close to Chandra's face and said something.

'Great! Now a language I don't understand,' Dhruva heard Chandra mutter. But, to her surprise, she understood the man!

'Who are you and why are you here at this hour?' the man was asking. One of Dhruva's maids, from the Vindhya region, used to speak to her in that dialect.

'They are Atavikas,' Dhruva tried to whisper to Chandra. But he had already charged at the man, disarmed him of his spear and now held him at sword point. The rest of the men, looking scared, retreated a little.

'We mean no harm. Let us go,' Chandra said to the group, holding down the large man with difficulty.

The men eyed him suspiciously, but did not reply. Chandra's tongue was as foreign to them as theirs was to him.

Dhruva, strangely unafraid, translated in a broken dialect what Chandra had just said. Chandra stared at her in disbelief.

The men seemed to understand her. 'Are you Shakas?' asked the man Chandra held in his grip. As her eyes adjusted to the dark, Dhruva noticed how gigantic the men were. Three horizontal white lines were painted on their foreheads. They wore long metal chains with skull pendants. Their spears looked like tridents. They were worshippers of Shiva.

'Har har Mahadev,' she bowed to them, eliciting a similar 'Har har Mahadev,' in chorus from them. The tridents went up in the air momentarily before they were pointed at Chandra again.

Dhruva decided to take a chance and tell these men the truth. Whether the Atavikas liked the Guptas or not, they hated the Shakas for the way Rudrasimha had killed their leader, Deva.

'No,' Dhruva said firmly. 'I'm the queen of Magadha, formerly the princess of Kamarupa. The Shaka king kidnapped me, and this warrior is rescuing me and taking me back to Pataliputra.' She decided not to reveal Chandra's identity. The Atavikas had reasons to hate Chandra as well.

She turned to Chandra and asked him to release the man. Chandra did so, but the look on his face told her that he was not happy about it. The man, probably the leader of the group, asked his men to step back.

'We respect your father, the king of Kamarupa. He's a devotee of Shiva like us. Though we're not fond of your in-laws, we will help you get back safely to Pataliputra,' declared the man gallantly.

'What is he saying?' Chandra's impatience was evident in his voice. 'Can't you translate as he speaks?'

'They are willing to help us,' said Dhruva.

'Can we trust them?' asked Chandra sceptically.

'Do we have a choice?'

The leader said, 'We hate the Gupta royals for what they have done to us. All our kings are slaves in your land. We will help you cross this forest, but will you help us in return? Will you get our leaders freed?'

Dhruva nodded. 'I promise you that I'll try my best.'

* * *

Once the Atavikas had left them at the edge of the forest, Chandra and Dhruva stood still and stared at the thick forest behind them and the river that flowed at a distance. Dhruva took the lead and started to walk towards the river.

Following her, Chandra asked. 'Now tell me everything. How do you know their language?'

Dhruva summed up the story for him and then urged, 'Please release the Atavika leaders. I don't want to be a liar!'

'They are not bad men. They were just greedy and sided with Rudrasimha. We will release them at the right time. So that their new friend doesn't become a liar.'

Dhruva laughed. She was feeling light after a long time. Standing ankle-deep in the river, she felt like she did when she was in Kamarupa, with her family. She hoped the feeling would last.

Standing next to her, Chandra said solemnly, 'It has been one strange night where so many things could have gone wrong. The Atavikas were a great help.'

'Oh, yes, they were. The men even carried me on a plank! Though I thought I was going to fall off it at some point!' Dhruva stared at the rising sun. *Is it morning already?* 'Where do we go from here, Prince?'

Chandra looked at her tired face. 'You mean, in life or now?'

'Both! First, answer the simpler question. What is our next destination? How far are we from Pataliputra?'

'It'll be a short walk to the nearest village where we can summon a chariot.'

Sitting on the sand that bordered the river, Dhruva

smiled. 'My brother Samu used to call me a chatting warrior, that I can beat even the most formidable enemy by just talking.' Dhruva laughed. 'And, I did that today, didn't I?'

Instead of laughing, Chandra was serious. 'I hope there never comes a time where you have to defend yourself. I was stupid to put you through this ordeal.'

'I too was stupid enough to go along! It was a crazy scheme but looks like we pulled it off. What doesn't kill you makes you stronger!' Dhruva leaned back on her hands and closed her eyes. All she needed was sleep.

'You didn't deserve any of this. You know what, to make up for all this torture, I'll win both Saurashtra and Malwa from the Shakas one day and offer them to you,' Chandra declared determinedly.

For some reason, Dhruva choked up, maybe because Chandra sounded so sincere. Managing not to burst into tears, Dhruva smiled and said, 'When you win Saurashtra and Malwa, I want *you* to be the ruler. And, I'll make Ujjaini in Malwa a literary haven!'

She couldn't help but notice that despite his valiant efforts, Chandra's eyes too had welled up. Shared hardships did bring people closer together.

67

Rama stared into the darkness blankly. It was way past midnight, and he was nowhere close to falling asleep.

Since his escape from the Shaka land of torture, he was healing physically, but mentally, he felt battered. He had nobody to call his own. Megha was the first to abandon him. Days had passed, but Megha hadn't met him.

Rama had finally barged into his house. 'I negotiated for your release along with mine. Is this how you pay me back? Why do I get the feeling you are avoiding me?'

But Megha's reply was more shocking than his silence. 'Because I am.' Megha had looked coldly into Rama's eyes. 'We are taught to respect and protect women. And we consider the queen a goddess. You betrayed her. I can't forget that.'

Rama's anger surged. 'She betrayed me! Now you are doing the same. I have no well-wishers in this world. I was a fool to think you were one!'

After that, the next blow, a much bigger one, was from Dhruva herself. After reaching Pataliputra, she'd fallen ill and had moved out of their bed-chamber. He'd visited her, but she'd refused to even look at him. When he heard that she was feeling better, he'd again gone to see her, but he was not allowed inside. She had sent word through Vasanthi that she would meet him when she felt better.

But he knew that everyone from Chandra to Kritavarma to Megha had met her. *Why is she belittling me in front of everyone? Can't we sort out our differences in private? After all, I should be the one angry with her for her deceit.* He had seethed in anger but remained quiet.

Then there was Atma – Rama felt both angry and depressed remembering his treachery. How could he have been foolish enough to trust him for years? Even before he'd reached Pataliputra, Atma, Vijaya and Shashi had vanished from their houses. Kritavarma had sent messengers to all parts of the kingdom to find them. He had even sent word to the neighbouring kingdoms to arrest the evil trio if they were ever spotted in their provinces.

Chandra had not tried to talk to him. But he was back to acting like king in the council meetings – making decisions, offering suggestions and ignoring Rama.

'Chandra is once again a hero, but this time, by burying me into the ground,' Rama had voiced his fury to Chandana, his only friend. Guru was still rotting in the Shaka jail.

'You are still the king. Once all this settles, take the administration back into your hands and prove that you are better than your father.' Chandana's words were, at best, patronizing.

Rama was to address people in the town square. 'We must do this to boost the morale of citizens. They've been shaken by recent events,' Kritavarma and Harisena had convinced him. Rama had agreed reluctantly. He was back in the clutches of the three old men and Chandra. He had no choice for the time being.

How will people react to me tomorrow? Will they throw rotten eggs at me this time? He let Kusha on the bed, who had been trying to snuggle next to him. At least, his dog still loved him. The rest of the night, his nightmares ranged from Chandra stabbing him with a stick and Dhruva pushing him off a cliff to Atma handing him a goblet of poison.

* * *

Humiliation. If a single word could sum up that day's public meeting for Rama, then that would be it. He had seen meetings turn violent, but that day, the rebellion and belligerence he saw were at an all-time high.

'We heard you traded the queen for your safe return.'

'If you can't take care of your wife, how can you look after us?'

'If Prince Chandra bailed you out, then we want him as our king.'

Rama had many comebacks to all these barbs, but he kept his mouth shut. Kritavarma and Harisena took over. When the demand for Chandra on the stage escalated, Kritavarma signalled him to come up. Rama, boiling with anger, watched Chandra make his grand entry. The entire gathering instantly went from accusing Rama to chanting Chandra's name.

'Yuvraj Chandra ki jai.'

'Yuvraj Chandra for king.'

Rama had to control his urge to punch that smile off Chandra's face when he began his speech. 'Our queen was never in any danger. Please don't believe the rumours. By Lord Vishnu's grace, we're again an impregnable empire.'

The audience quietened down. As Rama rode back to his quarters, he was not angry with Chandra. He hadn't talked about his own heroics or put him down. Then a thought struck him. Chandra hadn't said anything positive about him either. He could have said something to the effect that they were under an able king, at least to boost his image in people's eyes. *Why would he do that for me?* Rama thought bitterly. *The more I'm disgraced, the better it is for him.*

That night, as Rama waited for Kritavarma and Harisena in the private council chamber, the door creaked open. It was Chandra.

Feeling resentful, Rama narrowed his eyes. 'Who invited you here?'

'We need to talk.' Chandra took a seat and crossed his legs.

'What do you want to talk about? How you stole my wife and are now planning to steal my throne?' Rama's nostrils flared in anger.

'Brother—'

'Address me as king. I'm not your brother. Never was, never will be.'

'Fine. I'll address you with nothing. Let me jog your memory. You stole the woman I was betrothed to, and I donated the kingdom to you.'

'Get out of here, Chandra,' Rama screamed, pushing Chandra away with all the force he could muster.

Chandra got up and leaned towards Rama. 'Listen to me. I'm not going anywhere. If you make any decisions on your own from now on, I'll have you dethroned myself. Minister Harisena and the commander are too polite to tell you this, but your decisions are no longer unanimous. Today we will discuss how to get our kingdom back in order. The asinine policies you have put in place have to be reversed.'

'How dare you! I can get you arrested and throw you into the dungeon to rot.'

Before Chandra could reply, the door opened and

Kritavarma and Harisena walked in. They stood still for a moment sensing the tension in the room.

'Is everything all right?' Kritavarma asked, raising a brow.

'Ask the new king of the land,' said Rama, pointing at Chandra sarcastically.

Chandra, leaning against a chair, said grimly, 'I'm only the caretaker. I'll do whatever it takes to keep it safe.'

68

'Queen, the king seeks a visit.'

Dhruva paled. She had put him off for long. Couldn't he take a hint? Sighing, she gestured to the maid to send him in.

Rama, looking very unsure of himself, walked in and slowly closed the door behind him. Dhruva felt nervous. What she was going to say would send him into a fit of rage for sure. She should probably leave the door open to dash out if needed.

'How are you feeling now?' Rama asked softly as he neared her. He looked so pale that for a moment she felt sorry for him.

'Not too bad.' Dhruva involuntarily took a step back.

'Not trying to get away from me, are you?' Rama's voice dripped with entitlement. Dhruva's sympathy for him vanished.

'You've met everyone but me in the last few days. Why?'

She remained silent and sank into a chair.

'When do you plan to move back to our quarters?' Rama asked, sitting in the chair next to hers.

Dhruva hesitated but braced herself. She had to tell him the truth, for her own sake. 'I plan to stay here.'

'Don't be childish. You expect me to move in here? Into this hole?' The room had nothing more than a chest of drawers, a cot and a couple of chairs.

Dhruva shook her head. 'No ... I mean, we're going to live separately.'

'Enough of your drama, Dhruva. Move back now. Don't create more problems for me than you already have.'

Dhruva couldn't believe her ears. *Did I create problems for you? Isn't it the other way round?* She wanted to shake some sense into him, but silence seemed like a better option.

Rama grabbed her arm. 'Talk. Being silent won't solve our problems. Why do you want to live separately?'

'Because I don't want to be your wife anymore.' Dhruva extricated her arm from his grip. 'Common sense says if a husband pawns off his wife, he's no longer her husband. And the scriptures support that. A man who does not protect his wife's honour with his own life ceases to be her husband.'

Rama's face turned vicious. 'And what do the scriptures say about a treacherous woman? One who plots against her husband by siding with his enemy?'

'If the husband can prove that she's guilty of that crime, he can denounce her,' Dhruva replied calmly.

'Stop quoting the scriptures. Virtuous words from you are disgusting.' Rama kicked the table in front of him.

Dhruva watched as the vase on the table toppled, the flowers fell out, and water pooled on the ground. The space around her, immaculate only a few minutes ago, was now all muddied – just like her mind.

'I'll wait for three days. If you move back to our quarters, I'll forgive you and take you back. If not, get out of the palace.'

Dhruva felt exhausted when he left. This was a conversation she had dreaded since her return. Now that it was over, she felt both relieved and drained. She didn't want to think about her future. All she wanted was to forget the past.

* * *

Three days came and went, but Dhruva didn't return to their room. Rama's head ached with worry. Though he'd told her that she had to get out of the palace if she refused to be his wife, he knew that it was impossible. She was the queen of the land and people loved her. How was he going to handle this situation?

After a long hot summer, a spell of rain had cooled the night. Rama was plagued by miserable thoughts as he rode with Chandana, hardly noticing anything around him. This used to be his favourite part of the day, riding for hours on end on a chilly night. Not any longer.

Spotting a group of people warming themselves around a bonfire, Rama steered his steed towards them.

'Let's join them. I want to hear what everyone has to say behind my back.'

With the wine they'd bought from a nearby tavern, Rama and Chandana settled down with the group.

'What will happen to our crops this time? The summer has been harsh,' said one.

'We will die of hunger. We don't matter to our king,' another scoffed. 'What can you expect from a king who sold his wife to the enemy!'

Alerted, Chandana intervened. 'I heard it's a lie. The king planned to defeat the Shakas and get back the queen.'

There was laughter all around. 'You must be very drunk, brother. Who sends his wife to another man in the first place? That too, the enemy? Better to die. Our ill-luck that Prince Chandra gave up the throne to this selfish fellow.'

Another chimed in, 'Poll tax, income tax, celebration tax, war tax – is there an end to our king's greed? There will soon be taxes on death!'

People laughed as one of them added, 'There's a burial tax already! The new one will be a tax to sell your wife to your archenemy!'

Rama felt a surge of anger, the wine fuelling it further. He forgot that it was suicidal for him to speak. 'What is wrong with you all?' He stood up unsteadily. Wagging a finger at the men, he screamed, 'You are only paying ten per cent of what you earn. You are the selfish ones here.'

Some of them grew angry at the remark. 'Who are you? The king's crony? Ten per cent of what we grow is what we eat. Now even that goes to the pleasure pursuits of our king.'

Chandana pulled Rama away from the scene. It was a miracle that the men hadn't recognized Rama. As they mounted their horses, they could see an irate man spit after them.

'My troubles started the day Chandra was born. He has always done everything to come out looking like a hero and make me look like a loser. Now he has done it on a grand scale! What was that nonsense about dressing up as Dhruva? I could have won against that worm Shaka and brought her back. Chandra is a schemer, and nobody knows about it except me.'

They reached Rama's quarters. The king returning late at night, drunk, was nothing new to the guards. They simply looked away.

'Do you want me to stay here for a while?' Chandana asked. Rama declined. He preferred to be alone in his misery.

For the last three days, he'd waited restlessly for Dhruva to return. She hadn't. The way people spoke that night showed their complete disrespect for him. He had lost his wife and his kingdom, and both to Chandra! Rama gulped down more wine.

'Your cheap wine and lazy ways will never let you succeed, Rama.' His father's voice echoed in his head. He drank until he felt numb. That was when he decided that he was going to put an end to his misery.

69

Chandra stirred in his sleep. Something felt wrong, but he was too tired to wake up. He slipped once more into sleep, thinking it was a bad dream. The next instant, he was fully awake. The sharp pain in his thigh was no dream. He sprung up from his bed and reached instinctively for his dagger, Ajeya. He swiped the cold marble table-top frantically, but there was no dagger. That couldn't be right! For years, he had kept it in the same place. As he fumbled, his hand sent a silver pitcher of water to the ground with a loud clank.

'Don't bother. Ajeya cannot save you,' a voice slurred.

As his eyes got used to the dark, Chandra recognized the man wildly swinging a sharp, bloodstained knife.

'Brother!' Chandra's initial shock at seeing Rama quickly gave way to anger. 'Is this a joke? If you want to kill someone, you cut the throat, not the thigh.' He noticed that Rama smelt of ganja and wine more strongly than ever.

'Do I look like a joke to you?' Rama now hovered over Chandra, staring at him with bloodshot eyes. '*You* are the joke of the family. A cheap gimmicky joke.' The knife dangled too close to Chandra's throat for comfort.

'You are right. Saving you from humiliation has been my favourite gimmick.' Chandra pushed Rama aside, trying to sit up, but the soft, feather-cushioned bed made it hard for him to roll off. Rama, unusually quick tonight, pushed Chandra back on the cot and pinned him down with a knee to his chest.

'Behave like a king for once in your life. You are

no better than a drunk passed out on the street. I've had enough of your drama,' Chandra muttered angrily.

'The drama has just begun, you devil,' Rama stammered. The knife dangled unsteadily in his hand. 'It'll end soon with you dead. Magadha can mourn their hero tomorrow.'

Chandra felt his anger rising. He had had enough of Rama's nonsense. 'Then let us fight a duel in the morning. Except that this time, I won't be kind on your pitiful soul,' said Chandra.

'Always my saviour, aren't you? Did I ever ask for your help? You always jump in to save me to make yourself look good. There will be a duel now. If you can get to your sword, that is.' Rama's words were barely coherent. He looked like a man possessed.

Chandra had to escape the knife before Rama plunged it into his chest! He rolled off the bed. On the floor, Chandra held Rama's dagger hand in a vice-like grip. 'You want a duel? Let's have one, Brother. Prove to me that you at least remember how to hold a sword.' Chandra didn't attempt to hide his fury.

Rama's hard kick on his leg made Chandra wince in pain. But he tightened his grip until the dagger slipped out of Rama's hand.

'You should have shown this bravery when Rudrasimha demanded your wife. People would have respected you for that.' Chandra moved back, pushing Rama away.

'I would have, but did you let me? You had to be a hero, didn't—'

Mid-sentence, Rama made a strange gurgling sound.

As Chandra watched in shock, Rama slumped on the ground, making muffled noises. Alarmed, Chandra tried to support Rama. To his horror, his hands were sticky and wet with what he knew was blood.

He looked at the door only to catch a quick glimpse of a retreating cloaked figure. He must have thrown a knife at Rama! Chandra ran down the corridor, after the man, but could not catch up with him. Realizing that it was more important to help Rama than to catch the assailant, he looked around for a guard, but unfortunately, because of his own instructions, no guards were posted near his quarters.

Chandra ran back into his room. To his shock, the attacker was now standing astride Rama, stabbing him. Pouncing on the killer, Chandra pulled him back and took off the cover from his head.

'Megha! How could you?' Holding Megha's hand, Chandra bent to check on Rama.

'Don't bother, Prince. I've made sure he's dead.' Saying this, Megha threw away the knife in his hand. His dispassionate voice sent a chill down Chandra's spine.

'He was your best friend. Why on earth did you kill him?' Chandra whispered.

Megha was shivering uncontrollably now. Chandra guided him to the cot.

'He destroyed the empire. And sold the queen! Someone had to end his mad regime. You were too decent to dethrone him, and the others were helpless.'

'How did you know he was coming here? Did he tell you?'

Megha shook his head. 'I saw him swaying on his way

here. I followed him. I didn't come here intending to kill him, but I'm not sorry I did. The free knife training your father gave me came to use today.' Megha smiled wryly.

Chandra felt too numb to process what Megha had just done. It took him a while to find his voice. 'Megha, what you did is wrong. Very, very wrong. But ... I don't want to turn you in because you are a good man. Go away from here, now. I'll explain everything that happened tonight. But I won't reveal your name. I'll say that I couldn't see the killer in the dark.'

Megha shook his head. 'No, Prince. The blame could be levelled at you. Call the guards now. I'll confess.'

'No, Megha. Just go. I won't be blamed. Truth always wins. I didn't kill my brother, and I won't be blamed for it. Please go. Please.'

Megha slowly stood up. 'I will go for now. But I'll be around until you are crowned the king.'

Chandra knelt next to Rama's limp body. Shocked and dejected, he sat frozen like a statue, tears rolling down his cheeks.

70

A week after Rama's gruesome murder was the day of judgement to decide whether Chandra was innocent or guilty. An intense investigation had continued all week. Anubhuti, the royal chief of justice, was going to read out his verdict that day. All eyes were on Chandra, who stood below the podium.

Anubhuti began to speak in a deep baritone, 'We've heard Prince Chandra's account of what transpired in his room that dreadful night. Nevertheless, we investigated the crime because we don't want the slightest suspicion on our future king. So—'

The judge paused and looked around at the anxious faces. 'Having questioned the prince and after much deliberation, this is my verdict. Prince Chandra had no reason to murder King Rama. He'd surrendered the throne to his brother voluntarily. Looking at the past, we've never had an opportunity to mistrust Prince Chandra's intentions. I spoke to everyone who knew our late King Rama. Not one of them accused Prince Chandra of killing him. Finally, I spoke to Queen Dhruva. She too vehemently dismissed the charge. Thus, I declare Prince Chandra not guilty of murdering King Rama.'

The crowd went berserk. The sound of bugles, drums and cheers filled the air.

Megha walked away silently. He had betrayed his friend but not the kingdom.

* * *

The next day, Chandra sought a meeting with Dhruva. As he walked through the garden that led to her room, he felt nervous. How would she react to what he was going to tell her? Probably call him silly and laugh it off!

Dhruva answered his knock. He was taken aback when he saw her. She was dressed in a white saree, without bangles, nose rings, chains or flowers in her hair.

She's dressed like a widow. Sadness surged through him.

As they sat on the stone benches in the garden, Dhruva smiled. 'King Chandra. It has a good ring to it.'

When Chandra only flashed a small smile and looked away, Dhruva knitted her brows. 'Why are you sad? It's time for you to be happy.'

'My brother is dead, and you look like this.' He paused. 'I'm sorry, but I don't feel happy.'

'I agree that these are terrible times at a personal level. But I'm happy like the rest of the kingdom. Magadha is now in safe hands.'

Chandra looked at the sky. 'I'm nervous. Too much pressure to keep up with all that is expected of me!'

'You'll be a great king. Don't worry so much. Now please stop this I'm-so-sad drama and start looking happy! You are soon going to be crowned king!'

'Queen Dhruva! You are so bossy. You even tell me how I should feel!'

'Well, I won't be Queen Dhruva for long. I'm thinking of heading back to Kamarupa after your coronation.'

Chandra was taken aback. That was not part of his plan! 'What do you mean you'll leave Pataliputra? You are the queen of the land. In the absence of the king, you are the one in charge of the kingdom.'

'Of course. I'll stay until you are crowned. My responsibility ends there.' Dhruva's eyes were now moist with tears. 'Since I don't have a child, my only link to this land was through my husband. Anyway, you sent word that you wanted to talk to me about something. What is it?'

Chandra spoke after a pause. 'I came to ask if you'd

marry me.' He smiled awkwardly. 'Well, I wish I could ask you this in a better manner. But I can't gather my thoughts after the shock you've just given me about leaving the kingdom.'

Dhruva stared at him as if he'd taken leave of his senses. 'Of all your insane plans, this should be crowned the winner!'

Chandra didn't let her complete. 'Dhruva, please marry me and continue to be my friend and support.'

Dhruva shook her head. 'I can't. We can't. Being the king of the Guptas, you can't marry a widow, that too your brother's widow!'

'Then I don't want the kingdom,' said Chandra firmly. 'I can serve the country without being a ruler.'

Dhruva stared at Chandra in stunned silence for a moment. 'You can't do that! For a king, the kingdom should come before self. It sounded horrible when my mother said it, but it makes sense now.'

'Then, let me do this while I'm not yet crowned king. Listen to what I'm saying and think it over. Don't reject it right away.'

71

The large chamber was packed with people. In the front rows were the dignitaries – commanders, ministers, chieftains, nobles, guild-heads and Dhruva's parents. Behind them was a large open area where the citizens had gathered in thousands. Chandra had sent messengers to all the cities of the Gupta empire, notifying people of this meeting.

Chandra climbed on the stage, feeling nervous. Would people understand him or throw him to the lions? It was too late for such thoughts. If he were to be the king, people had to choose him willingly.

When he'd met Harisena the previous night, the minister had sounded confident and supportive. 'Don't worry so much. Truth always wins.'

Chandra tried to stay calm and focused. As planned, Harisena walked on the stage and stood next to him with a scroll in hand. A sudden silence and stillness fell over the crowd.

Anxiety shot through Chandra. He felt better when he looked at Dhruva walking towards him. She was dressed in a bright red saree, hair bedecked with flowers and jewels that gleamed. Dhruva took her place to the left of Chandra.

'I feel like an actor in a play! I want to run away,' she whispered to Chandra.

'Me too. I think it's best if we do,' Chandra whispered back.

Dhruva glared at him. 'Why do I always agree with your insane ideas?'

Murmurs were already spreading through the gathering. As per tradition, wives stood to the right of their husbands and Dhruva was dressed like a bride.

Before the crowd could become louder, Harisena began to speak, 'I'm happy to announce that Prince Chandra has married Queen Dhruva, the princess of Kamarupa, and the widowed wife of his brother, late

King Rama. If any of you have objections to him becoming the king because of this marriage, please voice them now. The rope barricade on your right side will be raised now. Those who support Prince Chandra for king, please move to the right of the rope. Those who object, please remain where you are. The prince has decided to ascend the throne only if there is a clear majority.'

The announcers were spreading the word through the audience. But everyone stayed glued to their places!

'Dhruva, nobody is moving!'

'I told you so. Who would agree to this plan?' Dhruva whispered back sounding desperate.

Chandra had thought he was ready to face this moment, but now his stomach turned with anxiety. *There goes my dream of taking the Gupta empire to new heights.*

Then he saw from the corner of his eye, Harisena crossing the stage and moving to the right. Kritavarma, Pranava and Vasanthi followed. Then Lakshmidhara, who had severe knee pain, hobbled to the right, leaning on his walking stick. There was a sudden buzz in the crowd with a steady stream of women crossing the barricade.

'At least some supporters! Now we don't look so foolish!' Chandra whispered to Dhruva. A joke somehow made it easier to bear the rejection.

'My parents! Why are they coming up here?' Dhruva sounded surprised.

But the moment her mother came near, Dhruva hugged her. Her mother's tears of joy brought out hers too. Dhruva and Chandra touched her parents' feet to get their blessings before they joined the group of supporters.

Most of the dignitaries moved to the right, but a large section of commoners remained glued to their places. After a brief lull, the head of the traders' guild walked up to the stage. The man, clothed elaborately in silk and jewels, oozed power.

'Why is this man coming up now? He is never good news.' Chandra was glad to have Dhruva next to him.

The man stood before Chandra without a hint of a smile. Then he bowed. A small relief surged through Chandra, though he made no display of it. When the man looked up, Chandra acknowledged his greetings.

'Do you promise to rule justly?' the man grunted his question.

'I promise to keep the people's best interests in mind.'

Chandra's reply seemed to please the man, who now turned to the audience. Raising his hand dramatically, he crossed over to the right and signalled his guild members to join him. After that, each guild-head pledged his allegiance to Chandra and joined his supporters.

The people began to cheer for Chandra and Dhruva.

'Queen Dhruva.' Chandra smiled, looking visibly relieved.

'No more of these dramas, King Chandra,' Dhruva muttered with a smile.

'Would you call that life?'

'You are right,' Dhruva chuckled, getting off the stage. She didn't know what the future had in store for her, but that day and that moment was something she would cherish all her life.

Acknowledgements

I thank Linda Jowsey, a dear friend whose feedback and encouragement helped me finish the book. My daughters, Akshara Mahesh and Neethi Mahesh, for all the brainstorming and their smart suggestions on the plot. A double thank you to Akshara for coming up with the book title. My editors from HarperCollins, Tina Narang for commissioning my book, Veena Wadhwani and Ateendriya Gupta, for their meticulous attention to detail and fabulous editing. Harshad Marathe for a gorgeous cover. Shinie Antony for her friendship and for finding the book a home. And, my husband, Kavi Mahesh, and my parents, Ramamani and Nagesh, for their support in everything I do.

Vani Mahesh has a deep-rooted interest in Hindu mythology and ancient Indian history. She is the author of *Stories of Creation – From the Brahma Purana* and *Saptarshi – The Seven Supreme Sages*, published by Amar Chitra Katha. She has written *The Glory of Shiva Purana*, Volume 1, published by Sri Ramakrishna Math. Her novel *A Kingdom for His Love* is based on a play by Bhasa, a first-century dramatist. Her latest novel, *Meet Me in the Middle*, has been published by Black Ink and HarperCollins.

A software engineer by profession, Vani owned and ran EasyLib.com, the first online library in India, for thirteen years. She lives in Bangalore with her husband and two daughters.